THE
GREEN
LINE

THE
GREEN
LINE

E.C. DISKIN

THOMAS & MERCER

Published by Thomas & Mercer, Seattle

www.apub.com

Amazon, the Amazon logo, and Thomas & Mercer are trademarks of Amazon.com, Inc., or its affiliates.

ISBN-13: 9781477818404
ISBN-10: 1477818405

Text design by Gwen Gades
Cover design by Derek Murphy
Cover photograph by David Pirmann

Library of Congress Control Number: 2013919402

Printed in the United States of America

For Jimmy and Caroline

THE
GREEN
LINE

ONE

A WOMAN'S voice, deep and coarse from thousands of cigarettes and too much liquor, roused Abby into consciousness. The woman, seated a few rows ahead on the opposite side of the aisle, was arguing with the empty seat across from her. Her gray hair, matted and kinky, sprang from her head in every direction.

"Git away from me!" the woman yelled, desperately clutching her plastic bags full of shoes and cups. "I know what you're up to. I kill you all." She scanned the car and locked eyes with Abby before continuing her rant at the empty seat. "If I had me a gun, I'd just shoot all them white people. That's what I'd do."

Abby looked around for comfort in the eyes of other passengers. Only three others were on board. They were not comforting. An older man, presumably homeless and drunk, was asleep. Two young guys, maybe twenty, covered in tattoos, gold chains, and baggy clothes, sat across the aisle behind her. Thugs.

Something was not right.

Abby fumbled for her glasses to read the train map. The green-colored chart of stops plastered above the doors confirmed her mistake. Her heart began beating faster and her body tensed. Shit. She was on the Green Line.

She'd been waiting for the Brown Line, watching as two Green Line trains came and went, silently cursing as her time for sleep slipped away. She had stood under the heat lamps, reading her cases and highlighting good quotes and relevant facts for her brief, when another train had finally pulled into the station. She had barely looked up—she just stepped into the empty car, took a seat, and kept reading. And, obviously, fell asleep.

Abby looked at her watch and realized she had been sleeping for about fifteen minutes. Given the time—11:25 p.m.—she was now several miles west of the Loop. She looked up at the train grid again, checking the stops to see if she could figure out how far she had gone and if there was a safe stop where she could turn around and wait for an eastbound train. She had no idea.

She wasn't from Chicago. Everyone she knew lived north of the Loop, along the lake, where the city was vibrant, full of restaurants, boutiques, and chain stores, and where she'd always felt relatively safe. All Abby had ever been told of the area west of the Loop was, "You don't want to go there." Last week's front-page story in the *Tribune* had highlighted this fact. The article, which described how Chicago had regained its dubious distinction as the nation's murder capital, having reached six hundred murders in 2003, illustrated where these deaths occurred, using red dots and a grid of the city. At the time, Abby had felt great relief. Her neighborhood had just two red dots. She had never been to any of the heavy red-dot areas, and she saw no reason why she ever would.

This train was headed into the heaviest red-dot zone. Her mother's warnings about the dangers of a big city began filling her head. She thought of the pepper spray her mother sent her years ago, which she'd laughed at, thrown in the kitchen junk drawer, and never touched again.

The rain-soaked windows framed blackness. There was no way to judge her surroundings. Staring at the window, Abby saw the thugs' reflections in the glass. One stared at her. She instinctively looked back at him. He smiled. The fleur-de-lis design on his shaved head was the symbol of her old Kappa Kappa Gamma. Many of her lily-white, southern-belle sorority sisters had rebelliously tattooed the same flower design on their ankles. He was clearly in a different club.

Abby remained blank-faced and looked away again, trying to avoid encouragement without pissing him off. It didn't seem to matter. Through the window's reflection, she watched him nudge his buddy, stand up, and head her way. He took the seat behind her, leaned forward, and whispered in her ear, "Hey, pretty lady." She could feel his breath on her neck and smelled the odor of too much cologne.

Afraid of appearing rude, but without turning around, she offered a weak "Hello."

"Whatcha up to?"

She glanced toward the window for its mirrored effect and watched as he touched her hair.

"Just going home," she said as casually as possible. She leaned forward and gathered her things.

"How 'bout I go witch you?"

His friend chimed in, "Yeah, how 'bout we both go?"

The man behind her laughed, "You know what they say 'bout redheads?" He didn't wait for a response. "They wild."

Abby's stomach was tightening in fear.

The friend laughed. "That's right. She look like she could handle us both, don't you think?"

Abby didn't turn around. "Thanks, but I'm married." She put her briefcase strap over her head and across her chest, grabbed her purse, and walked to the door.

"Hey, where you goin'?"

She stared at the door, avoiding any more eye contact.

"I don't see no ring! You 'fraid of me?"

Abby didn't respond.

The friend chimed in again. "I think she's rude."

The thug continued, getting louder. "Hey, I'm talkin' to you. You think you're too good for me, bitch?"

Abby shook her head.

The men laughed.

She continued to watch their movement through the window's reflection. They were together again. Both sitting with their hands on the grab bars in front of their seats, ready to pounce.

The train pulled up to the next stop, Cicero, and the doors opened. Abby remained still, feeling the weight of their intention. But as the automated ringing sound indicated doors closing, she jumped off. The doors shut behind her. She turned back. The thugs, now just a foot away, stood on the other side of the doors, waving her off, laughing. The train pulled away.

Abby finally exhaled, pushing out the air that had been trapped in her chest. She took several slow, deep breaths to calm her racing heartbeat and walked toward the heat lamps to wait for an eastbound train, while the passengers who had exited from other cars headed down the stairs off to her right. She hit the giant red button inside the enclosure and watched as the coils in the lamps above began to turn red. Calmed by the hint of warmth, she closed her eyes for a moment and let the faint sound of raindrops pounding the street below fill her ears. She pushed her hands deep into her trench pockets and cursed her rejection of the gloves, hat, and umbrella that had been perched by the front door this morning. A forty-degree day in January had seemed balmy, but now it felt more like thirty.

She stared at her watch and began weighing her options. At this point, it would take another ten or fifteen minutes to get back to the Loop, and then she'd have to wait for the Brown Line. It would be another twenty-minute ride and a five-minute walk home. It was no use. She would just go back to the office and hope for an available cot in the library. Like this train ride was just a break—a little joy ride. Maybe it would all seem funny tomorrow.

The sound of laughter came out of the distance to her left. At first, she could not see anyone. Much of the platform was unlit. But as the voices got louder, a group of about ten men came out of the darkness. She saw their silhouettes—the baggy clothes and the occasional reflection of light on gold chains. She held her purse tightly and looked away, panicking with all sorts of preconceived notions. She quickly countered herself not to assume the worst. "Not everyone is a criminal," she quietly repeated. But as she stood under the lamps, encased by three panes of glass, she felt like a department store display, waiting for observation.

She could feel them coming closer. The animated laughter, whispers, and high-fives told her that she was the subject of discussion. Stepping out of the enclosure, she peered west down the tracks for any sign of an approaching train. Nothing.

This was bad. "Don't just stand here and wait for an attack," she instructed herself. She walked with false confidence toward the stairs.

"Oh baby, don't go!" one yelled out. Others laughed.

Abby flew down the stairs, through the turnstile, and onto the street. Once outside, she could practically hear her thumping heartbeat. This was beginning to seem surreal. A quick scan of the neighborhood created more panic. The rain continued, but it was quiet—and not a cab in sight. Abby looked at her watch—11:40 p.m.

Standing under the stairwell for shelter, she flipped open her cell. *Low battery.* She hit the speed dial for David's cell. He was still number one on the phone and she didn't know who else to call. But after several rings and no answer, she closed the phone. The stairs above her began to shake from the pounding of feet on metal. It was time to move.

Abby crossed the street and began walking east toward the city. The tracks ran above Lake Street, and, at least downtown, Lake was a major road, riddled with businesses. There had to be a bar or liquor store or something that was open at this time of night. She hurried past a few industrial one-story buildings and a closed auto shop, before stopping for the traffic light at the end of the block. She wiped her now-fogged glasses and surveyed the street. It was like a ghost town. Streetlamps created only small halos of light. The train tracks above cast a shadow, adding to the darkness.

She knew she had gotten off at the Cicero stop, but that meant nothing. The stoplight changed and she kept moving. Doorways, blocked by heavy iron gates, were chained and locked, and windows were covered with lease and rent signs and plywood boards.

Two blocks later, Abby was soaked and shaking. She had given up trying to cover her head with her purse. She stood in what felt like an abyss. There was nothing. No people, no open businesses, no signs of life. The rain continued— thin now, but relentless. She stopped at a side street and looked north. A big piece of plywood with hand-painted red letters—"Reggie's Bar & Grill"—hung from chains off a balcony on the east side of the street about a block up. She ran toward the sign.

The building looked like it might have once been something special, a nice old brownstone with great architectural details. Buildings just like it, million-dollar properties, were peppered throughout Lincoln Park, the neighborhood she rode through every day while on the Brown Line, but this one, sandwiched between two boarded-up buildings, looked worn down by decades of neglect. A neon "Open" sign was lit in the front window. She quickly crossed the street.

A handful of people, mostly older, immediately turned to Abby as she entered. But after catching the glance of one woman, Abby realized she should not assume any kind of sorority. The woman scanned Abby from head to toe and turned back to her friends. Within seconds, everyone had resumed their conversations. Abby looked around at the folding chairs, the cracked plaster walls, the stained floor, the plywood bar, the lack of television or pool table. The place was homemade. A couple of old sports posters adorned the walls—the Bears in some Blues Brothers–inspired look and a Michael Jordan poster from the nineties. Abby hadn't even heard of the Bears or the Bulls back then, she realized. In 1991, she was finishing high school in Atlanta and just starting her focused quest for this life. Look where that got me, she thought.

Abby walked to the bar, noting the "Obama for Senate" placard propped up behind the vodka bottles, and wondered if her black friends became this anxious when they were the sole reps of their race in a room. She was sure it happened all the time, and it never seemed like a big deal. Now she felt it was. She was under the spotlight again.

There was no bartender in sight. Abby flipped open her cell. It wasn't on. She hit the power button. *Charge battery. Good-bye.* The phone died.

"Damn it," she whispered.

The faces of Martin Luther King and Malcolm X, both framed and covered in cracked glass, looked at her from their perch behind the bar.

An old pay phone hung on the wall back by the bathroom sign. Abby dug through her purse for change and headed to the phone. But after picking up the receiver, she went blank. She didn't know who to call. David was either asleep or at the new girlfriend's or maybe playing a gig. Besides, she couldn't call him. It had been five months. And now there was someone else. Abby strained to think of someone else she could call. This felt like an emergency— the kind of situation where you can call a friend for a rescue. But then again, maybe she had just been stupid and paranoid and racist. And it was all her fault. She never should have left the office.

Sarah, Abby's closest friend at the firm, was her only option. But Sarah had just moved in with her fiancé. Abby dialed 411 and asked for a listing for Rick Baker in Chicago. After a brief pause, the operator responded, "There are fifteen listings. What street, please?" Abby had no idea. "Fuck!" she said out loud. "Sorry," she mumbled into the phone before hanging up. She stared at the keypad. Calling her mother in Georgia or her best friend in New York would not help things. She dialed David's cell. After three rings, his voicemail picked up.

"David, I'm sorry. It's Abby." She paused, wondering what she could even say. She chose the path of calm and confident. "I'm in a jam and didn't know who to call. Uh, hope I didn't disturb you. Take care. Sorry again for calling so late." She shook her head in frustration for calling him again. Her mantra, *Move on*, filled her head.

She stared at the receiver for guidance and noted the Bluebird Cab sticker on the wall in front of her. Yes! But then she remembered that she didn't know where she was. She had turned off of Lake Street onto some side street when she saw the bar sign. Her stomach turned in knots. She hung up the phone and went back to the bar. Most of the people had cleared out. She sat down to gather her thoughts.

Where is the goddamn bartender? Abby's internal dialogue was reaching a scream. Trying to appear calm, she searched through her purse again—for nothing in particular, but the nervousness made her want to do something with her hands, and it was better to look busy. It would have been a good cigarette moment. She hadn't smoked since law school, when she smoked so many cigarettes while studying for the bar that she disgusted herself into stopping cold, but she thought it would make her look tough and confident—just what she needed right now.

Two people got up and left. An older, white man came up to the bar and sat two stools down. She looked around the near-empty room. It seemed like a good time to turn on the southern charm. She turned to the man with a smile and dialed up the accent. "Excuse me, sir. Do you work here?"

"Nope." He smiled. His teeth were as neglected as the building. He inched closer and moved his hand on the bar toward her. His long, dirty nails tapped the counter. She could smell the liquor seeping from his pores. "You need some help?" he offered.

"Oh, thank you. I'll wait for the bartender," she replied with unconvincing optimism.

Feeling his stare, Abby ranted in silence. What kind of plan is this? Stop staring at me, old man!

This was a mistake. She needed to get back to the train station. Those guys would be gone by now. She jumped out of her seat and headed for the door.

Abby tried to run but it was more of a jog as she held tight to her briefcase and purse and focused on keeping her two-inch heels from flying off. She passed a woman with a polka-dot umbrella, who was casually strolling down Lake Street. Abby nearly knocked her to the ground as she ran by.

"Bitch!" the woman yelled. Abby offered a small "Sorry!" over her shoulder, without slowing down. It took a second for it to register, but the outfit seemed like a giveaway—the plaid schoolgirl mini; the fishnet hose; the red patent-leather, three-inch heels. And then Abby giggled, realizing what sort of woman she might have just bumped into. It was better than crying. This was all so absurd.

In less than ten minutes, she was back at the train station. She ran to the top of the stairs, put her CTA card in the machine, and pushed the turnstile. It was locked. She looked at the readout on the machine. It said nothing. She tried again. It wouldn't work.

"*What the fuck?*" she yelled.

She looked up and saw the hours of operation—6:00 a.m. to midnight. She looked at her watch: 12:05 a.m.

TWO

TRIP grabbed the door of Reggie's and pushed it open with authority. He surveyed the room. It was just as he remembered—great potential. An old man sitting at the bar turned toward him. Their eyes met and the man grabbed his coat. Trip removed his gloves and held the door open as the man scampered out. He wasn't surprised at his ability to clear a room. Now he could get busy.

"Hello!" he called out, just to be sure.

A voice answered from the back room. "Yeah! Coming!" Trip went to the bar and sat, prepared to handle any delay. The bartender backed into the room, carrying a rack full of glasses. Trip grinned. He knew those dreadlocks.

"Sorry," the bartender offered over his shoulder. "Just doin' the dishes. We're about to close." He sat the rack on the back bar and turned toward the customer, offering his "What can I do …?" but stopped when he saw Trip.

"Hello, Leon."

The bartender backed up and grabbed the counter behind him. His gaze darted around the room. "What can I do for you, man?"

Trip tapped his finger to his lips and let the suspense build. This was fun. "Well, Leon, how about …a Stoli martini on the rocks with blue cheese olives?"

The man faked a laugh. "This ain't no hotel bar, man. I don't got that shit."

Trip erased his smile, leaned over, and commanded, "Well, maybe you better get it."

The man looked around again, probably wondering if the others had come back too. "What?"

"Leon, my good man, there's a liquor store just a mile away. Tell you what, I'll wait patiently." Trip sat back and folded his arms across his chest.

"I, uh, …"

"You don't want any more trouble, I'm guessing."

The man didn't answer.

"Don't worry, I'll watch the place for you. It's safe with me here," he offered.

The man looked around at the empty room. "Um, okay." He grabbed a jacket from the counter and went out the back, turning back several times to look at Trip.

Trip waved. "Take your time!" When he heard the back door slam, Trip pulled out his cell, hit speed dial, and barked instructions. "We're good. Yeah, hold him for about twenty minutes." He closed the phone, opened his jacket, and pulled a quart-sized ziplock bag from his inside pocket.

He placed it on the bar, put some newspapers on top, and turned to the door.

But he stopped, turned back, and stared at the newspapers. There was time. He pushed aside the papers and opened the bag for just a pinky-nail's worth. Or two.

He was wiping his nose when he heard the front door.

"Hey, baby. I thought that was you."

Trip turned toward the voice and tried to block the view of the bar with his body. "Oh yeah?"

Delia smiled. "Yeah. I saw that ass from a block back. I been looking for you." She raised one stiletto up against the door and smiled.

"Is that right?" Trip turned back to the bar, resealed the bag, and replaced the newspapers. Now he could talk.

She moved toward him in her most deliberate strut. "Well, it's been a while, but the last time I saw you, you were awfully kind to me."

He remembered well. He'd caught her doing someone in a black Mercedes near the United Center last fall. It was a great score. He loved the car, and the man's pockets had been loaded with cash and blow. And, of course, Delia had been happy to offer some service while they shared a few lines.

He leaned against the bar and welcomed the visual candy.

She caressed his chest and whispered in his ear, "I thought maybe you might be looking for some fun again."

Her voice, that breath in his ear, was hard to resist. Most of the whores were dirty and desperate, but Delia was a piece of ass. She had an innocence. Couldn't have been more than twenty. "What are you suggesting?" He could feel the coke ramping him up. He was ready for anything.

Her hands were all over him. She continued to whisper as though there were a roomful of people. "I think there's a bathroom right back there. Come on."

Trip looked around and checked his watch and smiled. He had twenty minutes. This wouldn't take more than ten. He locked the front door and followed her into the bathroom.

Delia was leaning against the stall door, unbuttoning her blouse. "So, baby, what's your pleasure tonight?"

"Well, I don't know. This is a good start, though."

She tried to take off his jacket, but he moved her hands away. "Well, how about this?" She knelt down and unzipped his fly.

Trip stood there, watching her, enjoying her tricks. But she pulled away and looked up at him. "Don't finish yet, baby. Let's both enjoy this."

He checked his watch again. "Okay." He pulled a condom from his pocket and gave it to her. She moved swiftly and then they were on the floor.

Delia began to moan. Trip was ready to finish.

"Hey, let's keep this party going," she panted.

It slowed him down. He opened his eyes and looked at her. "What do you mean?"

She offered a knowing look. "What was in the bag?"

Trip stopped moving. "What?"

"Oh, come on, baby. You know."

He tried to hide his irritation. "No, tell me."

She guided his hands to her breasts. "On the bar?" she hinted, squeezing his hands so he'd grab her with force. "Maybe we could take that back to your place and go have a little more fun."

15

He should have known. Addicts had a way of sniffing out drugs.

He stared at her breast and rubbed her hard as he processed the suggestion.

It only took a second. "Well, I don't know," he offered in a tease. "That does sound fun." He brought her leg up to his shoulder as he pushed harder.

"So, good idea?" She suddenly sounded desperate.

He kissed her leg as he rolled down her stocking and removed her spiked heel. She giggled.

"Okay, baby, but first, I need to finish." He let go of her foot and focused as he pushed harder and harder. Delia's eyes were closed and her mouth gaped open in pleasure.

Trip stayed inside her, motionless, as he readied himself for what was next. "Now," he said, wrapping the stocking around her neck, "let's see how you like this."

Her breathing became more labored, and Delia opened her eyes in confusion. Trip continued to twist the hose around her neck. She stared into his face. Her expression changed to fear. She tried to push him off, but his full weight was on her. Her legs thrashed wildly. She grabbed at his hands and tried to beat his arms away. She scratched at his coat. But she was no match. She couldn't yell. She couldn't breathe.

When it was over, he leaned down toward her ear and whispered, "Mind your own business."

THREE

TEARS welled in Abby's eyes. She crouched to the ground for stability, trying to gain control of her panic and her bladder, now begging for relief as well. Nothing, not those twenty minutes before the bar exam, not her first motion call, not even the breakup with David had created such anxiety.

She felt like she was losing it. Fuck. Okay, she just needed to breathe. Panic would do no good. No one was around.

She never should have left the office. Peter would never understand. She thought of his last comment as he'd walked out of her office at six o'clock: "You've got a spare suit, right?" They both knew it meant she was to pull an all-nighter. At the time, she'd just said, "I'll go get some coffee," having learned long ago that when a partner asked you to do something, you did it. Of course, her inability to say no was the reason that she'd spent most of her weekend at the firm and had slept only ten hours since Friday. She could just picture his face—the disappointment, the disdain, if she admitted leaving without finishing the draft.

She looked over the stair railing at the street below. It was still raining. Maybe criminals don't hang out in the streets when it rains, she thought.

She couldn't run home. It had to be at least six miles. It might as well have been sixty. She could not see anything along Lake Street from the top of the stairs. She looked north, but all she could make out were rooftops and street-lights off to the right along Cicero.

She rose and leaned over the railing for a bird's-eye view of the neighborhood. Small matchbox houses with uniformly pitched roofs lined several small streets to the west. She was desperate for a plan. She could ring the door-bell of one of those homes and ask for a phone. No. It was midnight. What if she rang some gangster's door? She couldn't get past her fear.

The bar was the only option. It wasn't too far. It had a pay phone. There had to be an owner or employee—someone who could help. "Most people are good," she assured herself.

Abby ran down the stairs and several blocks east toward the now-familiar side street for Reggie's, noting the address so she could tell a taxi where to go. Finally, the rain stopped. Things were turning around. Up ahead, someone was leaving the bar. The light by the front door lit his frame and wavy blond hair. The man was at least a block away by the time she got to the entrance. Please be open, she thought. She pushed open the bar door, praying the old man would be gone. It had been about twenty minutes.

The bar was empty, though the lights were all on.

"Hello? Anyone here?"

No answer.

She felt like a child, not knowing whether her fear of being viciously attacked or worse was unfounded. Of almost equal concern was her fear of screwing up on the motion she needed to turn in tomorrow. She had no time for getting lost, getting scared, getting attacked, and this almost brought back the tears. Worse, her nervous bladder could not be ignored. She headed for the toilet sign.

Abby pushed open the door and saw two stalls. She went into the stall directly in front of her and quickly pulled down her pants. Finally, she could breathe one sigh of relief. But there was no toilet paper. She bent down and looked under the stall to her right. She saw part of a high heel and sat up.

"Hello?" she asked. "I'm sorry, I have no toilet paper. Would you mind?"

No one responded.

"Hello?" She bent down again and saw part of a woman's leg. "Are you okay?"

The foot didn't move. In fact, it looked kind of odd.

She quickly dressed, flushed, grabbed her bags, and knocked on the stall next to her. "Hello?" The door bounced against her hand as she touched it. It was unlocked.

"Miss?" She pulled the door toward her.

A woman was slumped on the toilet with her head down, like she was unconscious. She had on only one stocking—fishnet.

"Can you hear me?" Maybe she'd overdosed. Abby crouched to the floor and looked up into the woman's face. Her eyes were wide open. Abby gasped. The woman didn't blink. She was frozen. And there was a red and purple mark on her neck.

"Oh, my God!" Abby fell back, scrambling to get up.

"Oh, God! Oh, God," she repeated, backing out of the stall.

She looked around for someone to help, someone to take charge of the situation.

Abby ran out of the bathroom, threw her things on the bar, and went around behind it to find a phone and call the police. The place was a mess. Open bottles, dirty glasses, full ashtrays, newspapers, dish towels. She didn't see a phone anywhere. She tossed the dish towels and papers aside and shoved some glasses out of the way in her search. Finally, she saw an old rotary-style phone.

Picking up the receiver, Abby noticed a large ziplock bag filled with white powder sitting right there on the bar. What the hell? Something else to mention to the police, she figured.

She dialed 9 and waited for the dial to unwind itself. The front door flew open, slamming into the wall. Abby jumped.

Several men entered the room. They looked at her and then each other. Abby was speechless. Were these the same guys from the train? She saw the same gold chains and oversized clothes, though she assumed this was the uniform of the streets, of thugs everywhere.

The short one walked toward her with a swagger and a smile. "Hey, pretty lady. You don't look like Leon."

Others followed. "She a lot prettier than Leon," said one.

"Got that right," said another.

There were seven of them. Five got comfortable on the stools in front of her. The other two hung back by the door.

They were all in good spirits, smiling, looking ready for fun. Or something.

The receiver was still in her hand, but she could not look down at the numbers. She dropped it and moved out from behind the bar.

"Oh, hi guys. Help yourselves—I have to get going." She grabbed her purse and briefcase. The leader put his hands on her bag.

Abby stared at the man and faked confident irritation. "I have to leave." She pulled her bags away and went toward the door.

The two men by the door stepped into her path, blocking the entrance. She tried to push her way through. One grabbed her from behind, pinning her arms and lifting her off the ground, while the other one ripped her bags from her grip. Abby screamed, but the man immediately covered her mouth. He was only about five foot nine, but solid, and he laughed at her struggle. The other one went to the bar and began going through her purse.

The door opened. A huge man, as black as night, maybe six foot four, built like a bouncer, entered and surveyed the situation with authority. He wore a black leather coat and a giant gold chain with a cross medallion. A thick, pink scar made a jagged line from his right temple to his cheekbone. He looked past Abby, like her being held captive was nothing, and addressed the short man at the bar. "D, what's this?"

"Hey, bro'! Just having a little fun." Like a kid busted for bullying on the playground, the short man then motioned to Abby's captor, who suddenly released her. Abby grabbed the briefcase by her feet, pushed past the giant man, flung herself through the front door, and practically fell onto the concrete sidewalk. She regained her balance and ran.

Once on Lake Street, Abby turned back to the bar. The giant man was leaving and heading her way. She turned east toward the Loop and kept running.

Sirens wailed in the distance. There were huge warehouses ahead and still no signs of life. She was heading straight into darkness. She did not know what else to do. If she turned away from the train tracks, she would lose her sense of direction. At least now, running under the tracks, she had her bearings. She passed a few solitary people, mostly men and a few women who looked like hookers or crackheads, or both.

After several blocks, she slowed to a walk to catch her breath, wiped down her fogged glasses, and looked back again. A figure about a block back was coming toward her. Within another second, she could see that he was running. She started to run again.

A convenience store appeared up ahead on the corner. She wasn't sure what street she was coming up to now, but it looked like a pretty big intersection. The store was open. She sprinted—as well as she could in her heels—and ignored a red light to run across the street. A passing car screeched its brakes and honked. Abby reached the store, grabbed the door handle, and looked back again. The man was about one block behind, waiting for a car to go by in order to cross the street. The doorbells chimed wildly as she yanked the door open with force and ran into the store.

Abby turned to the attendant at the counter, breathless. "Please help me. There's a man chasing me."

The man dropped his book. "Come with me."

He came around the counter and guided Abby to the back storage room. His reaction was immediate, as if he'd dealt with this kind of situation often. Once in the back, he took her by the shoulders and pushed her up against the wall, where she stood sandwiched between a storage shelf and some boxes. It was dark. He looked her in the eyes and put his finger to his lips, suggesting silence. He left and shut the door behind him. Abby sank immediately to a crouched position and hugged her briefcase. Like a video, images raced through her mind—that woman's dead face, the drugs, the men, her purse. It felt like ten minutes before anyone came back. It was probably three.

The door opened, and Abby held her breath as light poured into the dark storage room.

"Hey." It was the clerk. He looked calm. "He's gone."

Abby exhaled. "What did he look like?"

The clerk offered his hand to help her up. "Black guy, black leather coat, giant gold cross, big scar on his face. He looked around, bought some cigarettes, and left. He's having a smoke on the corner."

Abby tried to explain. The tears were coming, though she wiped them quickly, trying to maintain composure. It was hard to make sense. "I can't believe this is happening to me. I got on the wrong train. There was this guy, and these thugs, and then my cell phone died, and they grabbed me and stole my purse." She couldn't even say "dead body." She could barely speak. "I need to get home," she whispered. She couldn't look at the clerk, embarrassed by tears that kept escaping.

"Hey, hey, calm down." His English was good, with a hint of British influence, but his accent told Abby that he was from somewhere far away. "It's okay. I'll help you. I know this neighborhood can be scary. I spent the first two years here looking over my shoulder every five minutes. And you, well, I can see why a woman like you would be nervous around here. You're quite the spectacle."

Abby did not know whether he was trying to be funny, but she looked up at his face, and they both smiled. He put her at ease.

"It's okay. I'll get you home. Where do you live?"

"Wrigleyville."

"By Wrigley Field? You are far from home. We can't call you a cab—they won't come to this neighborhood at this hour. I live upstairs with my friend. I'll have him come watch the store while I give you a ride."

Abby hesitated. It was a generous offer, but she had never considered getting in a car with a complete stranger.

She looked at him and tried to read his face. She had spent all last summer working on these skills during her first jury trial. She sensed earnestness, maybe a hint of insecurity, a reserved quality. But he was a stranger.

He obviously sensed her concern. "Listen, it's not every day I meet a beautiful damsel in distress—besides, I'd be happy to get out of here for a while."

She took the "beautiful" comment as a way to be kind, because there was no way she looked beautiful right now. She could just imagine the mascara smeared all over her face.

She looked into his eyes. Dark, long lashes. Something about his expression was calming. "I need to call the police."

"Can you describe who stole your purse?"

She shook her head. "I don't know." She began thinking about what she needed to tell police—the dead body, the drugs, those guys. It could take a while. It could cause a scene. She just wanted to get home. For months, being at home had done nothing but depress her, but right now, she wanted to be there more than anything, to be safely behind her front gate, her locked door, her security system. She would talk to police in her own neighborhood. It was now twelve forty-five. She looked at him again, at his genuine concern.

"I guess I'll take that ride. I can figure this all out at home." He had just saved her life, after all. Abby wiped her face.

"What's your name, anyway?" the clerk asked, putting on his coat.

"Abigail."

"I'm Ali," he said, leading her out a back door that went to the alley. "Come on." He locked the store and pulled a brick from the side of the building. The mortar had fallen away and the brick was chipped away at the back. He slipped the key into the crevasse and replaced the brick.

"Quite a security system, right?" he offered with a smile. "My friend will be right down."

She tried to make conversation as he opened the door to his car, parked by the exit. "So, 'Ali,' as in 'Muhammad Ali'?" What a stupid comment, she immediately thought.

"Well, I'm no boxer," he laughed. "It's Ali Rashid."

Abby nodded. He seemed harmless, and as he had alluded, he wasn't an intimidating figure—maybe five foot seven, barely taller than Abby, and probably 140 pounds. She felt safe. "Can you get to Ashland?"

"No problem."

"Okay. You can take Ashland north all the way to Belmont, and then turn right. I'll show you from there." This was enough information to keep Ali going for many miles and probably ten or fifteen minutes, so she took off her glasses to rub her eyes, rested her head, and stared out the window, hoping he would not want to make conversation during the ride home. The evening's events already seemed like a bad dream. She just wanted to pretend it had never happened.

"So what do you do?" Ali asked after allowing silence for a couple of miles.

"I'm a lawyer."

"Ah, yes. You argue to judges, then?"

"Sometimes." It sounded more interesting as a one-word answer, and Abby didn't feel up to explaining that most lawyers like her spent a lot more time in their offices, dealing with mounds and mounds of papers, than they did arguing to judges.

"I was a chemical engineer in Iraq, but no one would hire me when I got here. I had to start over."

"That's too bad." She tried to focus on Ali and his story. It was better than thinking about that dead woman's face, those men and their laughter, the drugs. She closed her eyes hard, trying to erase the images.

Ali continued. "Yeah, but then I thought I'd live the American dream and be an entrepreneur!"

Abby gave him a half smile. She was exhausted. She looked back out the window for signs of home.

"And it's been pretty good." He obviously didn't need her for the conversation. "It's been tougher since 9/11, of course. I mean, now everyone from my country is a possible terrorist, right?"

She turned to him and cracked a nervous smile. He was obviously used to the fear. His monologue continued, and she offered slight responses to suggest she was listening.

The Dunkin' Donuts and Linens 'n Things appeared up ahead. Chain stores, the comforts of home. She began thinking about the large coffee and warm blueberry muffin she'd pick up in the morning. She needed to be up and out in about five hours.

"You are not from Chicago either, I imagine."

"No."

"You have just a hint of an accent … like … maybe you're from the South?"

Abby nodded. "Georgia."

"Where is that?"

"Pretty far away, out east, about a fifteen-hour drive from here."

"You must miss your family."

Abby continued staring out the window. "I do."

"Me too."

She advised Ali to head north on Clark and soon saw people on the street and her favorite restaurant, Mia Francesca's, up ahead.

"You can let me out right here." She was already grabbing for the door handle.

Ali's arm shot out across her chest. "Wait a second," he said.

Abby's whole body tensed.

Ali pulled back and smiled. "You look like you're going to jump. We're still on Clark. Let me take you all the way to your place."

"Actually, I live right up here on Roscoe, just down the block." Abby was pointing east. "It's one-way heading west, so it will be much faster if I just jump out here. Really."

"No problem. Let me just pull over," he said. "You're obviously relieved to be home."

"You have no idea," she said, as he pulled to a complete stop.

Finally sure that he was going to let her get out on Clark in the midst of people and streetlights, she was overwhelmed with gratitude.

"I can't thank you enough for taking me home. Please give me your address, so I can send you some money for the ride."

"Don't worry about it."

"No, really. I insist on repaying you. Please."

He looked around the car. "Well, here's a flyer from the store," he said, grabbing a coupon from the back seat. "The address and number are at the bottom."

"Great. I'll be in touch."

"Take care, Abigail," he said with a tone that sounded like he never expected to hear from her again.

She got out and leaned back into the door. "Thanks again, so much." She slammed the door and watched him drive away.

ABBY trudged to her townhouse, weighed down by physical and emotional exhaustion. She would have to ring Mrs. Tanor next door in order to get in. It was now after one o'clock.

The buzzer on the gate was disarmingly loud. Abby looked up to the second-floor windows of all the other units, fearing that all the neighbors' lights would immediately come on. A faint and scratchy "Hello?" came through the speaker.

"Mrs. Tanor, I'm so sorry to wake you. It's Abby. I've lost my keys and I can't get in."

"I'll be right down, dear." The buzzer went off again, releasing the heavy iron gate so Abby could enter the courtyard. When Abby reached her front door, Mrs. Tanor came out in her trademark floor-length nightgown, matching robe, and fuzzy slippers. It was the uniform Abby had come to expect any time before eight in the morning or after eight at night.

"Is everything okay, Abby?"

"Oh yes. I had a really late night at the office and I misplaced my purse."

"Honey, you look wet. Were you crying?"

"Oh no. I got caught in the rain. I'm just a mess. I'm so sorry to have woken you, but I'm so grateful that you have my spare."

"That's what neighbors are for. Get some rest, dear." Mrs. Tanor unlocked Abby's door and gave her the key. She still had that worried look, the one she'd had when David moved out. She was never satisfied by Abby's brief explanations. But Abby was never willing to share more, for fear of the motherly advice she was sure would follow.

"Don't worry, Mrs. Tanor. And thanks again. Goodnight."

Abby headed inside and pulled out the three-year-old laminated neighborhood information sheet Mrs. Tanor had presented her when she and David moved in. She found the local precinct's number and took a wine glass down from a cupboard, hoping the police and the wine could calm her nerves enough so she could get some sleep.

FOUR

MARCUS watched as officers went in and out of Reggie's. There were three cop cars on the street. Neighbors had streamed out of their homes to find out what was going on, and Marcus blended in with the crowd. An ambulance pulled up, without lights or noise, and parked in front.

They all watched as two EMTs carried a covered body out on a gurney and pushed it into the back of their vehicle.

He had waited just beyond the entrance to the convenience store for about ten minutes, smoking a cigarette and watching the door, but the girl never came out. And now, watching the scene at Reggie's, he didn't think he'd get any answers here either. He would have to find out more tomorrow.

"Hey, dawg!" Marcus turned to see Darnel running up to him.

"Hey, Darnel."

"You catch up to that girl?"

"No."

"Too bad. Look like that coulda been fun."

"Yeah. So, what happened here?" He gestured to Reggie's.

"Dude, we were in the wrong place at the wrong time. You got out just in time. Maybe two minutes after you left, we heard sirens. Some of the boys headed out the front. Little D and I ran out the back. The place was surrounded in minutes. Looks like some bad shit went down in there."

"Whatchu mean?"

"Fuckin' dead body, man. Drug bust too, I think. Saw some cop carry out a big ziplock o' smack."

"Huh. And you didn't know nothin' 'bout that?" Marcus was doing his best older-brother-style grilling.

"Nothin'! I swear! We just got there. Saw the white girl behind the bar, and we was just playin'." He chuckled then. "She was scared shitless, dude. That's when you came in."

Marcus gave him an unconvinced look.

"Swear!" Darnel held up his hand.

"All right. Well, I got to head."

"Yeah, me too. 'Night, Marcus." They did the handshake and parted ways.

Marcus walked another two blocks and headed west on Colfax to his apartment. He pulled out the five keys it took to get in and climbed the stairs to the third floor.

His sparse, beaten-down apartment greeted him with typical silence. He should have brought Lucy, he thought for the hundredth time. She always ran to the door like a dog would, and rubbed up against his legs. At the time, he couldn't bear the reminder. But it was hard to walk in the door without thinking of that damn cat.

The apartment didn't look much different than it had seven months ago when he moved in, other than the mounds of papers and files that now covered the coffee table. There was no point in trying to make it homey. It would never be home.

He opened the fridge, surveyed the leftover take-out containers, and grabbed a Budweiser. Moving some papers around, he found a pen and took some notes about the evening. There wasn't much to say. He sat back and closed his eyes. The silence of this room, even of the street outside sometimes, was suffocating. New York was always loud. Every minute of every hour of every day there was something going on down on the street. Horns, cabbies yelling, music, metal trashcan lids, dogs, even screeching cats. Here, he heard only sirens in the distance and the occasional argument from his neighbors next door.

He undressed, brushed his teeth, and caught a glimpse of himself in the mirror. The scar was changing colors. It was less pink now, healing. He wasn't healing. Without even closing his eyes, he could still see the smoke, the tears, the screaming, that deafening crack. The day his world imploded. He touched the discolored pink skin that would forever remind him, and his eyes filled with tears. He closed them hard, shook out his hands, like he could rid himself of the thoughts, and headed for bed. He watched TV until he couldn't keep his eyes open any longer.

FIVE

ABBY was running down the street, running from something, scared, confused. She heard a ring. She kept looking around to find the source. It happened again. And again. Why wouldn't it stop? She opened her eyes. The phone was ringing. She quickly sat up, rubbed her eyes, and surveyed the damage. A box of Wheat Thins and a half-empty bottle of red wine sat on her bedside table. The television was on and Matt Lauer was chatting with the crowd in New York City.

"Shit!" She jumped up to answer.

"Hello?"

"Abby!" Sarah was yelling in a hushed voice. "What the fuck? Peter just came by. Looked pissed. Said you're due in his office in a few minutes and he hasn't seen you this morning."

Abby was already out of bed, trying to pull it together. "Damn it. What time is it?"

"Eight o'clock—what's going on?"

"Fuck! I was supposed to pull an all-nighter."

"So why didn't you?"

"Oh, fuck. Fuck, fuck. I can't explain it all right now." Her mind was racing, trying to figure out how to control the situation. It was hard to focus. She spoke softly and slowly, trying to lessen the pain in her head and carefully consider her actions. "Listen, I'm never going to make it to the meeting. Please do me a favor. Tell Peter that I'm terribly sick—throwing up or something—and I'm running late. But I'll be there in an hour. My draft is on the system if he wants to review it now. Oh shit!"

"What?"

"No, I can't do that. I need more time. Please go tell Neil that he may need to pick up the slack for me."

"What? Why would you get Neil involved? That won't look good. You don't want Peter to think you're blowing him off."

"I know. It's complicated. But I have to do some things first. It's an emergency. Listen, I need to go. Thank you so much for calling."

THE hot water pouring over her felt intensely relaxing and with repeated deep breaths, Abby began her mental checklist for the day. She had to call her credit card companies. The police had emphasized that she needed to act quickly regarding her finances. They didn't seem too worried that anyone would come find her and rob or kill her, but she was also going to call a locksmith right away. With house keys and her drivers' license in the hands of those criminals, she couldn't feel safe, and as the wine had kicked in last night, her imagination had gotten the better of her. She tossed and turned and drank until at least four in the morning, wondering whether the thugs in the bar had murdered that woman and whether they were now after her, or whether they were just guys who thought it would be fun to find her and rape her, or whether the man who chased her was a drug dealer and was searching for her.

Now, under the vise grip of her pounding headache, combined with the hot water attempting to shock her system into a new day, some of her fears sounded pretty far-fetched, and she just wanted to try to forget all of it and fix things at work. The officers last night had been comforting. They had not criticized her for coming home before calling, and they assured her that the information would be passed on to the appropriate district. Another officer would probably contact her to follow up, but for now, she had done all that could be done.

A LITTLE more than an hour later, Abby sat on the train, looking out at the rooftops of the neighborhoods she knew so well, and wondered what to tell Peter. This was bad. Peter was a hothead on a good day. He would blame her for trying to go home last night. Neil had probably stayed all night. That's what any dedicated lawyer, certainly anyone nearing partnership, would have done. She leaned up against the window and looked out at the neighborhood. She pictured the conversation and thought she'd come off looking like an idiot. Being sick seemed better. That woman's face, the blank stare, kept popping into her thoughts, and Abby shook her head, trying to erase the image. She looked up at the brown chart over the door and realized she couldn't read the stops.

She'd forgotten her glasses. It only took a second for her to remember: She had left them in Ali's car.

ABBY waved at the receptionist without an explanation and headed for her office. It was now quarter to ten and life appeared to be business as usual. Like last night never happened. Just a bad dream. The mail guy was rolling the cart down the hall, stopping at all the in-boxes with the new daily dose of stress, and several paralegals and secretaries were gathering in the break room for coffee and whatever sweet treat might have been brought in for another birthday. Abby slowed as she approached Peter's corner office and strained to listen for voices inside, praying he wasn't there. She rushed past the empty office, turned the corner down the south hall, and made it to her office without being spotted. She hoped to find a note or an e-mail or voicemail from Peter berating her. At least then he'd have gotten the initial rage out, and she could go from there. But there wasn't anything. No voicemail, no e-mail, no notes. She tried to pull up the draft motion, but she couldn't. The document was open on someone else's computer.

She checked her e-mails and saw one from Neil. When she opened it, she cringed. It was actually from Neil to Peter, but he had blind-copied Abby. *"Don't worry, Peter. I've got it covered."* The next one was from David, wondering what her voicemail message had been about last night. She sent a short reply: *"Nothing. Sorry about that. Take care."*

ABBY was ignoring all work, staring out her office window at the traffic on Lake Shore Drive, when Sarah showed up.

She entered quickly and shut the door behind her. "So? You ready to tell me what happened to you last night?" She sat in one of Abby's guest chairs before Abby had a chance to respond.

Abby had to laugh. "What's this?" Sarah had gone from jet-black hair to platinum blond overnight. Abby was used to Sarah's tricks. She was a master of adding funk to an otherwise conservative pinstripe suit, but now she was going even further.

Sarah laughed. "What do you think? I thought the blond might be fun for the wedding!"

"Sure!" Abby couldn't imagine changing hair color with the ease of changing a sweater, but that's what was fun about Sarah. "You'll be like Marilyn Monroe. Oh, and I love the red."

Sarah's bright red lipstick was a perfect match for the red satin blouse that was trying to get out from under the black suit. "Yeah, blondes do more red, don't they?" Sarah pretended to ask. "So, anyway," she leaned forward, obviously bursting for a good story.

Abby sat back. "I'll tell you all about it, but not right now. I'm just trying to dig myself out around here," she said, acknowledging the piles of work on her desk. Sarah would enjoy the drama, but she would chastise Abby for working that late to begin with, and begin her diatribe regarding Abby's priorities. Sarah would have found a way to turn down the assignment. She believed all-nighters were the result of disorganized partners and she'd rather leave their messes to be cleaned up by over-eager beavers. Of course, such comments always made them both laugh since they both knew Abby was one of those over-eager beavers. But Sarah had always been blunt with Abby. Her personal life came first. She didn't care about partnership. She'd do good work and keep clients happy, but she had no fear of refusing work. Lawyers like that didn't last, but Sarah only cared about paying off her law school debt with a fat big-firm paycheck. She had no intention of submitting to a lifelong sentence. Abby wasn't in the mood for the lecture.

"That assignment for Peter took over the last seventy-two hours of my life. You know how things just pile up," Abby added, while checking her clock. It was now lunchtime.

"So, no lunch, then?"

"Not now. I've got to go see Peter and try to explain."

"Well, I'm curious as hell, but obviously you seem okay now, so I'll be an adult and let you decide when to tell me." They both chuckled. When it came to juicy stories, Sarah was like a kid at the candy counter, begging for more.

Sarah began to stand, but stopped, sat back down, and leaned forward. "Hey, I'm sure this isn't a good time to do this, but I've been anxious to catch up with you today for another reason."

"What is it?"

"I need to tell you something." She gave it a dramatic pause. "David and that girl are engaged."

For a second, Abby tried to remain cool. It would never work. She was too sleep-deprived. She swiveled her chair toward the window as the tears began and wiped her face over and over and tilted her head back, as if she could stop the leak.

Sarah continued. "I hope you don't think it's terrible for me to tell you this right now. I know you're swamped and you look tired, and I don't even know what happened last night. But I just thought that you are bound to run into him, especially if you end up going to court to file that temporary restraining order for Peter this afternoon. I thought you could use a warning."

"No, I know. Thanks for telling me." She was still looking at the ceiling, as if she had a bloody nose. She wiped her eyes and looked at her friend with an embarrassed smile.

"I shouldn't be surprised. Obviously, we knew he wanted to get married and start having kids. It's just that it's only been a few months. Who gets engaged to someone five months after breaking up with someone else?"

"I don't know."

"The sad thing is," Abby began while attempting some levity, "I assumed that he wasn't over me yet." She began organizing stacks on her desk, as if to move on. "So much for me being the love of his life."

"Abby, I have no doubt he still loves you. But you gave him the ring back. I'm sure he thought there would be no reconciling. And we're not getting any younger, girlfriend. He's definitely not." They both smiled, and Abby wiped her face again.

Abby's phone rang. She looked down at her caller ID. "It's Peter."

Sarah stood to leave.

"I'm leaving early for a dress fitting. Lunch tomorrow, yes?"

"Yes."

THE call with Peter, though uncomfortable, was well-timed, as it forced Abby to focus on work and put David out of her mind for the afternoon. She tried to explain herself, but before she got started, he said, "These things happen." He was not interested in hearing her excuse. He told her Neil could handle this one, so she was off the hook. Not what she wanted to hear. Getting removed from a case, regardless of the reason, was not good.

She plowed through a few of the piles on her desk for the rest of the afternoon. By five o'clock, she felt like she had put in a full day. She was exhausted. Rubbing her eyes, Abby thought of how she needed her glasses. She also needed to repay that man, Ali Rashid. Shuffling through her bag, she found the coupon sheet and picked up the phone.

"Quick Mart. How can I help you?"

"Hello, this is Abigail Donovan. Is this Ali Rashid?"

"Yes, hello." His voice made it clear that he remembered her.

"I just wanted to thank you again for getting me home safely last night."

"Not a problem. But I'm glad you called. You left your glasses in my car."

"I know. I realized that today. If you don't mind, I'd like to get those from you, but as you might guess, I'm a little nervous about coming to your neighborhood again."

Ali laughed. "It's not that bad, you know. In the daylight, you'd probably see that it's just people. It's a pretty poor neighborhood and there's a good bit of crime, but mostly good people. We've just got some crackheads here and there," he added lightly.

Abby laughed. "I'm sure that's true. I'm just a little freaked out. And unfortunately, I can never seem to get out of the office before dark. What if you came to the Loop and I took you to lunch?"

"Well, I'd be pleased to have lunch with you, but I cannot let you pay for my lunch."

"Please, I insist on repaying you for your kindness."

There was a moment of silence and Abby waited, hoping she had not somehow insulted him. Would a woman ever buy a man lunch in Iraq? She had no idea.

"Okay, that would be great," Ali finally said. "When?"

"How about tomorrow?"

"Unfortunately, I don't have help at the store tomorrow. I could do it Thursday."

"Great. Let's say twelve thirty at Italian Village. Do you know where that is?"

"That's by the Daley Center, right?"

"Yes."

"That would be lovely."

Just the sound of his voice, his sincerity, his formality, put her at ease. She was actually looking forward to seeing him again under much better circumstances.

SIX

AFTER a good night of sleep, Abby settled back into her daily routine: a full day focused on her caseload, a short dinner break with other associates in the cafeteria, followed by some Norah Jones in her office while the cleaning crew vacuumed the halls and she caught up on returning e-mails. At eight thirty, she grabbed her fourth coffee and settled in to do a bit more research for a case, planning to be out by ten. And get a cab, she thought.

She was deep in concentration when the phone rang. The call was from an outside line.

"Abigail Donovan," she said in her typical business tone.

"Abigail? It's Ali Rashid."

"Oh, hello…how did you get my number?"

"I checked my caller ID for your call from yesterday. I'm sorry to bother you so late."

"No problem. I'm working, unfortunately."

"Actually, I'm calling because I think I need a lawyer."

"Why's that?" Abby sat back, almost welcoming the distraction.

"I've been having problems with the police. They're trying to shut me down and take my building."

"Hold on." She sat forward and grabbed a pen and paper. "What happened?"

"I don't even know if I should have called you. Where I come from, you don't fight police." His fear was palpable.

"Ali, it's okay. Just start at the beginning."

"About eight months ago, the police arrested a boy for dealing drugs in my store. And then a couple of months ago it happened again. The officer said he found a bag of drugs behind the coffee maker as well." He paused. "Hello?"

"I'm here. I'm just taking notes. Go on."

"I was in the store both times. I never even saw anything happen. I've always cooperated with police, but they don't like me. They brought me to the station one time and questioned me about drugs in the store, and they asked about my legal status, and..." He stopped.

"And what?"

"They just made some jokes about deporting me."

"Are you legal?"

"Of course. But today the police officer returned and put a notice on my building that says it's been 'constructively seized' pending a civil forfeiture action."

She could tell he was reading from the notice.

"I didn't understand and protested to the officer. I said, 'This is my building,' and he just smiled and said, 'Not for long.'"

Abby circled the word *forfeiture* in her notes.

Ali continued. "I didn't know who to call. I don't know any lawyers. I don't know how it works here. I don't do drugs.

I don't sell drugs. I don't know how they found drugs here or where the boy came from who they arrested."

"Jesus."

"Can they do that?" Ali sounded like he was getting more hysterical by the moment.

Abby spoke calmly, hoping to slow him down. "I'm not sure. I really don't know much about criminal law cases. I do commercial litigation—contract disputes, product liability, stuff like that."

"I've been struggling with this all day, and then I thought of you. I hope you don't mind."

She began jotting down some names of fellow associates. "Well, this is a big firm. We don't do any criminal work, but we have some former district attorneys here. I'll ask around tomorrow for some names and see if I can get you a good referral."

"Thank you, Abigail."

"Call me Abby. Besides, you saved my life. This is the least I can do. Let's meet for lunch tomorrow, as planned, and I'll have more information for you. You can tell me exactly what happened."

After hanging up, she wondered if she should call David about this. The state's attorney's office would be a good source for criminal-defense attorney references. But just the thought of having a conversation, of pretending that she was okay about everything, was too much.

ON Thursday at twelve fifteen, Abby walked over to the Italian Village. The restaurant was packed with the typical business-lunchers along with a few tourists who had found their way over from the Marshall Field's on State Street. The hostess led Abby to the table where Ali was waiting.

Though his face was a bit of a blur until she got close to the table, she noticed for the first time that Ali was cute in a wholesome, nerdy way. He looked clean-cut, wearing a stiffly starched light-blue dress shirt and khakis. He stood as she approached the table. His smile revealed perfectly straight, bright white teeth and his obvious relief mixed with embarrassment. The familiar eyes made her feel instantly comfortable. They began with polite hellos, Ali returned Abby's glasses, and they ordered their drinks. He sat forward and shared his tale in a hushed tone.

"Abby, I feel like all of a sudden, out of nowhere, the whole life I've been building here is going to be destroyed."

Abby pulled a card from her purse. "I asked around this morning. This guy I work with was with the DA's office for five years. He gave me the name of a lawyer who is well-known in defense circles." Abby handed him one of her business cards with the lawyer's name and number on the back.

"Is he expensive?"

"Probably."

"I don't have much money."

"Don't worry about how to pay yet. I'm sure he has creative billing options. What's most important is that you get great representation. You need to meet with him and get some proper legal advice."

"Yes, you're right. Thank you so much."

"I haven't really done anything. But I'll be happy to call him and give him the heads-up that you'll be calling."

"Okay, that would be wonderful."

Abby sat back then and offered a smile. "Try not to worry. This will get sorted out." She had no idea if it would get sorted out, but she didn't know what else to say.

Ali nodded in agreement and caved into silence, scanning his menu.

They ordered pasta, and Ali quickly returned the subject to his store. "Abby, do you understand this law? Taking my building when I have done nothing wrong?"

"I don't know as much as the lawyer you should call. I do know that there are two ways police take property—criminal forfeiture and civil forfeiture. In criminal, they go after someone's property after getting a criminal conviction. In civil actions, the case is actually against the property, so it doesn't matter if the owner is proven guilty of anything. Often, the owner isn't even arrested."

"But how can that be?"

"I know it seems crazy. I researched it years ago in law school. The theory is that the property is an instrument of the crime—in this case, I'm guessing drug trafficking—and so it's the property's guilt at issue."

Ali shook his head in amazement.

"It's weird, I know."

"So, it doesn't matter if I'm innocent?"

"It depends. There are usually innocent owner defenses in these types of cases, but again, Ali, I'm not qualified to tell you whether this is a weak or a strong case."

"I used everything I had to buy that building. If I lose that, I lose everything."

"You own the building?"

"Yes. I bought it several years ago. It was actually pretty cheap at the time because it was so run-down. But I've fixed it up. Last year I replaced a lot of windows and repaired the roof. Now it's probably in the best shape of the buildings on the block."

"And you have a roommate?"

Ali smiled. "Yes, his name is Miguel. We've lived together for three years now. He's like my only family in this country."

"Well, try not to worry, Ali. I'm no expert, but this attorney that you're going to call, I'm sure he'll be able to ease your mind." She then looked at her menu to avoid his eyes.

She wasn't an expert, and it was possible that the laws had changed in the last six years, but what she knew was disturbing. Seizing property was a great moneymaker for police departments and the system was not set up to protect people like Ali. Abby looked at him as he buttered his bread. She could tell he was worried.

"As soon as I get back to the office, I'll call that attorney, Ted Gottlieb, and advise him that you'll be calling. And don't wait to call. It's important to get someone working on this right away."

Ali nodded at her instructions.

"Oh," Ali added, "there's something else I should tell you. The same officers who appeared yesterday with the notice were in my store on Tuesday also, asking about you."

"What?"

"They had a picture of you. Looked like an ID card of some sort?"

"Really? What did you say?"

"Actually, I lied. I got nervous because I realized that you might have committed a crime, which would mean that I had helped you escape somehow."

"Don't worry. I didn't commit a crime. But I did stumble upon a crime scene. And I ran away because I was scared." Her mind instantly returned to the dead woman's face. "The police must have found my purse—that would actually be a relief. So I guess there's no reason to worry. I've already given a statement about everything I saw."

"Were you at Reggie's?"

"How did you know?"

"Well, word in the neighborhood the next day was that police pulled a dead prostitute and drugs out of there."

"Yes. I found her. I went in there looking for a phone, but before I could call for help, this gang came in and I ran." Abby took a sip of tea and added sarcastically, "What a great night."

Ali sat back and smiled. "Well, I feel like it was a great night anyway. I met this lovely woman who, as it turns out, may be my guardian angel."

"Thank you. I think I was pretty lucky to have met you too."

WALKING back to her office, Abby was struck by Ali's kindness, her good fortune in meeting him, and the bizarre string of events that led to their meeting. She felt a sudden fear for Ali. He felt like a friend. More than a friend, really. Now he was in big trouble. She knew well enough that he could actually lose his building over the drug bust. She began to recount all those cases she'd researched years ago. The details were still in her mind: the woman who lost her car because her husband solicited a prostitute while driving it; the parents who lost their home because their son secretly grew some pot on the property; the yacht company that lost one of its boats because a single joint had been found on board after a renter had used the boat. There were countless tales of innocent owners losing property. Antiquated laws, re-energized in the seventies to combat the "war on drugs" that only gained momentum as law enforcement realized the power and revenue created in taking property. It had infuriated and baffled her back in law school when she was simply focused on writing a good law review article. Now, as she came face to face with a potential victim, she just felt scared for him. Her cell phone rang, and she stopped in mid-stride to answer.

"Ms. Donovan?"

"Yes?"

"This is Officer Reilly. I got your number from Officer Tunney out of the twenty-third district."

"Oh, yes."

"He sent me the police report regarding Monday night. We appreciate your cooperation, and we'd like to ask you some more questions. Also, I believe we have your purse."

So this was the same officer who'd served notice on Ali.

"Oh, sure. And I'm so relieved about my purse. Does that mean you've arrested the men who took it?"

"We found the purse at the scene, Ms. Donovan. There was no one there."

Something about his tone put her off.

"I don't see any cash in here, but otherwise, I'm guessing it's all in order. Wallet, keys, ID. Can you come to the station?"

"Of course, but can I come tomorrow? I've got a full day and a required work function at five."

"Well, we do have your statement, so I suppose we could wait until tomorrow."

"Thanks so much. And where is the station?"

"Pulaski and Division."

"I'm a little nervous to come to that area. Could we meet somewhere else?"

"We'd really like you to view some mug shots and see if you could identify anyone you might have seen that night."

"Oh. I guess that makes sense."

"Why don't I pick you up at your office and bring you in? No reason to feel nervous when you have a police escort."

"Yes, except, of course, I'll feel like a criminal," she added lightly, envisioning herself getting into the back of a police car in front of her office.

"Well, Ms. Donovan, there has been a crime. We need your cooperation."

"Of course."

"Why don't I come to your office tomorrow at noon and bring you in? I'll give you a lift back to the office afterward."

"Okay, that would be great." She wondered if that was standard procedure.

After lunch, Abby stared at the Dalcon Laboratories interrogatories for about two hours. She read the inquiries, drafted responses, stared at the computer screen, lost her thought, and tried again. It happened over and over. She decided to put it off and turn to her correspondence. The same thing kept happening. Her mind was wandering. She couldn't get Ali and his new problems out of her head. She dialed David at work twice but hung up both times.

ABBY was staring out the window when Sarah popped her head into Abby's office.

"Hey, you ready?" Her lips were a fresh coat of dark purple that matched the burgundy knit sweater clinging to her shape. She looked ready for a night on the town.

"For what?"

"Where is your head these days, girlfriend? We've got the associates' dinner tonight."

"Oh, yes, of course. Is it time to go?"

"Yeah, let's just freshen you up for the brown-nose fest."

Abby laughed. She always looked like she'd been rolling around on the ground by the end of the workday. She habitually played with her hair and rubbed her eyes while researching, ruining her makeup. Her hair was now in a loose bun, held up by a pencil.

"Okay." She grabbed her purse and pulled a small mirror out of the drawer. "Oh, jeez, look at me!"

Sarah came around behind her like a hairdresser and pulled the pencil from her hair, allowing it to fall to her shoulders. "Relax. Just brush those gorgeous auburn locks of yours, and here, have some lipstick." She offered her burgundy color.

"Uh, not so much," Abby laughed, pushing it away.

"Okay, so maybe it doesn't go with your hair. Here," she pulled another from her bag, "a beautiful nude for the natural beauty."

It was perfect. "Thanks."

"I heard Peter say he'd be coming."

"Ugh. Whatever happened to 'associates only'?" Abby dreaded seeing him. If she ignored him, it would probably be bad, and if she tried to make conversation, it would be terrible.

"Who the hell knows? I've seen at least three partners today who plan to attend. The Neils will be tripping over themselves. We should bring a wet nap for their shit-laden noses."

Abby laughed. They had made Neil a description of all the up-and-coming, hundred-hour-billing, born-to-schmooze go-getters. "Well, if nothing else, free cocktails and a three-course meal," Abby offered as she turned off her computer and grabbed her coat.

Sarah did a final lipstick check. "Damn straight. I'm ready for some good vodka. What do you think—cosmos?"

"No, ma'am." At work functions, Abby always stuck to white wine and wouldn't dream of having more than a couple of drinks for fear of letting loose in front of the wrong people. Sarah did not share her burden and always relished getting tipsy and telling people what she really thought— about Republicans, religion, the firm, lawyers. It was entertaining to watch.

They took a cab to Bistro Margot on Wells, where they were ushered upstairs for cocktails. Abby scanned the room for anyone with whom she'd care to catch up. There had once been several associates Abby would have considered friends. When they'd joined the firm after law school, it was like a group of pledges, all green, starting out together. But as the years had passed, most of her class had left, either for other firms, career changes, or family issues. She and about four others from her class remained. They each worked eighty- to one-hundred-hour weeks and, other than the chitchat at dinner in the cafeteria, kept to themselves. There didn't seem time for friends anymore. She noticed some younger associates. They were still green and giddy about their jobs. Too cheery. Then there were the Neils and a few quiet lateral hires that kept to themselves. And Sarah. Thank God for Sarah.

Sarah, now at the bar, waved Abby over. When Abby arrived, Sarah handed her a cosmo and cut her off before the protest. "Just drink it, *b-e-otch!*" She was bursting. "Okay. I've been mature about this long enough. There's no one here we need to talk to. Tell me what the hell happened on Monday night."

Abby smiled and acquiesced. "Well, you remember how it was raining on Monday?"

"Yeah?"

"And you know how you can never find a cab when it rains?"

"Yeah?"

"Well, when I gave up on pulling the all-nighter, it was like eleven o'clock. I was so wiped. I'd spent the whole weekend on that damn brief for Peter, and I just knew I had to get a few hours of sleep."

"Sounds reasonable."

"When I didn't see a cab, I decided to take the L."

"Okay."

Abby continued on with all the highlights. Sarah's jaw dropped and she gasped at the details. Abby realized how crazy and unbelievable it all sounded. She needed to keep it that way. To think of them as characters in a play. That was the only way to keep that woman's face and those men out of her dreams. She and Sarah toasted to her safety and tried to joke about her saga.

"Hey, who's that tall drink of water?" Sarah asked. She was pointing to a man talking to some of the younger associates. Thirty-something, tall, maybe six foot two, with wavy dark hair and some funky glasses, or so it seemed from his profile.

"I don't know."

"Me likey," Sarah purred. "Let's go introduce."

"Aren't you the flirtatious one, Miss 'I'm getting married in a week'?"

"Well, I'm not dead, and besides, I'm only suggesting that we say 'Hi,' O Uptight One."

"Yeah, yeah," Abby replied with a smile. She followed Sarah toward the stranger.

Sarah paid no attention to the conversation in full swing in front of her—they were first-years, after all. She tapped the stranger's shoulder, and he turned around.

"Hello there," Sarah offered. He was even better from the front. His hair was a little long on top, swooped across his forehead, and his funky, rectangular neon-green frames were a great complement to his green eyes. So Sarah's type. "I'm Sarah Voight, senior associate, Chicago office. This is Abigail Donovan," she said with a nod toward Abby. "And who might you be?"

The man studied Abby's face. "Abigail Donovan...Abby?"

"Yes?"

"It's me. Nate. Jesus, I don't think I've seen you since..."—and then his face darkened as he remembered— "Denny's funeral."

The newfound style hadn't looked familiar, but those green eyes and the dimple on his right cheek—how had she not recognized him?

"Nate!" She grabbed him and hugged hard. He hugged back like he had found a long-lost family member.

"Well, what's this reunion about?" Sarah asked.

"I'm sorry," Nate said, pulling out of the embrace and returning to a professional stance. "The name is Nathan Walters. I practically grew up at Abby's house. Abby's big brother was my best friend."

"Was?"

Abby's gaze stared straight through Nate. She was lost in thought as she muttered, "He died in high school."

"Just before graduation," Nate chimed in. He turned back to Abby and offered a subject change. "Now, are you an attorney? I would never have guessed!"

Abby smiled. She knew his comment was not meant as an insult. "Yeah, I know, but we all have to grow up."

Sarah joined in. "Are you kidding? She's the golden girl—definitely one of our best and brightest."

Abby nudged her friend. "Shut up, Sarah."

Nate was all smiles. "Really? That's great, Abby. But what about your music?"

Sarah was obviously confused, but Abby turned her attention back to Nate. She was not up for a trip down memory lane and changed topics.

"You can't be a new associate then, right?"

"No, actually, I'm here to present to all of you. I'm running a legal aid clinic these days, and I'm on one of my recruiting missions to get all the fine big-firm associates to do some pro bono hours for me."

Sarah interjected. "Haven't you heard? We don't really do much pro bono around here. It was good recruiting talk, but we only get fifty hours of credit toward our billing minimum for pro bono. I did a pro bono matter a few years back and it required about two hundred hours of my time. I had to do the work, of course, but it meant that I didn't hit my two thousand–hour target that year. Advisors weren't too pleased. And now we're expected to hit twenty-one hundred a year, so it's hard for associates to get excited about doing pro bono."

"Well, not to worry, Sarah. It's Sarah, right?"

She nodded.

"I've got a way to deal with that. These are major litigation pieces, not so much small matters that associates handle on their own. So I just need the help. Warm bodies. I can rotate people in and out once they've hit their fifty."

Abby and Sarah were nodding with some enthusiasm. This sounded promising.

"And," he added with some more excitement, as some of the younger associates listened in, "I've got it on good authority that if you're getting exposure to some good skill building, like depositions or trial prep, you can get more credit toward your minimum billables. And this is really interesting stuff. A little more scandalous and intriguing than some negligence case for a spill."

"Like what?" one of the young men nearby asked.

"Like police brutality. Like immigration issues, sex discrimination."

"Nice," the kid offered with a smile.

Sarah chimed in. "Okay, so maybe we will be doing some work together." She and Abby knew it wasn't easy getting trial experience at the firm as an associate. They did all the prep, and the partners swooped in and did all the fun stuff.

"Anyway, that's why I'm here." He looked at Abby again. "Jeez, Abby, I just can't believe I've run into you after all these years. How're your parents doing these days?"

"Oh, they're great. Dad's actually contemplating retirement, and Mom's still busy trying to save the world."

Nate smiled. "Your parents are awesome."

Sarah looked intrigued by all this new information. "So, you and Abby's brother were tight? Does that mean you saw our little Abby as a preteen study bug?" she asked, laughing at her friend.

Nate smiled Abby's way. "Well, I certainly knew Abby back in the day, but I'd never call her a study bug. She was the cool one. Friends, parties, singing in a band."

"What? Abby, what happened?!"

Abby just shook her head in embarrassment, hoping the *This is Your Life* would end.

"Yeah," Nate added with laughter. "Denny and I were the geeks. All about grades and college. We were ridiculously focused little goof balls."

"And where did you go?" Sarah asked.

"Yale for undergrad. University of Chicago for law. Denny and I were going to room together at Yale, actually. In fact, I credit Abby's brother for getting me into Yale."

"Why?" both women asked.

"Abby, you must know." Nate turned to explain more to Sarah. "Denny was the one with all the big ambitions in high school. I didn't know what to do with my life. He talked about law, and getting into an Ivy League, and actually kept us both pretty focused. I was lucky to have been his friend."

Abby was getting a headache. She downed her drink and looked around for a quick exit.

"Nate, it's so great to see you. But I've got to run to the ladies' room before they round us up. Excuse me." Nate didn't have a chance to respond before she had walked away. She heard Sarah behind her adding, "Well, Nathan, we'll talk later!"

BACK at home, Abby climbed into bed and opened a book. The words on the page dealt with a dysfunctional family, but she could only focus on her own. Mom, sitting perfectly still, legs crossed, posture sure, staring at the coffin—no emotion, no sound. Dad, wiping back tears that Abby had never thought possible. And Nate, sobbing for his best friend. Though she remembered that there were hundreds who'd come out for the service, she couldn't remember more faces. The image of Denny's face was as vivid as it had been fourteen years ago. His confident smile. That look he always gave her when she was making fun of him. She never knew how he could be such a dork and so confident at the same time. The ball was rising into her throat, and the stinging behind her eyes began for the millionth time. Abby slammed the book shut, grabbed the remote, and searched for an episode of *Friends* or *Seinfeld*.

SEVEN

O N Friday morning, Abby floundered from one task to the other, unable to concentrate. She looked at the clock every thirty minutes, wondering when Officer Reilly would arrive. She hoped no one would be in the lobby at the time. She could just imagine the gossip.

By eleven thirty, she gave up on getting her own work done and focused on Ali's problems. She ran a quick search on the Westlaw database for the Illinois and federal civil forfeiture laws. Back in 1997, when she was researching these laws for school, Congressman Henry Hyde had been trying to get a bill passed to change the laws and give property owners more rights. She wondered what had come of all of that.

She found a federal statute—the Civil Forfeiture Reform Act of 2000—and the Illinois version, and hit "Print." Maybe the laws had all changed. Her phone rang, and the receptionist, Barbara, advised Abby that she had a delivery. Flowers. Abby walked to the lobby with a smile of anticipation, wondering who might have sent them, and picked up her printout en route. When she got there, Barbara was speaking to a uniformed officer. They both turned to Abby.

"Abby, this officer says you're expecting him?"

Barbara's raised eyebrow signaled her hope for some scoop. Abby ignored the unspoken request and reached out to shake hands with the officer.

Officer Reilly was tall, at least six foot four, but he didn't have an intimidating look, other than the crew cut. He looked like a true Irishman—strawberry-blond hair, fair skin, freckles, and blue eyes.

"Hello, Ms. Donovan. Nice to meetcha. You ready?"

His accent was pure South Side Chicago. Just like the mayor's. A true Chicago boy, for sure.

"Actually, I need to grab my purse. I didn't realize you were here. Barbara called me about some flowers," Abby said, turning her attention back to the desk and the small assortment of daisies and lilies.

"Oh, yeah," the officer added. "Is it your birthday?"

Abby smiled. "No." She silently read the card attached to the vase: *I feel so blessed to have met you. Thank you, Abigail, for everything. Sincerely, Ali Rashid.*

Barbara wanted the scoop. "New boyfriend, Abby?"

Abby shook her head and felt a sudden awkwardness, with the man who was going after Ali's building standing right behind her. She picked up the vase and turned back to Reilly.

"Let me just run these back to my office, and I'll grab my purse." She headed off before he could respond, but within a few steps fumbled with the printout, and several pages went sailing to the floor.

"Here. Let me help," Reilly offered, as he joined her in gathering the papers.

"Thank you. I haven't even read this yet."

"Research?"

"Yeah."

Reilly read the title of the bill out loud as he passed the papers back.

Abby didn't look at him, unsure what to say. "Thanks, I'll be right back."

THEY made small talk on the way to the station. Reilly was obviously saving the real questions for later. He asked about her heritage, talked about his own Irish roots, and mentioned that his grandparents' best friends in Ireland were the Donovans. Abby's own family had been in America for several generations, but she laughed and played along. He seemed nice.

Once at the station, Officer Reilly and his partner, Officer Trask, asked Abby to review what had happened, which she did: the train mishap, the gang on the platform, finding Reggie's, the woman, the drugs, the men, the mugging, the chase, and Ali's kindness.

"So, you know Mr. Rashid?"

"Well, yes, he gave me a ride home, and I just met with him yesterday too."

The officers looked at each other.

She knew what they were thinking. "He told me some officers came into the store and asked if he recognized my picture. I guess that was you?"

Reilly replied, "Yeah."

Abby continued. "He was just nervous. He was afraid I had done something wrong and he would be in trouble for giving me a ride. But actually, we only met again because I left my glasses in his car." Abby thought it best not to mention the legal assistance.

The officers nodded and seemed to accept her story.

She looked through three binders of mug shots, but it was fruitless. The only man she really remembered was the big one with the scar on his face who had chased her into Ali's store. And other than the scar, she didn't think she could describe him well. It had been so dark and he'd worn black. She didn't know anything about the drugs or the woman.

There were no inconsistencies with her written statement, and after about forty-five minutes, the officers thanked her for her help, and Officer Reilly drove her back to work. Abby wished him luck on the case.

THE alarm went off at eight o'clock on Saturday. Abby smacked the "Snooze" button. It happened again. She snoozed again. Three more times. Finally, she turned it off and pushed off the covers. But she couldn't get out of bed. She stared at the ceiling for what seemed like an hour, replaying her week, thinking about that night, which already seemed like a bad dream; thinking about Ali, and the real problems he now faced; thinking about David marrying that woman. It seemed impossible to think about work. Fuck it. She grabbed the covers and rolled over.

At ten, Abby finally got up. She read every page of the paper but saw nothing about the dead woman at Reggie's. She hadn't seen anything in the paper about it all week. Too many crimes to report, she figured. Just another senseless death in that neighborhood. No one cared.

She spent the day in her pajamas, listening to music and cleaning out closets. She found some of David's T-shirts, books, and CDs, and stared at the phone, wondering if she'd ever get the courage to call. She put his things in a bag and left them in the spare bedroom.

WHEN the alarm went off at eight again on Sunday, she only hit "Snooze" twice. She really needed to get to the office. There was so much to do. The Amro deposition was Wednesday. She was so behind. She sat on the edge of the bed, staring at the wall, unable to get up. Where was her drive? That will and determination that had served her career so well? That dedication that had alienated David? She fell back onto the mattress as if she weighed too much to stand. She wasn't sure if it was because of her near-death experience, her new friend, Ali, or David's engagement, but that singular focus was failing her. She finally got up and showered, but when she went into the bedroom to get some clothes, she reached for her sweatpants.

ON Monday morning, inquisitive associates, the ones who were always at the office on weekends, popped in her doorway at what seemed like regular intervals, wondering what event had finally kept her away. They knew it had to be something big—a death or a wedding—and they each hoped for a good story, a distraction, a delay from their own start to the new week. Abby brushed them off and enjoyed the surprised reactions as she told them all she had done nothing.

It was around ten thirty when the phone rang. It was an outside caller.

"Yes, Ms. Donovan. This is Ted Gottlieb. You referred Ali Rashid to me for help with a forfeiture matter?"

Abby looked at her flowers, now wilting on the desk. "Oh, yes, hello. What can I do for you?" She sat back and turned to the window, away from her work.

"Well, I met with Mr. Rashid on Friday morning. We've taken on his case, and I'm having trouble getting hold of him. I'm wondering if you have heard from him?"

"No, actually. Not since lunch last week when I gave him your name."

"Well, the prosecutors have moved forward with the in rem proceeding."

Shit.

Mr. Gottlieb continued. "I'm sorry, are you familiar? I mean they're going after the property."

"Oh, I know *in rem*—'against the thing.' In fact, I was just reviewing the reform bill on forfeiture this weekend, and it looks like there have been some improvements in the law."

"Well, that's true in federal cases, but this is an Illinois state case, and, unfortunately, the law is still pretty pro-police. The burden on the state is quite low—they only need probable cause, and they can use hearsay evidence in support."

"So any dealer on the street or person facing their own charges can give the police a statement about drug trafficking, and that'll do it?"

"Pretty much."

"And then Ali is forced to prove what? That he couldn't have known about the drugs or couldn't have done more to prevent the trafficking?"

"You got it. It's pretty difficult for an owner. In fact, as I told Mr. Rashid, relatively few owners of seized property even contest the forfeiture in court."

"Why, because they never win?"

"Because they can't afford the cost of litigation, or they fear criminal prosecution or having their sworn statements used against them in other matters."

"Ali told me he wasn't sure he could afford you."

"True, but we worked it out. In fact, I'd like to file something tomorrow that I hope will convince the prosecutor that this is not a good case to pursue."

"I'm so glad you got involved. Thank you again for taking on his case."

"Not a problem. I'm pretty confident. We just need to get this moving so he can get out from under this as soon as possible. Otherwise, these cases can drag on for quite some time."

Abby relaxed back into the chair. "That's great."

"Yes, except that I need to find Mr. Rashid. I was unable to reach him all weekend. You don't have a cell number for him? No one is answering the home phone number he gave me."

She instinctively turned back toward her desk, the location of all answers. She shuffled papers around like some magic phone number would appear. "I am so sorry, but I don't know what I can do to help." She stopped the search and looked at the lilies again. Her favorite flower. "I really hardly know him. The store phone number is all I have."

"Okay, well, if you do hear from him again, please tell him to call me right away."

"I will. And thanks again for taking on his case."

She hung up and rested her hand on the receiver. This would all work out. Ted Gottlieb obviously knew what he was doing. But what a racket. It was still baffling how this whole process was legal. She just hoped Gottlieb could reach Ali soon.

ABBY crawled into bed at ten o'clock and began leafing through her *Rolling Stone* magazine. She flipped the pages, scanning for good stories on her favorite bands and half-heartedly listened to the local news on TV. The reports were typical: fifteen seconds of information, depressing and shocking but for the fact that every day's news was intended to shock. A rape in River West, a robbery in the Loop, a semi turned over on the expressway, an apparent murder-suicide in the West Garfield neighborhood. Abby had heard enough. She grabbed for the remote to hit "Mute." Looking at the TV, she saw a picture of a convenience store that looked familiar and quickly hit "Volume" to hear the story:

"Two men who lived above a convenience store at Lake and Pulaski were found dead in their apartment early this morning. Police have determined that this was an apparent murder-suicide. One of the men, Mr. Ali Rashid, had recently been detained in relation to a drug-trafficking charge, and the government had begun forfeiture proceedings against the property. It is unknown whether there is a connection between that matter and today's events."

Abby sat up, grabbed her glasses from the side table, and stared harder at the screen, at a picture of Ali. She felt sick. And then his face was gone. The newscast moved on to the weather report.

EIGHT

"ALI is dead?" The words rang in her head over and over. She couldn't process it. She didn't know how to feel. Her stomach ached. She reached for the bedside phone, her hand trembling, but she stopped. She didn't know who to call. She couldn't even think of anyone to talk to. Both hands, as if they knew she might scream, clamped over her mouth as her head shook back and forth in disbelief, and tears fell down her cheeks. How could this happen? She pictured his face, those soulful eyes, that warm smile. It was just a week ago that they'd met.

She tossed around most of the night, unable to sleep as she recalled Ali's face, relived her night in that neighborhood, and reviewed every detail about their lunch at Italian Village. It didn't make sense.

At work the next day, she remained distracted, wondering if she should do anything about this new information. She pulled out Officer Reilly's card and dialed the number.

He answered on the first ring.

"Officer Reilly? It's Abigail Donovan. We met last week?"

"Oh, yes. How can I help you?"

"I was just watching the news last night and heard about Ali Rashid and his friend's death."

"Oh, yeah. Quite a mess."

Abby immediately imagined his dead body and the blood. She struggled to continue.

"I'm sorry, Ms. Donovan. I'm not sure how this relates to you."

"Officer, it's just that I met Ali. Like I told you. Actually, we had become friends, kind of."

"I don't think you mentioned that before."

"No. Sorry." There was no point lying now. "He told me all about the seizure of his store. I just can't believe this happened. Can you tell me anything?"

"Well, Ms. Donovan, the evidence looks pretty clear. Mr. Rashid appears to have shot his friend and then himself—"

"No!" Abby interrupted. She just didn't believe that Ali would hurt anyone, especially the man he considered family.

Reilly continued. "Perhaps he found out about his friend's drug dealing. We found a lot of drugs at his store. We'd been investigating that location for quite some time. It was a haven for trafficking, and we knew at least one of them was involved. I'm sorry, Ms. Donovan. People are not always as they seem."

Abby had nothing else to say. She was dumbstruck. She couldn't believe it. Any of it. They hung up and she immediately hit the caller ID to find Gottlieb's number to tell him the news.

Gottlieb sounded surprised but dispassionate. Perhaps his criminal law practice made him that way. He advised Abby that obviously he would quit pursuit of the matter. After all, he had no client. The forfeiture proceeding had already been instituted, and with the owner of the property dead, there was no one to come forward and fight against the process. The court would undoubtedly declare the property forfeited and auction it off.

No one seemed to care.

Abby spent the next hour searching the Internet for more stories about the shooting—anything to make sense of it. She found nothing. She stared at her e-mails and the stack of files on the desk, but she could not begin. Nothing made sense. Something about the last week's events felt important, like she needed to pay closer attention. She stared up at her framed diplomas and moot court awards. She had always known she was living a charade, pretending to be someone she wasn't. But now she wondered if she was actually sitting in that big-firm office for another reason. She would never have met Ali had she not been on that train. She would never have been on that train had she not worked at the firm. Maybe there was a reason she found herself in the middle of these two horrific and mysterious deaths.

The phone rang; it was one of her clients. She closed her eyes and shook her head as if to turn on her professional voice. She picked up the phone and defaulted into work mode.

LATER that afternoon, Abby turned to face the window and recharge. Her office on the forty-ninth floor provided a great southeast view. She soaked it up as she never before had. The Lake, Buckingham Fountain, the Planetarium, Soldier Field, the traffic along Lake Shore Drive. There was a lot going on outside her little box. She wondered where all the people on Lake Shore Drive were heading. She wanted to trade places with any of them.

By six thirty, Abby clocked her eighth billable hour and called it a day. There were still ten unanswered e-mails, a few voice messages to return, and countless projects to be done, but no one would die if she put off the work until tomorrow. And if she stayed any longer, she'd just stare out the window. She grabbed her coat, turned off the computer, and hit the light switch.

THE next morning, Abby got to the office by eight o'clock and was just beginning her routine when the phone rang. The caller ID read *J. Hadden*.

"Shit," Abby said as she picked up the phone.

"Abigail Donovan," Abby offered in her professional voice.

"Abigail. Jerry. Can you come to my office?"

"Sure. When?"

"Right now." He hung up the phone.

Fuck.

She grabbed a notepad and headed for the fiftieth floor.

"HEY, Jerry. What's up?" Abby was leaning in the doorway of his massive corner office, trying to appear casual and confident.

He didn't look up at her. "Come in. Shut the door, please."

Abby obliged. Her warm and lighthearted partner-advisor looked anything but. Unlike so many of the senior partners who often chose to tear down and rebuild associates as if they were in an army boot camp, Jerry was a great mentor. Every time she'd visit, he'd have some joke or story to share, and his big belly would shake with laughter.

There was nothing light in his expression today.

He motioned to the chairs in front of his desk. "Take a seat. Abigail, is everything okay?"

Abby obliged. "Why do you ask?"

Jerry removed his oversized glasses, revealing the painful-looking indentations they left behind. He rubbed his nose. He did not look pleased to be having this conversation.

"Abby, you have long been one of my favorites. As I've told you during past reviews, you have done stellar work here for years, and your future looks bright."

"And?"

"And all of a sudden, I'm hearing things that give me serious concern."

"What things?" Abby sat straighter in her chair, on the defense and eager to show that she would take any criticism seriously.

"Well, Peter mentioned that you bailed on an assignment recently, and that sounded out of character."

"Jerry, honestly, it couldn't be helped. I just didn't bother with my explanation because I could tell that Peter was stressed and wasn't in the mood for any excuses."

"Well, that may be, but I just hung up the phone with Steve Prince, and he said he sent you two e-mails and left you a voicemail last week and never heard back from you."

"Jerry, I'm really sorry. I'm just sort of swamped right now, and I've had some personal issues." Her voice began to trail. She knew it was sounding like a poor excuse. "Calling Steve was at the top of my to-do list today."

"Abigail, we're in the midst of a multimillion-dollar lawsuit. If the client calls you or e-mails you, I don't care what is going on in your life or in other cases. You drop everything, and be sure to respond before the sun goes down. You know that."

Abby nodded, conceding her screw-up. "I do. I do. I'm really sorry."

"Well, unless you want to be removed from that case too, which I'm sure you realize is career suicide, I suggest you get on the phone as soon as you leave here, apologize profusely, and do everything in your power to regain Steve's confidence. You're the lead attorney on the case, for Christ's sake."

"Of course. I'll go call him right now. Jerry, I'm really sorry I let you down." She was ready to escape and braced her armchair to stand.

Jerry raised his hand to stop her. "Remember, it's your job to delegate work if you get overwhelmed. It's your job to let me know if you can't find some junior associates to help you out. If you don't speak up, I can't help you."

"Thanks, Jerry. It won't happen again."

Abby walked down the stairs, silently berating herself. Fuck. Fuck. Fuck. Snap out of it, she thought. Focus. Do not lose everything over this.

Her gaze remained fixed on the carpeting as she walked down the hall. She ran right into someone.

"Jesus, I'm so sorry," Abby offered as she bent down to grab the files that had fallen to the floor.

"Well, hey there, Abby. That's quite the 'hello'!"

Abby looked up and saw Nate smiling down at her.

"Hi, Nate. I'm sorry. I was deep in thought."

"A big case?"

"Kind of. What are you doing here?"

"I've found my first warm body," he said, nodding in the direction of Becky's office, a first-year associate.

Abby leaned into Becky's doorway and waved.

"Listen, I'm so glad you bumped into me. I was just about to come find your office. I really want to catch up."

"Nate, that sounds great, but ... I, uh ..."

"You can't have lunch with me?" He was mocking her.

"It's just that—"

"Okay, I get it. It's a busy day for you. How about Friday? Unless you have a serious prior engagement that can't be broken, you are not allowed to blow me off. Dinner. An early one. I want to get home to kiss my baby."

"Excuse me?" It was an odd thing to say about a girlfriend.

He pulled out a photo. "Lizzy. She's extraordinary." Abby looked at the picture. A precious baby wrapped up in a tiny pink blanket. It was one of those hospital photos taken moments after birth.

"Oh! Wow! Nate, you're married? And a baby?"

"Yes and yes. Now let's catch up."

She couldn't resist. She had to eat after all. "Okay, Friday."

ABBY was just getting settled into work mode, with her mental checklist in overdrive, when there was a knock on her open door.

"Hey, dollface." Neil was already helping himself to a seat in her office and getting comfortable before she could respond. He leaned back and began propping his feet up on her desk. Abby shooed them off.

"Listen, Neil, I've got the Amro dep in the conference room in an hour, so I don't have time—"

"Abby, Abby. This will just take a second." And then he leaned forward like he had a secret to tell. "Word is you were escorted out of here by the police on Friday."

Looking into his pointy face, she wondered how he had such an attractive and apparently normal girlfriend. Abby rolled her eyes. She knew this would happen.

"Hot date? Or maybe you've been a bad girl?" he said in his most provocative tone.

"Is there anything work related that you need to discuss with me, Neil?"

He leaned back and settled in. "Of course, my lady. I just thought you might be interested in the status of our motion for that temporary restraining order."

"Yes. Where does all of that stand?"

"We didn't get it."

"I knew that much."

"So we just moved forward with filing the complaint, and we're hoping to fast-track it, but of course these bastards just filed a motion to dismiss."

"Seemed like there was easily a basis for a suit, from what I recall. Do you think they can get it kicked out?"

"No. I'm sure they don't think so either. They're just stalling and trying to run up our client's costs."

"Of course."

"Now here's the good news. I just came from Peter's office, and he suggested that I ask you to take a stab at opposing counsel's motion. Pull up his cited cases, see what we can do to chop up their brief."

Abby grabbed a pen and paper. "Sure. What's your timeline?"

"Well, we need to get a draft response together by next week so we can discuss what we need with the client. How's your schedule?"

"I'm busy, but I can make time. I'll take a look at it tomorrow."

"Great. Thanks, babe." She didn't even bother to cringe at the "babe." She was used to it, and it was the least of her problems right now. There was no way she could turn him down. She wasn't even sure Peter had suggested bringing the work to her. Neil had a way of pawning off grunt work. But at this point it didn't matter. She needed to get Peter back in her corner.

Neil's five-foot-five frame stood to leave. He gestured to the flowers on his way out, now wilting in the vase, and teased like a fourth-grader, "Nice flowers, Ms. Donovan. Perhaps they're from Officer Friendly?"

"Ugh. Get out of here!"

He saluted her, as though his mission were complete, and laughed aloud as he walked away.

Abby looked at the flowers. The water was starting to darken, and a few petals had fallen to her desk. She couldn't toss it.

She turned back to her mounds of files and the forty new e-mails and searched for Steve Prince's number.

THREE hours later, Abby had finished the deposition for Amro, talked to her pissed-off client, and successfully checked a few things off her to-do list. It felt good to lose herself in the tasks.

"Time for a pop-in?" Sarah queried from the door.

Abby knew she shouldn't break her rhythm, but she couldn't forget this was a big day. "Always for you, girlfriend. Come, sit. So, are you excited?"

Sarah sat on the edge of the chair. "Are you kidding? I'm freaking out. It's my last day! Tomorrow, spa treatments with my sister and mom. Friday, we pick up the dress and check on the details, and then Saturday! I've been looking up things to do on the island all morning. I just don't know if I'll ever come home."

"Please do. I couldn't last a day here without you. Just having to be here two weeks without you is going to be a bear."

"Come on. You mean that you won't replace your lunch buddy immediately? Maybe Neil is free?"

"Ha ha. We had a nice little chat this morning. I've got to do some work with him—for Peter. He talks to me like I'm working for him. Anyway, I think I'll be eating lunch at my desk until you come back to me."

Sarah returned the conversation to the wedding. "Do you know what you're wearing?"

"Actually, I haven't decided, but I've got a pretty good selection at home."

Abby had been to eight weddings in the last two years. It seemed everyone she knew was getting married. Even thinking about why she had so many dresses led her to think of David, which made her want to think of other things. She turned the focus back to Sarah.

"I'm so excited to see you in your dress and see this shindig in action. It's going to be spectacular. Your mom really knows how to throw a party."

Sarah laughed. "I know she's a little over the top, but hopefully, we only do this once, right?"

"Yeah, I just hope I get to say hello to you. With four hundred guests, you might be tough to spot!"

"Well, you know that at least two hundred of those people will be over fifty. Just keep the visual for the young 'uns.

75

And of course, I'll be in the big white dress! You'll see a few cool people from the firm who you can hang with."

"Got it. I'm kidding, you know. It sounds like a fairy tale. I couldn't be happier for you guys."

"Thanks, babe!" Funny how it sounded so much better when Sarah said it. "Now you can still change your mind if you want to bring a date."

Abby tried to speak, but Sarah held up her hand, ready to defend herself. "I just think it would be nice to have a built-in dance partner."

"It's not necessary. And really, what am I going to do, hire an escort?"

"That would be hot!"

"Yeah, right. I promise not to break down and cry or cause some scene with David and his girlfriend. Excuse me—fiancée."

Sarah smiled. "Are you going to talk to him?"

"I don't know. I think I won't make a point of it. I don't want to make them uncomfortable. But if they approach me, I'll be very sweet, of course."

"Well, back to work." Sarah stood to go. "Have you eaten lunch yet?"

Abby checked her watch. It was one o'clock. "No. Let's meet in the lobby in thirty minutes."

Working another thirty minutes now was easier said than done. The image of David standing at the front of that church next to Rick on Saturday was fixed in her head. It had been five months, but still, she wondered every day if she could have held onto him. She was not looking forward to this wedding.

NINE

WITH hands in pockets and a black knit cap pulled down over his ears, Marcus walked the littered sidewalks for ten blocks through bitter cold over to Carter's BBQ on Madison, just a few blocks west of the United Center. He looked forward to the snow. They were predicting six to eight inches over the weekend. At least then the grime and trash would be covered for a while. The neighborhood would even look peaceful.

Carter's was a good place for the neighborhood scoop. Regulars hung out the way they used to at barbershops. The typical crowd was there, bullshitting the day away. Marcus grabbed a plate of wings and took a seat at an open table.

"'Sup, Marcus?" It was Darnel, seated at the next table.

"Hey brotha." Marcus reached over for the required fist bump.

Darnel waved around the room like this was his party. "Marcus, you met these muthefuckas yet?" Everyone in the room smiled.

"I met a lot of muthefuckas lately, but none of these," Marcus offered.

"Hey, muthefuckas, this is Marcus. Moved here from New York last spring." Marcus gave them each a simple nod. "That's Rickie, Tomboy, Fat D, Mikey." Each of the men nodded as his name was called.

"Fat D, huh?" Marcus offered with a smile. The man was about six feet tall and one hundred and fifty pounds.

"It's ironic," Darnel offered with a proud nod, like he had created that one.

"So, Marcus," Tomboy began, "I got a cousin in New York. Where you live?"

"Queens."

"Oh. My boy Tyron's in Harlem. Guess you wouldn't know him."

"Oh, yeah, Tyron. I love that dude!"

"You shittin' me?"

Marcus held up a finger so he could finish the wing. He had their attention. He dropped the bones on the plate. "Yeah." They all broke out in wild laughter, and Marcus licked his fingers.

Darnel threw his napkin at Tomboy. "You dumbshit. 'Course he don't know your cousin. New York's fuckin' huge."

"So why'd you come to Chicago, Marcus?" Rickie asked.

"Just needed a change." He focused on the food.

Darnel was glad to fill them in. "He was there when the Towers came down."

Fat D spoke up. "No shit. You see that happen, Marcus?"

"Yep." Marcus didn't offer more, and they left it alone.

The bells on the door chimed as the front door was pushed open. A white man, late thirties, dressed in business clothes, walked in and surveyed the room with confidence. He went to the counter and addressed the fry cook by name, like they were old friends, and ordered a platter to go.

Darnel looked at Marcus, nodded toward the man, and mouthed, "Cop."

Marcus looked him over. He had the right air, all swagger, no fear, but the clothes weren't typical of the undercover look. They were too polished.

The room fell silent, and they all waited for the white man to leave. The man smiled, nodded at them, and left.

"Watch out for that one, Marcus," Darnel began.

Marcus turned and watched the man through the glass front. He got in a Mercedes parked illegally out front.

"Yeah, why's that?"

Mikey was quick to join in. "Crooked as they come, that's what I hear."

Tomboy stuffed a bunch of fries in his mouth and garbled, "Johnny told me that he jumped him two weeks ago." There had to be thirty fries in there. It was disgusting. He put up his index finger for a moment to chew, wiped his face, and continued. "Pulled the gun, acted like he was going to arrest him. Johnny was carrying big that day. He was on his way to Darrel's place."

The others chimed in with a knowing "Shit."

Tomboy continued. "Grabbed his entire wad and the stuff. Five large and three pounds."

"Five hundred bucks?" said Fat D.

"No, dumbshit. Five thousand."

"So, I guess I gotta worry about cops here too, eh?" Marcus offered.

They each added their own version of "Hell, yeah."

Rickie continued. "Some of 'em act like we their fuckin' ATM machines. Just pat you down, take your cash, and move the fuck on. Who gonna stop 'em?"

Marcus didn't respond.

Fat D offered his bit to the group. "Jenny said she saw that dude with Delia before."

"Who's Delia?" Marcus asked.

"You 'member last Monday they pulled a body outta Reggie's?"

Marcus nodded.

"That was Delia."

WHEN Nate called on Friday morning to confirm dinner, Abby suggested they meet at Mia Francesca on Clark at six o'clock. With snow coming, she wanted to be close to home. Plus, she had work to do. The Prince Industries case was heating up. She had to prepare for next week's depositions and deal with all the discovery that had come in from the Dalcon Laboratories case.

They ordered cocktails and an appetizer while Abby learned that Nate had married just two years earlier to a fellow lawyer, a woman he met at school. His wife was on maternity leave for six months. He shared a picture from his wallet. She looked like the girl next door: shoulder-length, straight brown hair, an Abercrombie T-shirt, a lovely smile, and not even a hint of sorrow or sarcasm. A perfect match for him. Abby couldn't believe it. She and Nate were only two years apart, but he seemed so adult. It sounded as if his life had been going according to plan: great education, great job, great girl, and now a beautiful baby. If he didn't remind her so much of Denny, she would have hated him.

Nate grabbed the bread, smearing it through the olive oil and parmesan. "I can't believe we've both been in Chicago for all these years. Both lawyers and we never connected."

Abby just grinned and nodded in agreement.

"If I had known you lived in Chicago, Abby, I would have insisted you come to the wedding!"

"I would have loved to see that." She looked at her menu then, hoping he didn't sense the false sincerity. Until now, Chicago had been a great escape from all reminders of her childhood.

The dinner was entirely enjoyable while she grilled Nate for information on his life. She found out that he lived up on the North Shore in Wilmette, in an old house, built in 1927, with a view of the lake. She laughed at the swanky address, since he'd gone into public aid work, and he joked back that it was nice to have a rich wife. Actually, he explained, she had chosen the big-firm route like Abby, but she'd also lost her parents years ago and they'd left her some money.

She watched him savor his martini, both of them enjoying this little reunion. But then he had to go and turn the tables. "What about you?"

"Brown for undergrad, DePaul for law, now working at Simon & Dunn. Not much else to it."

"I still can't believe you did it in the first place. I know it's been a long time, but I would have guessed you'd go to New York or L.A. or something—hit the big city."

"This is a big city!" Abby smiled with justification.

"Oh, I know." He continued to press. He wondered aloud about her school choices, her major, why she chose big-firm work, which firms she considered, her practice area. And, of course, he wanted to know about her love life, of which there were only charred remains.

It seemed pathetic to have nothing to share, so she told him stories of David, of their meeting in law school, and of their steamy affair that had begun almost by accident. She had chosen a study group that seemed the most focused, being older students, and it was there that she'd met David. She had assumed it would be a brief affair, but it had ended up lasting for years.

It was fun to talk about him like this. He was the best person she knew. So she gave Nate some of the highlights, like how he was nothing like the other guys in law school. David had been twenty-seven when they were first-year students. He had spent years as a musician—he played the acoustic guitar and saxophone. He had tried to make a living at it, but after five years, two bands, and six waiter jobs, he had succumbed to the "grown-up world," as he used to joke. He wasn't sure what to do, but he was smart and had always done well in school. He enjoyed reading and writing and figured that he might actually be able to find an intellectually fulfilling career, as he couldn't seem to make the creative one work out.

Nate was nodding, laughing, and enjoying her tale. Abby could tell from his expression what he was thinking: This guy sounded perfect for little Abby. She needed to set him straight.

"But we broke up a while back, and now he's engaged to someone else. In fact, I have to see him and his bride-to-be at a wedding tomorrow night."

"Oh, God. Abby, I'm so sorry. The way you just spoke of him, I would have thought you'd be next to get married."

"Yeah, well, timing is everything, and it just didn't work out."

That's what she had been telling herself for months. Of course, she didn't know what she was talking about, and it seemed like Nate could tell.

When Nate started reminiscing about Denny and "the good ol' high school days," Abby knew it was time to call it a night. The snow had started, and they walked out to a fresh inch of powder already on the ground. They hugged on the sidewalk, promising to e-mail soon and keep closer contact, and she walked up the street to her place while he waited for the valet to retrieve his car.

Abby drafted deposition questions for the next couple of hours. By about ten o'clock, she needed a break. She looked outside at the tree branches now fully blanketed with snow. Wearing a baseball cap and heavy coat over her sweats, she ran around the corner to the liquor store that sold some snacks and ice cream. It felt pathetic to be making a run for ice cream at this hour, in this weather, and on a Friday night. The streets were alive, and everyone seemed to be meeting new people or hanging with friends or having dates—acting like twenty-somethings. Most of Abby's twenties, except when she had been with David, had been spent like this. All she could think about right now was getting some ice cream. She settled on Ben & Jerry's—Chunky Monkey, of course. Tomorrow's dress had an empire waist, so she could handle a little "chunk."

Coming out of the store, she glanced across the street at a police car, briefly wondering if she'd recognize the officer inside—she'd met a lot of policemen lately. The door of Johnny O'Hagan's flew open, and a couple walked out holding hands and stood momentarily under the light before turning away from her and heading south on Clark. They both had blond hair, pulled back. Like matching Barbie dolls.

The wind picked up, and she pulled her coat tighter and walked home.

Abby settled on the couch with her ice cream and stared into the lit courtyard, watching the snow fall. She began drowning in a pool of images that kept coming at her—David and his fiancée, Nate and all that he represented, Ali, a dead woman—then, like a flash, she was back in that neighborhood, reliving her own fear, running down the street, bumping into that hooker, heading back to the bar, spotting that blond coming out.

"That guy!" Abby sat up, as if there were someone in the room listening to her. She stood and paced the floor, sorting through the images. She hadn't told the police. She ran to her purse, grabbed the note with Officer Reilly's number, and called.

He answered after three rings. "Officer Reilly here."

"Hello. I'm not sure you remember me. It's Abigail Donovan. We met a week ago?"

"Oh, yes, I remember you. How can I help you?"

"I was just sitting here thinking about that night, the night of the murder at Reggie's, and I just remembered something. I saw a man leaving the bar as I turned up the street to Reggie's."

"Really? Did you get a good look at him?"

"Not really. He was about a block away. But I could tell that he was white because I saw light wavy hair."

"Are you sure it was a man?"

"Yes. He was broad. He walked like a man. I'm sure it was a man. I'm guessing around six feet tall. That's just a guess. But bigger than a woman, for sure."

"Okay, well, I'll update the file with this information. Thanks for calling, Ms. Donovan."

"Wait. There's more. I had bumped into a prostitute on the street a few minutes earlier. I don't know why I didn't think of it before, but she was the same woman I found in the bathroom. I'm sure of it. I remember the skirt and the fishnets. Those red high heels. I had noticed the outfit when we bumped into one another and that's how I realized she was a prostitute. So, whoever I saw, he had to either have seen what happened to her or been her killer, right?"

"Well, that may be a big leap. But I'll add this information to the files. I really appreciate you calling this in, Ms. Donovan. We rely on the watchful eye of the community in many cases."

"Well, I just can't believe I didn't remember to tell you before."

"It's not surprising. It's common to remember some details days and weeks after an event. After the shock goes away. Listen, I'm in the middle of something right now, but thanks again. Please call if you can remember anything else."

She hung up the phone. "He thinks that's a big leap?" Abby wondered aloud. "That guy came out, and a few minutes later I found a dead body. There was no one else there. That's not a big leap!" Her stomach turned. She didn't know if it was from the pint of ice cream, now in her belly, or the idea that she had been so close to a murderer.

TEN

TRIP paid his bar tab, finished off his martini, and checked his watch. It was time. Tonight he'd hit Englewood, where there was always a good supply of kids on street corners. He took Halsted south a few miles from downtown to Sixty-Third Street, took a right, and slowed down. His windshield wipers were on low, just enough to clear the giant snowflakes that were quickly building up around him. The flakes on the ground reflected the street lamps, creating an aura of light. He watched the street activity. The soft glow and blanket of snow failed to create any serenity on the streets. It was eleven o'clock, and the punks were out in full force. Perfect timing.

He pulled over to the curb near a group at the corner, hit the button for the passenger-side window to come down, and waited. He knew the signals. So did they. He watched as the boys looked at his car, at the tinted windows. This kind of car always meant one of two things: a visit from a boss or a good customer. Within a moment, the obvious young leader approached the window and leaned in. He couldn't have been more than fifteen, but the strut went a long way.

The boy bent down to look in the window. "Sweet ride."

Trip smiled. Everyone loved a Mercedes. "Thanks."

"Can I help you with something, mister?"

"I'm sure you can," Trip responded.

"What's your pleasure?"

"Coke. How much you got?"

"How much you need?"

"A lot more than you're carrying right now."

"Well, how 'bout I sell you a taste and if you're happy with my product, we can go from there?"

"You're a good business man. I like that." Trip cleared a jacket from off the passenger seat. "Hop in."

The boy looked around, unsure what to do.

Trip continued. "This street's too busy. Let's not make a deal right here. I'll drive around the corner and buy a sample."

That was enough for the boy. He got in and pulled his black hood back off his head, revealing the tattoo on the side of his neck—the letters B and D and a six-point star. Black Disciples. Trip smirked at the boy's subtle message.

As they pulled away, Trip watched as the boy's friends tried fruitlessly to see into the car. He drove a few blocks farther, turned right onto a side street, and pulled over. They were surrounded by run-down two-flats.

The boy pulled out a sandwich-sized baggy with several little baggies inside of it.

"That's it?" Trip had to laugh.

"It's been a busy day, what can I say?"

"How much?"

"Fifty bucks."

"Let me try first." Trip stuck his pinky finger in the bag, scooped a tiny amount into his nail, and snorted.

"Good stuff, right?"

"Yeah, that'll do. Now, here's a hundred dollars. Where'd you get this?"

The boy stammered.

"I need a lot. I told you that." He flashed a stack of hundred-dollar bills at the kid. It looked like thousands. "Now, you bring me to your supplier, and I give you another hundred. And he probably gives you a promotion for bringing in the business." They both smiled.

The boy instructed Trip to continue north to Sixtieth Street, take a left, and pull over in front of an apartment building. Trip then followed him up the stairs to the second floor and down the beaten-up hallway.

The boy knocked on door number 212 and yelled out, "It's Billy! Come on, let me in!"

The chain unhooked and the door slowly opened. *Wheel of Fortune* was on in the background.

The boy stood between Trip and the man. "Hey bro, I brought you a customer."

The man, maybe twenty-two, wearing an undershirt and boxers, pulled the boy in by his head. His bare arm revealed his own version of B and D and the six-point star.

"Get out of the fuckin' hallway."

Trip entered without invitation and shut the door behind him.

"What the fuck is this?" The man gestured to Trip but focused on Billy.

Trip began scanning the room. It was typical of the neighborhood—in need of paint, repairs, air freshener.

"If I may? Your young worker here sold me a bit of cocaine, and as I explained, I need a lot more. Apparently, you're the man who can handle my needs." Trip reached for his inside coat pocket, but the man grabbed his arm and twisted it up behind his back. Trip winced. It would snap if pushed any farther.

The man's face was inches from Trip's. "Who the fuck are you? I don't know you. I don't know what you're talking about."

Billy started in to foster the deal. "It's cool, Jake. He's not a cop or anything. I saw his car—jacked-up Mercedes. He's got a lot of cash. Show him." The man held Trip's arm tightly. Billy waited for Trip to help create the trust.

Trip stood perfectly still and remained calm. "Billy's right." He offered his available hand to the man. "I'm Trip, by the way."

The man looked at him and ignored the hand. Trip just smiled and continued. He knew how to turn this around. "Listen, I work the North Shore. Lots of rich high school kids. Big market. My old source has dried up, and I saw your boy here and thought he could bring me to a decision maker. Someone I might be able to work with."

The man didn't budge. "I don't know what the fuck you talkin' 'bout."

Trip continued. "I have cash. On me. Now, you could just rob me and throw me out of here, or we could actually do some repeat business."

The man released him. "How much?"

Trip slowly reached into his pocket again and pulled out a stack of hundreds and handed them to the man.

The man leafed through the stack to confirm.

Trip was making progress. "I need a few pounds to start. Can you handle it?"

"Well, well, well!" The man's tone had turned. "Let's just hold on a second." He turned Trip back toward the front door and pushed his hands against the wall. "Let's just be sure here." He patted around Trip's chest, his pants, his crotch.

Trip squirmed slightly and offered a small giggle like he was being tickled. "Hey now, let's keep this professional."

The man stopped and pushed Trip toward the couch. "Have a seat." He tossed the roll of bills onto the table and hit the "Mute" button on the remote control. "Let's see what we can do here."

Trip and Billy looked at each other and smiled. They both sat on the couch. The boy turned his attention to the muted *Wheel of Fortune* and began guessing at the puzzle.

The man headed for the kitchen, yelling back over his shoulder. "It's coke you want, right?"

"Yes."

Pots and pans banged around, and then a cabinet door slammed. He returned to the living area and dropped a quart-sized bag of cocaine on the table.

"That's about two pounds. And it'll cost you about five thousand. Can you handle that?"

Trip smiled. "I can." He leaned toward the table and leafed through the roll of bills. "Ah, this isn't quite enough." He stood to reach back into the coat as the man relaxed and sat next to Billy.

Trip bent down, pulled a revolver from his ankle holster, and pointed it at the man's head.

The man sat back, exasperated. "Motherfucker. You're fuckin' dead, Billy."

Billy looked away from the TV when he heard his name and froze to see Trip standing in front of them with the gun.

"So, little Billy here was wrong. I am an officer of the law and, as I'm sure you're aware," he said, grabbing the bag of cocaine, "this is enough coke to get you for trafficking and put you away for a long time. Now, since I entered your home with your permission and have now been given probable cause, please get up."

"What the fuck?" The man slapped his hands to his thighs. He didn't budge.

Trip stepped forward and smashed the side of the gun into the man's head.

The man fell forward and grabbed his head. Blood poured out of the gash. "I ain't listening to a thing you say, muthefucka."

Trip bent down, cocked the revolver, and lowered his tone. "I don't think you understand, my friend. I will blow your fucking brains out. I don't give a fuck if you live or die. Now where's the fucking cash?"

The boy began to cry.

Trip continued, gesturing to the sobbing child. "I'll kill the kid too. But if you cooperate, I'll just walk away. I don't even care about arresting you today. But I'm taking your stash, with your help or without."

The man stood. Trip directed the boy. "You too."

They headed to the kitchen and Trip followed.

The man bent over to reach into the cabinet.

"Wait a second." Trip stopped him. "Have the boy do it."

The boy bent over and pulled out a cash box and opened it on the counter.

Trip reached in and grabbed the gun that was in the box and put it in his ankle holster.

"Now, let's see here. Looks like about twenty thousand. Not too bad." He left the small bags of drugs and led Billy and the man back to the couch.

"Sit down." He grabbed the bag of coke and the cash from the table and began backing out of the room. They sat and watched. Vanna White smiled on TV.

Trip reached for the door. "Sorry boys. Maybe you should start fresh, change your ways!" he said with a sarcastic smile.

TRIP drove off with the satisfaction of a decent score for thirty minutes of work. That was easily a down payment. He checked his cell messages. There were two. His mother, asking him to come home for dinner on Monday. And Mike, who was panicked and yelling into the machine. "She saw you! That woman from Reggie's said she saw you coming out of the bar! What the fuck do we do now? Call me!"

Trip slammed the phone against the steering wheel. Bullshit. Mike needed to calm the fuck down. There was no way anyone saw him. It had been dark. No one was around. But he'd check it out. And then he smiled, remembering the ID card from the purse Mike had showed him. He smirked at his own reflection in the rearview mirror. "Might even be fun."

ELEVEN

ABBY sat in a middle pew along the aisle to get a good view. Waiting for the service to begin, she focused on the architecture, to avoid any unintentional eye contact with David, who was ushering people to their seats. Fourth Presbyterian was sandwiched between all the shopping of North Michigan Avenue, and Abby had walked by it hundreds of times, but she'd never been inside. The limestone brick walls must have been forty feet high. She counted fourteen angel statues, each at least seven feet tall, propped on piers along the sides of the sanctuary. Massive arched timber supports, each painted with more angels, graced the ceiling. Gothic pendant lights suspended by old black chains hung from above. As the organ music began, all eyes turned toward the back.

The setting sun cast light through the stained glass windows, creating a multicolored spotlight on the action at the altar. Abby focused on David, who stood beside Rick, serious and engrossed in the moment. David was always a casual guy, but she had loved seeing him in suits when they went to weddings together, and now, to see him in a tuxedo, he took her breath away. His typically disheveled hair, longer now, with a few natural curls at the ends, had been tamed for the occasion. And when the priest instructed Sarah and Rick to kiss, David led the cheers and wiped his eyes. He was always sentimental, never embarrassed to cry. She remembered the tears they'd both shared the night she had finally said yes. She scanned the pews, guessing who might be taking her place in his life.

The guessing was over once the cocktail hour began.

Though David and the rest of the bridal party were taking horse-drawn carriages from the church to the Drake Hotel, Abby and the other guests had hurried, en masse, the two blocks to the reception, where they were greeted with champagne at the entrance of the grand ballroom. After a few minutes of soaking in the space—marveling at the forty or so round tables draped in satin, the second-level balcony encircling the room, and the hundreds of guests already there—Abby had convinced herself she might not even notice David and her replacement in this crowd. But when the wedding party walked in, they stood out against all others. They seemed taller somehow, and once she saw a groomsman, her gaze quickly found the others among the crowd.

David was escorting his future wife up to the bar to get a drink. They were holding onto each other tightly. He looked happy. She was beautiful. She did not look anything like Abby. Olive skin, dark hair, taller. Maybe Latin or Italian or something else exotic. Suddenly, Abby's dress felt like a tent and her up-do felt like curlers in a rag. Her stomach ached. She felt incredibly thirsty.

She grabbed a champagne glass off the tray of a passing waiter and walked toward the exit. Collapsing onto a big upholstered chair by the grand piano on the mezzanine level, she secretly freed her feet from their torture devices under the ottoman directly in front of her, and sipped her champagne. She was already exhausted by the small talk, her spiked heels, and the David-spotting. She still could not believe that he would marry another woman.

"Marry me," he'd said to her so long ago.

She'd had a spicy tuna roll in her mouth and had started choking when he said it. She smiled, thinking of that ridiculous moment. They had been talking about work. Abby had just shared some gossip about that brown-noser, Neil, who unfortunately for her had an awesome handicap in golf; partners were already lining up to play with him on the weekends, even as a first-year associate. She'd been waiting for David's reaction to her tale. Instead he'd said, "Marry me."

Luckily, he had understood the apparent absurdity of the moment, and they'd both laughed. But he was serious. The dinner had been to celebrate their one-year anniversary, and David had made a reservation at Le Colonial. Of course, Abby had called with a work crisis and suggested that they hook up at his place later and walk up to Kamehachi's on Wells.

"Let's just live together," Abby had suggested.

"Don't we do that now?"

"But not really. We can make it official."

David had smiled. "Okay, I'll live with you. But you're going to have to marry me at some point, you know."

"Of course." Abby did love him. She didn't want to lose him.

That was five years ago.

With a deep breath, she braced the arms of the chair and sat up straight. She couldn't stay in the lobby forever. She put her shoes back on and looked around for a restroom to do a vanity check.

A man standing by the bar caught her eye. He was tall, blond—very Matthew McConaughey—a little unshaven, jeans, black turtleneck, camel suede coat. Yum. He was leaning against the bar, looking out into the crowd and smoking a cigarette. Once he saw her, his gaze remained fixed. It felt good to be looked at that way.

She acknowledged the silent compliment with a smile in his direction.

He grinned and waved.

She waved back.

He patted the barstool next to him.

The three drinks she'd already downed gave her a little courage. Maybe you can come be my date, Mr. Marlboro Man, she thought. She was still giggling to herself as she approached.

"Do you have another?" Abby asked as she hopped up onto the barstool next to the stranger. He was smoking a Marlboro Light, her old brand. This was meant to be.

"Sure. Need a light too?"

"Yes, please." It had been six years, but suddenly it seemed like a great idea. She turned to the bartender and ordered another champagne. The man insisted on buying her drink, and she thanked him.

"I'm Trip."

"Trip? Is that a nickname?" she asked.

"It's what friends call me."

"Is it short for something?"

"Kind of." He smiled.

"So? Are you going to tell me?"

"Maybe at some point."

It was annoying, but then again, he was really cute. She put the cigarette to her mouth and let him light it.

"And you are?"

"Abigail."

"You're stunning, Abigail. Are you here alone?"

This was just what she needed. "I'm at a wedding reception. There." She pointed toward the ballroom door.

"So, why are you out here?"

"Oh, just trying to escape the crowd for a moment."

"I see." He examined her from head to toe.

His intensity was unnerving. She looked around the bar and felt his eyes on her.

"And what brings you here this evening?" she asked.

He took a drag from the cigarette and looked around. "Business."

"Oh, are you in from out of town?"

"Sort of."

She waited for more information, but he offered only a smirk.

"You sound like you're from…Memphis, perhaps?" he asked.

"Georgia, but I thought I'd lost the accent."

"There's just a hint." He looked into her eyes. "A beautiful southern belle. How did I get so lucky?"

She shrugged. "Thank you," she said, focusing on her cigarette. It didn't taste good, but she couldn't look at him.

After a final drag, he put his cigarette out. "Hey, maybe you'd like to get out of here?"

Abby was startled. It was a bit much. "Oh, thanks for the offer, but I can't go. It's a big night for a good friend." She put out her cigarette and stood up.

He stood too. "Wait. I didn't mean to scare you off. I'm just a straightforward guy. It's just like in business. When I see something I want, I go after it. No apologies. And you're lovely." He looked into her eyes, right through her. It drew her in. His eyes were a piercing ice blue, surrounded by long lashes. He had a slight tan and dimples. It was a killer smile. He was probably a master salesman.

He put his hand on hers. It was hard to resist. She imagined running her hands through that hair. But the non-champagne-soaked part of her brain kicked in. She snapped out of the trance. "I'm flattered. I just can't leave."

"We could stay here?" he said with hope. "Have some more drinks?"

"No, I really should be getting back in."

"Okay, well, if you'd like to go out sometime, I'd be honored." He grabbed a pen from the bar, wrote his number on a cocktail napkin, and handed it to her.

"Thanks. It was nice to meet you."

As she neared the ballroom entrance, she could hear the band playing "At Last," that old bluesy Etta James song she loved. The song, the only song, she'd ever sung to David. She smiled, remembering that night all those years ago.

But as she got to the doorway, she saw David—on the dance floor, holding her replacement. She braced the frame of the door for support. She felt sick. It could have been the cigarette or the drinks. But it felt more like she was getting punched in the stomach every time she looked at him.

Abby looked down at the recently acquired cocktail napkin. The Marlboro Man could take her mind off of David. At least for the night. She looked back toward the lobby bar. He was still there. She stared at him for a moment. Maybe she should just do it. Have a fling. Go roll around with that beautiful man and forget everything. He turned and saw her. He raised a glass to cheer. She waved. Just do it. She went in the ballroom to grab her coat. This was just what she needed.

"Abby!" Sarah was shuffling toward her with open arms.

It stopped Abby in her tracks. Seeing Sarah brought tears to her eyes. She felt surprisingly choked up and whispered, "You look beautiful," embracing her friend.

Sarah twirled proudly in the dress, enjoying the compliment. "Are you having fun?"

Abby put on a big smile and lied with gusto. "Of course! Sarah, this dress—it's so amazing. You're just radiant. And this place—my God—are you a Rockefeller?" They both laughed.

Sarah scoped out the room and nodded toward her new groom. "Did you see Rick during the ceremony? I thought he was going to pass out! You would have thought he was standing in court waiting for a judge to determine his punishment. Hilarious!"

Abby laughed. "I've never seen him look so speechless." She spotted him holding court among friends. "Clearly, he's feeling better."

"Yeah, we had a martini after the service. He relaxed."

"Well, I couldn't be happier for you guys. You make a great pair."

"Hope so!" Sarah said, already ending the conversation. "I'll try to find you again. I've got to go say hello to two hundred pseudo-friends of my parents."

"Have fun!" Before Abby could even think, the lights dimmed, indicating time for dinner. She grabbed her table assignment card and looked over at table eight. Two young attorneys from the firm, second-years, and a few strangers were already sitting at the table. The singles table. She looked at the exit sign again. If she were going to go, now was the time. A waiter walked by with a tray full of white wine. Abby grabbed a glass and crumpled the assignment card in her hand.

TRIP motioned the bartender for his check. The excursion had proved reassuring. Nothing to worry about here. In fact, maybe she'd call. He should be spending time with women like that. Smart, beautiful. Mom would love her. Enough with the whores. His mind wandered to the last woman he'd fucked. "Useless," he muttered. He looked around the opulent lobby. This was where he belonged. He turned to leave. Abigail was heading toward him.

"Well, well!" He smiled.

She took a seat next to his. "I hope you're not leaving."

"No. No. Sit! Shall we have another drink?" He was already waving the bartender over.

"Yes, please." She put down the near-empty wine glass. "I can't drink any more wine. How about...?" She smiled and tapped her finger on those full lips, pondering the best choice. "A cosmopolitan, please."

"You got it." Trip turned to the bartender, now waiting for an order. "She'll have a cosmo, and I'll have a very dry Stoli martini, straight up, with three blue cheese olives."

"Oh, yum. I love blue cheese olives."

"Make that six blue cheese olives," Trip ordered.

Trip smiled at Abby. Things were looking better and better.

She grabbed another of his cigarettes, and relaxed. "So ..."

Trip sat back too. "So." He knew he had her.

TWELVE

SUNLIGHT streamed through the open vertical blinds, creating stripes across the bed. A thick stripe of light across Abby's face pulled her into the morning. Her head throbbed. Her tongue felt covered in soot. Her mind was blank. She rolled to her back and felt the sheets against her skin. She looked down at her naked body. "Fuck," she said softly as she braced her head and tried to piece it together. She looked around the room. Her dress was in a ball on the floor. She was alone. She counted the champagnes, the wine, more wine. Out to the bar. With Trip. Trip who? Did she even get a last name? Cocktails. Many cocktails. No dinner. She remembered pulling him into the ballroom for a dance. She remembered spinning and stumbling before he caught her and they laughed. Had David witnessed this? Did she do anything else? She remembered beer. And lemon-drop shots. She closed her eyes and remembered a kiss. They were in the lobby. It was passionate. She remembered touching his hair. Oh, God. She couldn't remember more. She didn't know how she'd gotten home. Or why she was naked.

Abby put on a robe, went to the bathroom, and peeled the contacts from her eyes. She looked at her mascara-smeared face and wondered if she were alone. She went down to the kitchen, half expecting to find Trip sitting at the table, drinking coffee. But there was no sign of him. She stood at the butcher-block island and searched her brain for details. If only she had a friend she could discuss this with, who might have seen something, who would jog her memory so the whole story would come to her. But there was no one. She looked at her watch. Sarah was probably boarding the airplane right about now. And David. God, she hoped he hadn't seen them together. Of course, why not? He'd moved on. He loved someone new. That beautiful Amazon. But it would hurt him. She'd hurt him enough already.

Mrs. Tanor was in the courtyard, grabbing her newspaper, when Abby opened the front door to do the same.

The cold air shocked her system. "Morning," Abby said in her best attempt to be pleasant.

"Well, hello, dear. How are you?"

"Oh, I've been better." She went for the paper.

"How was the wedding?"

"It was fun. I'm just really tired." Abby's foot was already back in the door.

"You don't look like yourself, dear. Is everything all right?"

"Of course, Mrs. Tanor. I just got in pretty late." She turned to go inside.

"Abby, is there a new beau I should know about?" Mrs. Tanor had a devilish look.

"Excuse me?"

"Oh, that handsome man."

Oh, God. She must have brought him home.

"He came here to see you yesterday. I told him you had already left for the Drake."

What? Her head hurt, and listening to Mrs. Tanor was more exhausting than usual. "I don't know who that was, Mrs. Tanor. Don't know too many handsome men," she offered with a smile.

"Too bad. Well, maybe he'll come back."

"Maybe." Abby shut the door.

ABBY got to work at nine o'clock on Monday and read through the twenty new e-mails. She had put in a few hours in the office on Sunday but was still behind. An outside line rang.

"Abigail Donovan."

"Yeah, hi. Ms. Donovan? This is Detective Henton."

Abby turned from the computer. "I'm sorry?"

"Detective Henton, ma'am. Ms. Donovan, I'm working on a matter related to the Reggie's Bar homicide. I believe you were there a couple of weeks ago?"

"Oh. Are you working with Officer Reilly?"

"No. It's kind of complicated. I'm on a different case. Is it possible for me to meet with you today? I'd like to ask you some questions."

"I don't understand. I told the police everything. I really can't do any more." She looked around at her increasing piles of paperwork. "I want to cooperate, but I'm really swamped here."

"Ms. Donovan, I'm sorry to bother you. But I'm calling because you called Officer Reilly on Friday with some more information about that night."

So, perhaps someone had thought her revelation was significant. She turned her back to the desk and looked out the window. "Yes, I remembered seeing a man."

"Right. I'd like to show you some pictures and see if you might be able to identify the man."

"Okay. Officer Reilly didn't seem to think too much of my description."

"Well, I do. Would you mind if I came to your office?"

Just what she needed, another officer showing up at work. But it was better than going to the police station again. She quickly reviewed her agenda for the day. "Yes, that would be okay. How about four o'clock?"

"Great. See you then."

IT was nearing five o-clock when an inside line rang. Abby picked up.

"Abby, it's Barbara. You have a visitor. A Marcus Henton?"

"Oh, thanks, Barbara. I'll be right there."

She walked into the lobby, and Barbara pointed to the waiting area by the windows. A tall black man, wearing khaki pants and a black leather jacket, was looking out the window at the view of the park and the lake. She was relieved he wasn't in uniform.

She walked toward the man. "Hello? Detective?"

The man turned around. Abby's breath caught in her throat and her heart pounded.

She couldn't speak. She stared at his face. At the scar.

The man smiled. "You recognize me?"

Abby looked around. Attorneys were walking by; Barbara was still at the desk. She couldn't be in danger.

He obviously sensed her fear. "Don't worry." He offered his hand. "I am Detective Henton. When you saw me, I was working undercover." He looked different, not scary. His clothes were straight out of Banana Republic.

Abby tentatively extended her hand in return. "I don't understand. You chased me."

"I realize that may be how you perceived it. But actually, I followed you because I was concerned. I wanted to find out what happened in Reggie's. And I wanted to be sure those boys didn't follow you."

Abby sat in one of the lobby chairs and put her head in her hands. The detective took the chair next to hers and lowered his tone. "I've been working undercover in that neighborhood for about seven months. I'm getting to know the kids, the gangs, and I've gained some trust. I couldn't just bust in and arrest those kids for messing with you."

She didn't know how to feel. Relieved? Angry?

She went with angry. "Why are you telling me this? Why are you here?"

He looked around. There were several people in the lobby now. "Can we go to your office?"

Abby tried to process this. "Could you show me some identification?"

He smiled and leaned back. "Sure." He offered his badge and police ID card.

Abby examined the picture carefully and then looked at the man again. It was definitely him, though the picture looked old and he didn't have a scar.

She stood up. She felt safe at the office. "Okay, come with me."

They walked, she leading by a few paces, down the long corridor and turned right down the south hall. Her door was open, and she gestured to the two guest chairs by the door. "Take a seat." Abby went to her desk and sat. She was glad to have the desk between them and to feel the comfort of her own territory. "So, what's going on?"

"You mentioned seeing a man leaving the scene." The detective reached into his coat pocket and pulled out a copy of a photograph. "I was hoping you might be able to give more of a description. Does this man look familiar?" It was a blond man, wearing blue jeans and a black leather jacket, coming out of a store and talking on a cell phone. The picture was obviously taken from across the street. The man did not seem to know he was being photographed. The picture was grainy, and the man's face was partially covered by his sunglasses.

Abby took the picture and studied it. "I don't know. I don't think so."

Henton looked disappointed. "I realize it's not very clear. Can you tell me again who you think you saw coming out of Reggie's?"

"Well, it was dark, but like I told Officer Reilly, I feel sure it was a man and that he was white, and he had kind of wavy light hair. Blond, dirty blond—not like white. There's a street lamp right outside the doors, and he turned up the street, and I saw the blond. That's how I knew it was a white guy. He was dressed in dark clothes, so I couldn't tell you much. I didn't see his face."

"But you don't recognize this guy?" He pointed out the picture again.

She studied it again. "I couldn't say."

"Would you say the man was tall or short?"

"Neither. It was kind of far away." She pointed to the picture. "Who is this?"

"This man," he said, pointing to the picture, "was seen with the woman who was found dead. I was hoping you might recognize him."

Abby shrugged. "Sorry."

"Okay. Well I appreciate your time, Ms. Donovan." He stood to leave but then turned back. "Oh, and Ms. Donovan, I'd appreciate it if you didn't mention our meeting to Officer Reilly should you speak to him again."

Abby stood. She felt unsettled. "Why? He was the officer who brought me in to the station."

The detective sat again. He took a moment, like he wasn't sure what to say. "Ms. Donovan, I'm working undercover. It's important that no one knows I'm an officer."

This just seemed strange. The hairs on the back of her neck started to tingle. "Well, if you're actually a police officer, other officers would know you."

"Actually, that's not the case. I came here from New York last spring. You could say I'm on a special assignment. Officer Reilly is ... well, we've never met. That's why I came to you today. I have never been to his station house."

It was a wild tale, and Abby wasn't sure she should believe it. "I'm sorry, but how do I know that you didn't just come in here with some fake badge and identification. Maybe you're the one I saw leaving Reggie's. Maybe I should call Officer Reilly right now." She knew that didn't make any sense, but now she had the creeps. She grabbed for the phone.

The man reached forward and put his hand over hers. She looked up at him.

"First of all, you said he was white. Do I look white to you?" Obviously a rhetorical question. "Listen. I'm telling you the truth. I was hired directly by Robert Duvane. He's the assistant deputy superintendent of the Internal Affairs Division. If you are nervous about trusting me, you can call him." He reached into his wallet and offered her a business card. "I'll give him the heads up that you may be calling.

But no one else knows about me. It's important to keep it that way."

"Internal Affairs? So you're investigating police officers."

"Yes."

Abby was intrigued. Questions began whirling in her head and she didn't know where to begin. It was almost as if the detective sensed this, because he quickly rose to leave.

"Anyway, thank you for your time, Ms. Donovan. And I trust we can keep this conversation between us?"

"Sure. Oh, wait." She grabbed the picture of the man from her desk and studied it again. "So this guy, he's a policeman?" There was something vaguely familiar, but she just couldn't put her finger on it.

"Perhaps. I'm looking into it." He took the picture. "Well, thanks, Ms. Donovan. And please call me if you think of anything else about that man you saw walking out of Reggie's."

"Will do."

AFTER the detective left, Abby's head spun with all sorts of unanswered questions. Was Reilly a bad cop? Why did that detective pause when he spoke of him? Why didn't Reilly care when she called in the description of a man? Was he the target of this man's investigation? He was white. He was the one who was investigating Ali's store. Maybe she should have told the detective about that. But he had a crew cut. She wondered who to trust.

She looked at the flowers on her desk. The water was completely brown now. The petals were crisp and fragile. Ali. So nice, so afraid. Nothing about his case or his death felt right.

She pulled her research from the drawer. Research she had tossed aside after that meeting with Jerry. She read through the state laws related to trafficking and forfeiture again and then studied some pages from a website put out by a watch group called the Forfeiture Endangers American Rights Foundation, a.k.a. FEAR. She had highlighted some of the FEAR facts, and they caught her attention again:

Eighty percent of property forfeited to the U.S. during the previous decade was seized from owners who were never even charged with a crime... Under civil asset forfeiture laws, the simple possession of cash, with no drugs or other contraband, can be considered evidence of criminal activity.

She turned to an article from the International Society for Individual Liberty. It was the story of a woman stopped at the airport because a drug dog scratched her luggage. The agents had found thirty-nine thousand dollars in cash, money she had received from an insurance settlement and her life savings. Even though she'd documented where she got the money and had never been charged with a crime, the police had kept the money, and four years later she was still trying to get it back.

There was a *USA Today* article about police in Washington, D.C., who stop black men on the street in poor areas and routinely confiscate small amounts of cash and jewelry, most of which is never recorded by the departments. The article spoke of the continued incentives to expand forfeiture because the police departments benefit by keeping the goods for use on "official business" or receiving some of the profit from the auctions.

And now, Ali's property would be sold off to the highest bidder, just ripped from under his dead body. She scanned the local listings. There were twenty upcoming real estate auctions listed. No descriptions, just addresses and pictures. And then she saw it. *Quick Mart.* What? How could it be sold already? Ali's body was barely cold in the ground. The auction was set for Tuesday, February 10, 2004, 11:00 a.m. Tomorrow. It would be held at the property location.

THIRTEEN

AT six forty-five, Trip left the city along with the tail end of rush-hour traffic and drove up Sheridan Road toward Lake Forest. It would have been faster to take the expressway, but he loved going up along Lake Michigan, winding his way up the shore under the canopy of oak trees that lined so much of Sheridan. There was a good six inches of snow on the ground, and it clung to the tree limbs as though painted with the grace of an artist's brush. The street was lined with beautiful old homes, most built in the early 1900s. "Soon," he muttered.

As he drove through Wilmette, he noticed some construction going on at an old place on the east side of the street and a "Weber Design" sign in the front yard. Of course. It looked like they'd done an addition in the back. It was blending perfectly with the limestone facade and slate roof of the original structure.

He continued up the north shore through Glencoe, Kenilworth, and Highland Park and finally veered right into Lake Forest. Once he got to Deerpath Road, he made the instinctive right toward the lake and wound around the fifteen-foot hedges that blocked views of the massive homes behind them. Many were still covered with Christmas lights, creating a glow under the snow. He made a left into the long gravel driveway and parked in front of the entrance. He looked at his watch: 7:35 p.m. Oh, well.

He rang the bell and waited. Father answered. Trip smiled at the red pants. It made his father look like Santa Claus with that huge belly hanging over. Even his cheeks were red. But, of course, nothing about his face was jolly. And those dark eyes and his mostly bald head dispelled any chance of being mistaken for the world-famous children's hero.

"Hi, Dad." Trip extended his hand.

His father didn't take it. "You're late."

"Sorry, just busy at work. You know how it is."

"New car?" He was looking past Trip into the driveway.

"Yeah," Trip said with satisfaction. "What do you think?"

"A tad flashy, isn't it?"

Trip laughed. It had those spinning hubcaps; not exactly Trip's taste either, but he hadn't had time to change them. It was a recent acquisition.

"My baby!" Trip's mother was walking toward the men in the front hall with arms outstretched to hug her youngest child. "I've missed you! Oh, look at my handsome boy!" she said, cupping his face in her hands.

"Thanks, Mom. You look beautiful, as usual." Another round of Botox was doing well to prevent her from looking anywhere near her age. Her hair remained golden blond without a hint of gray, and she had a nice tan.

"Oh, my sweet boy, how I love to hear that. Your father and I just returned from Florida. I just had to get out of this cold for a while. Now, come in, come in! Let's eat." She locked her arm in his, and they walked toward the dining room. "Cassie fixed a lovely dinner for us."

The table was dressed with the china, crystal, and place settings for seven.

"Sit anywhere, honey. Your sister just called and the kids are sick, so they're not going to come after all."

Just as well. The little shits were a pain in the ass.

"So, tell me, how's work these days?"

"Oh, it's good, Mom. Really good."

She dropped her fork then and put her hands to her heart. "I'm so happy you're not a police officer anymore, Trip. That was so dangerous."

Trip sighed. He'd heard it so many times before. "I know, Mother."

His dad joined in. "Yes, Margaret. Everyone at this table knows how you and I feel about that little career choice."

Trip looked at his mother, who appeared sorry she'd started this conversation.

His father continued. "We could not have wasted more money if we tried, right, Trip?" He didn't wait for an answer and continued, addressing his wife. "The boy got kicked out of some of the best schools in the country."

Trip had heard the insults so many times that it didn't faze him. And, of course, his father had no idea how well being a cop had served him.

"Well, Dad, you told me to stand on my 'own goddamn feet,' and I've been doing that for a while now. You ready to let it go?"

His father ignored the question and turned to his wife. "Looks like he's finally on the road to success, Margaret. The boy drove here in a cherry-red Porsche."

"Oh, my!" Trip's mother responded, with exaggerated approval. "Didn't you drive a Mercedes up here last month?"

"I did." He paused to eat some salad and enjoy the moment. "Hey, Mom, I saw a new project of yours in Wilmette on the way up. Looks like a big job."

"Oh, yes, the Walters' house on Sheridan. It's lovely. Great bones, but so out of date. I'm having fun with that one."

"I might have a new project for you if you're willing to head to the city."

"Well, of course. Where is it?"

"It's not too far from the United Center."

"But, honey, that's not a good area. From what I remember, the United Center is in a depressed part of the city. A good bit west of Interstate 94, right, Thomas?" She looked at her husband for help.

"It's changing, Mom. Up and coming."

His dad let out a chuckle and joined in. "Sounds like a risk, Trip. You know real estate. It's all about location. And I just read that some analysts are predicting a massive slowdown. Some people think this is a bubble just waiting to burst." He gave Trip's mother that look. That look Trip had seen for thirty years. That "Trip is an idiot" look.

Trip dropped his fork. "Please, Dad. I know what I'm doing. I'm making a killing."

Trip's mother chimed back in with more support. "It's wonderful, honey. Let's talk next week. I'd love to see what you're doing with your business." Her smile never wavered until she looked at Trip's dad and gave him that "cool it" look.

Cassie served the dinner, and Trip's mother gave updates on his sister, the kids, his brother-in-law, his aunt, the neighbors, old friends—all the gossip for the month. When his cell phone rang as they were finishing their meal, Trip excused himself to the hall and scanned the caller ID: *M.R.*

Trip walked through the kitchen, stepped out into the solarium, and took a seat in a lounger among Mom's flowers as he picked up. "What's up?" He knew Mike would be panicked.

"You never called me back. Did you get my message on Friday? That woman saw you."

"First of all, calm down. She didn't see me."

"She described a white male with light hair leaving the scene."

"Hardly cause for panic, as I found out. She can't pick me out."

"How do you know?"

Trip paused. He wondered if he should even tell him. Mike didn't seem to have the stomach for all this. "I just know. Now, what else can you tell me?"

"Nothing. Listen, I don't think I can do this."

Trip rolled his eyes and began the pitch. "Mike, you sound stressed. There's nothing to worry about. I'm not asking you to do anything you haven't done before."

"Things have changed."

"Like what?"

"Like now there are dead bodies."

Trip was irritated, and he knew better than to talk about murders on a damn cell phone. "Mike, you sound hysterical. We have no connection to anything that has happened."

Mike didn't respond.

"Hey, Mike, I've got your back. Now, I know you need the cash. It's the last one, I swear."

"Really?"

"Yes. I'm nearly done anyway. I don't need the stress. This little venture has served its purpose and I'm nearly set, so I won't be able to help you in the future. Tell you what: How about I give you a five percent cut on the back end this time?"

"That would be great."

Trip relaxed, satisfied. "How's your investigation of the Madison brownstone coming?"

"We've checked out the title. The owner has a mortgage for ten thousand. The property appears to be worth a hundred and twenty thousand."

"Good news. Now why don't you make that "10" a "100" in the paperwork? Just a little typo to ward off my bidding competition."

"Okay."

"Good man. Now what about the owner?"

"He's illegal."

"Perfect. It's a slam dunk. I've got big plans for that place. Let's make it happen."

"Sounds good."

Trip hung up and smiled. He was born for sales.

He went back to the dining room and joined his parents for coffee.

ABBY watched the train's reflection in the building windows along Lake Street as she headed west through the Loop. Once the train crossed the expressway, the scenery went through a rapid change. Before long, she saw shabby and boarded-up buildings. As she got closer to her stop, there were more and more abandoned buildings, graffiti, trash-laden yards, barbed-wire fences, and burned-out cars. But Ali had been right. In the light of day, it wasn't really scary, just kind of sad. She and several other riders stepped off the train at the Pulaski stop. The wind was whipping along the platform, and she quickly pulled her scarf up around her head.

Looking around, she was struck by the difference between night and day. It did not feel like a ghost town anymore. It was loud and full of life. The kids on the street looked too tough for their age, but they didn't look like criminals. She could hear children playing a block away, and cars poured down Lake Street with seamless energy.

It was probably a waste of time, and it was bound to make her lunch hour entirely too long, but Ali had worked hard on that building, on creating a life here, and now his life and his friend's life, and all his dreams, were dead. She needed to know that someone would take good care of the building for him.

She opened the door and heard the familiar bells clanging against the glass and frame. She pulled off the scarf, opened her coat, and looked over to the counter where he had sat, reading his book that night, only two weeks ago. Now the room was empty. It was quiet.

Just then, two men and a woman came out of the back room. They walked toward her, and the man in charge introduced himself and asked her to sign in. Abby did so quietly and studied the potential bidders. A young white woman, maybe twenty-four, with long brown hair spilling out from beneath her wool hat, was taking notes and managing to look fashionable. The other bidder looked about forty-something. He had an accent like Ali's.

The auctioneer toured everyone through the store space and up the stairs. It wasn't even cleared out yet. Abby mentioned this, and the auctioneer, displaying some annoyance with the comment, read her name off the sign-in sheet with formality, and pointed to the listing sheet, which indicated that the value of the goods had been ascertained. They were going with the property, of course. Abby felt adequately chastised and followed along in the back. She watched the woman. She couldn't imagine that a woman her age was an investor in commercial real estate, particularly in this neighborhood.

They saw the living space. There were no personal items, but it was still filled with furniture. The furniture would go with the property. It was a nice, two-bedroom apartment. The kitchen had been updated, and there were hardwood floors throughout. The auctioneer asked if anyone had any questions. Abby didn't feel she should speak. She really shouldn't even be there. The middle-eastern man asked a few questions about the age of the building, the roof, and the plumbing. The bidding started at sixty thousand dollars. Both bidders were willing. Then sixty-five, then seventy. At seventy-five, the man dropped out, and the woman was awarded the building. She turned over her earnest money and was told to be downtown at Chicago Title on LaSalle the following Friday for the closing. These matters usually took thirty days, the man explained, but because there was no mortgage or lien holders and the title looked clear, they could fast-track the process.

Abby had no idea about the value of real estate in this part of town, but she assumed the price was considerably under market value.

• • •

MARCUS sat by the window waiting for his boss. Duvane had told him they'd meet at Erik's Deli in Oak Park for lunch on Tuesday. It was just fifty feet from the Green Line stop on Oak Park Avenue, and Marcus had spotted the red awning with no problem.

The people on the street were bundled in their long coats, hats, and gloves, with just enough of their faces exposed to allow them to see and breathe. The wind whipped down the street, forcing them to move at an angle. Marcus knew cold weather, but nothing like this wind. He cupped his coffee, relished the warmth, and marveled at the change in scenery of just two train stops across the Chicago border. Kids were running around a beautiful park on the corner, making snowballs and snow angels. An enormous public library, a fresh bread shop, restaurants, coffee houses, a popcorn shop, and an antique furniture boutique filled the avenue around them. It was as if he had entered another world.

He spotted Duvane coming in the door.

Duvane pulled off his hat and brushed off the snow before removing his heavy coat. "I see you found the place." They shook hands. Duvane's hand was as massive as Henton's, though his size didn't appear related to weight training. More likely, pies.

"Yes, it was easy. But why the change?"

"We can't meet in the city anymore. I was at that diner we went to the other day, and four officers came in. We can't have that." Duvane patted Marcus's back and guided him up to the counter to order sandwiches. They found a table away from the door and the cold air that swept in with all the entrants.

"So, how's it going these days? You got some new leads for me?"

"Well, I'm definitely getting to know the players, and I've found a few chatty kids who love passing on the neighborhood gossip."

"That's promising, but remember, I don't want gossip. I want you to eyewitness."

Marcus nodded. "Well, I've got two cops on my radar right now. Michael Reilly, he's with the eleventh district."

"Sounds like a white guy."

They both laughed. "Of course."

"What do you got?"

"I don't know yet. You know that murder and drug bust we talked about at Reggie's? Turns out he was the first cop at the scene. I know some of the kids that were at Reggie's when that went down. Not sure what would have tipped him off to go there. Also, he supposedly found drugs at this Quick Mart down the street where the kids in the hood say drugs were never sold. And then a week after they go after the building, the owners were found dead. He found the bodies. I don't know. It just feels odd. But I don't have anything real yet."

"Okay. Have you pulled him up on the system?"

"Clean as a whistle. He's pretty young. Eight years on the force."

"What else?"

"I've been hearing stories of this other cop that comes around every now and then. Roughing up some street kids, taking drugs and money, but no arrests."

"Who is he?"

"Don't know yet. I've pulled the pictures of the cops in that district and the neighboring districts. He's not one of them. But one kid said he'd seen him with that prostitute a few times, the one that turned up dead at Reggie's. Here, I got a shot of him."

Duvane studied the photograph as Marcus continued.

"Yesterday, I met with the woman who walked into Reggie's that night. She called Reilly on Friday with information that she remembered seeing a white guy leaving as she got close. But she didn't recognize this guy," he said, tapping the photograph.

"It's not much of a picture. Can't really see his face."

"I know. But I've seen him up close. I just couldn't get a shot at the time. Whoever he is—I think he's worth checking out. One kid told me he busted up a drug deal down the street a few weeks back, took a bag of heroin and five thousand, and let the kid go."

Duvane slammed the table with satisfaction. "Now this is the shit I'm talking about. I want to know who he is."

"Me too."

"Well, we gotta get a better picture, for one."

"I'm working on it."

"I know you are. And obviously I'm grateful that you've already nailed four bad apples for me."

"Well, that kind of just fell in my lap. I mean, they beat the living shit out of some punks, without cause, right in front of me."

"Yeah." Duvane smiled. "That's why I like this little operation of ours. My little secret weapon."

"Well, I wouldn't say I'm little, but the secret remains."

Duvane finished his burger and re-salted his fries for the third time. "Nothing would surprise me anymore, Marcus. I mean we've got sixty-eight active street gangs in Chicago, with over five hundred factions. Did I mention that?"

Marcus nodded. He'd been reading all he could on this city, the force, the scandals, the crime.

"We estimate gang membership at sixty-eight thousand. That's five times the number of police officers in the department. It's a war out there. And I get it. Some police abuse seems to be routine. I mean, once in a while, you're gonna have to fuck someone up. But I'm telling you, brutality is a sport for some of these guys. There are some really racist motherfuckers running around in uniforms. I read reports of officers shouting 'niggers,' 'monkeys,' 'hood rats,' all over the PA systems of their cars."

Marcus shook his head in disgust.

"It's a small wonder that I was actually promoted to this post. Maybe someone up there knows it's gonna take a black man to bring down these shits."

Marcus raised his Diet Coke to toast.

"I'm starting to think that some of our guys may be as bad as the gangbangers. Maybe worse. I mean, what's more dangerous than a criminal with total immunity?"

Marcus sat back, pushed his empty plate away, and listened.

"I told you about that officer convicted last year of running a drug operation? Drugs found in his locker, for Christ's sake. Balls, I'm telling you. These fuckers think they are above the law."

"And if it's anything like New York, I'm sure you don't get much internal reporting. Snitches were terrorized in New York."

"Exactly. These cops know the system, where the holes are. It's mayhem. I've got to attack this from all angles. That's why I need you on the street. The residents are not reliable witnesses. Too many criminal records, too much fear. They're too vulnerable. But I'm cleaning house, my friend, and you're going to help me catch some of these motherfuckers."

Marcus smiled.

"And once we get through the districts on the west side, I'd like to move you to the south side and do it again. If you're willing."

Marcus could tell it was a question, but he wasn't ready to answer yet. It was hard to think about the future. He just wanted to get through each day. But he could see why his old boss was friends with this guy. Both were good men at the core; both loved saying *motherfuckers;* and obviously both loved food.

Duvane wiped the ketchup from the corner of his mouth, pulled an envelope from his inside pocket, and leafed through his notes as he continued. "Now here's another one to look into. Some woman that lives in one of the projects by Cellular Field said she was attacked by four plain-clothed white officers a few weeks ago. They were apparently wearing bulletproof vests. Said they made her tell them where she lived, brought her to her apartment, put a gun to her head, and ransacked the place, looking for drugs. She filed a report with OPS, but two weeks later they were back for more."

"What's OPS?"

"Office of Professional Standards. It's where residents are encouraged to report police abuse. But it's not doing great in my book. Says right here ..."—Duvane looked at the notes again—"'*From 2001 to 2003, OPS received over seventy-six hundred complaints of police brutality.*' And guess how many of those complaints ended in discipline against the officers?"

Marcus shrugged.

"Thirteen."

"Shit."

"Granted, there are some bogus claims filed, but come on. This is the problem, Marcus. This means that the officers know there's less than a one in one thousand chance of being fired for their actions. And honestly, I think you and I may be the only ones in the Chicago Police Department who are concerned."

"Well, it's a good thing you got the job."

Duvane sat back, drank his soda, and wiped his mouth. "Yeah, well, I never would have if it hadn't been for that trial last spring. When a ten-person jury finds the City of Chicago guilty of systematically covering up criminal violence of its officers, heads are gonna roll. And you've seen our mayor. You knew he'd put some pressure on the force to improve—at least public perception, anyway."

"Like maybe promoting a black commander to take over the Internal Affairs Division."

"Cheers to that!" Duvane raised his glass. "Now this woman, she's filed suit against the department and has named three of the officers involved. They've been put on leave for now. That's three less pieces of shit I need to worry about. But the fourth one, I need a name. I want you to see what you can find out. Her claims, if true, are just the sort of shit I need to deal with most. Apparently, the cops around the projects are terrorizing the residents. Planting drugs, stealing money. Some even show up on the first and the fifteenth of the month."

"Payday," Marcus added.

"Exactly. I want to create a criminal case against all of them. Send a message that we don't tolerate this shit."

"Got it."

FOURTEEN

TRIP stared up at the city map, a blown-up version of the west side that stretched three feet across the brick wall behind his massive glass desk. With little flag and circle pins on the various properties, he could easily survey his acquisitions and targets. He'd already sold ten properties to other developers who were doing as Trip was, sort of. Quick profits had been parlayed into more capital for further buys. He now had seven properties around both United Center and Cellular Field, at least ten more under investigation, and he was finally operating on his own profits. Things were going well. He just needed to get Reggie's and the Madison property, and he'd have the necessary diversity. A little commercial, a little mixed-use, a little residential—all with great potential in emerging neighborhoods.

"And who says you need money to start a business?" Trip said to himself with a satisfied smile as he looked around his loft with its mod/chic interior, as his mother had called it.

The front door flew open. "Morning!" Lisa said, with that sultry voice that had been part of the reason he'd hired her. He looked over at the twenty-four-year-old by the door as she shook off the snow and removed her coat and hat, revealing her super-snug, cashmere V-neck—a Christmas gift from Trip—and a suede miniskirt, which would provide optimal viewing once she sat at her desk. She shook her hair and let it fall down her back, just as Trip had requested. "All men love long hair," he had advised in the interview. "Don't hide it." She had seemed flattered at the time and had always worn it down. After trading her Ugg boots for three-inch heels, she headed to the kitchen and offered, "Coffee?"

"Yes, please!" She was a good hire—right out of college, smart enough to do the work, eager, and naive—a great combination.

Lisa put a napkin on his desk and handed over his coffee.

"Thanks. So, how did the auction go yesterday? Did we get the building?"

"Sure did. Seventy-five thousand."

"Nice. Any competition?"

"Not really. There were only three of us there, and one woman didn't even bid. The man dropped out at seventy."

"Woman?" That didn't sound right. People who went to auctions investigated the property in advance. Potential buyers came with checks in hand. No one went unless interested.

"Yeah. A redhead. Maybe twenty-nine or thirty, I'd guess. Pretty. She asked about the stuff. She didn't know the process."

"Did you get her name?"

"Something with a *D*, I think, and Irish sounding…Donolley, maybe?"

Trip sipped his coffee.

Lisa walked to her desk and then yelled over her shoulder, "No, Donovan. That's right."

Trip nearly choked. "Abigail Donovan?"

Lisa was sitting at her own smaller, glass-topped desk not twenty feet away, pulling up the e-mails. "Yes, that sounds right. Do you know her?"

"Yes, I do," he said only to himself. He looked back up at the map of the city. He removed the circle pin that had been on the corner of Pulaski and Lake, the Quick Mart building, and replaced it with a small flag pin. What was she doing at that auction? He thought back to the other night. He'd been so hopeful of the potential, but she'd already proved to be disappointing. The thought of it pissed him off. He looked over at the circle pin on the Reggie's Bar & Grill address. "You've got no business there, Abby."

Trip sat in silence as the wheels began to turn. He made a note to call Patrick. Just for insurance. "Don't fuck this up for me, Abby."

The phone rang and Trip livened up with the confident air that this latest disturbance could be handled. It was his mother.

"Hey, Mom, so you want to look at my property today?"

"Honey, that's why I'm calling. I know I said I'd come downtown today, but my car wouldn't start this morning. Your father dropped me off at my Wilmette job, and I've got maybe forty-five minutes left of work. I was thinking you could pick me up, and we could go into town for lunch. Bring me some pictures of the property, and we can talk about what you have in mind."

"No problem. It's on Sheridan, right?"

"Yes, it's at 1014. Limestone facade, tile roof, lake side."

"Yeah, I remember it. I'll be there in forty-five."

ABBY sat at the conference table, staring at the clock. The Prince Industries deposition was scheduled for nine o'clock. She had worked late into the night Tuesday, to make up for the two-hour field trip to Quick Mart, and had spent most of the night tossing around with questions and worries and thoughts and depression at the realization that there was no one to talk to. She was exhausted.

Opposing counsel called just after nine with some crisis, asking to reschedule, and Abby breathed a sigh of relief. She went back to her desk, paralyzed with indecision, lack of focus, distraction. She'd lost her rhythm. She couldn't get into her day.

After staring at the phone number in front of her for ten minutes, she finally decided to make the call.

A half hour later, she grabbed her coat and headed to Starbucks. It felt great to get outside and breathe some fresh air. The sun was making an appearance for the first time in what seemed like weeks, and Abby needed to feel its warmth on her face, even if it was only thirty degrees outside.

A man came up behind Abby in line at Starbucks, and she quickly turned around to see him. Just a stranger. They both gave embarrassed smiles. She felt paranoid, jumpy—so strange about everything.

She grabbed her latte, sat by the window with a good view of the people outside and the customers inside, and waited.

Detective Henton arrived about fifteen minutes later, looking nothing like that night she first saw him, except for that scar. It was hard not to stare at it. Now that he was here, she was nervous. Would he be angry about this frivolous meeting?

His smile relaxed her. "Hello again, Ms. Donovan," he offered, extending his hand. "Shall I sit?"

"Please, thanks so much for coming. I feel a little stupid for calling you. I just needed to talk about this, and I really didn't know who else to call."

"I'm glad you did. Let me just grab some coffee."

Abby watched him walk to the counter. He was massive. Obviously, he worked out, something she'd never found time for. She sipped her latte and smiled nervously as he took a seat next to her.

"So, did you remember something else about the man you saw at Reggie's?"

"No, I didn't. I'm sorry, I just…well, I guess…" She hesitated, wondering what she could possibly say to justify this meeting. "I just want to know that someone is looking into Ali Rashid's death. And, of course, that woman I found. I wonder about her too. I can't believe that I stepped outside my little bubble, just by accident, and I ended up here."

"And where's that?"

"Wondering about a dead prostitute, dreaming about gangbangers grabbing me, meeting a sweet man like Ali, and then hearing that he's a murderer and maybe a drug trafficker. And then you—you show up and tell me you're investigating police officers and show me a picture of some guy and tell me not to mention our talk with Officer Reilly, and now I'm just paranoid. I mean, is Officer Reilly…?" She hoped he might fill in the blank.

The detective sipped his coffee.

Maybe he was contemplating a response, but she didn't wait to find out. "It's all just insane. I'm a senior associate at a big firm, and my whole purpose in life is supposed to be representing my clients. Working their cases, billing ridiculous hours," she said with a roll of the eyes. "But I can't do it. I'm screwing up at work. I can't focus. I'm preoccupied. I keep coming back to all of this."

"Ms. Donovan—"

"Please, call me Abby."

"Abby, listen. I'm really sorry this happened to you. But you need to put it out of your mind."

Yeah, right. "I went to the auction yesterday."

"What auction?"

"The auction of Ali's Quick Mart building. You know the government seized it, right?"

"I did, though I'm surprised it would be up for auction so quickly. Why would you go?"

"I was surprised too. According to the rules, it should take months, even if no one protests the proceeding."

"But why'd you go?"

It seemed silly and hard to explain. She took a sip of coffee to regroup her thoughts. "I guess I wanted to know that someone was going to take care of it. It just seemed like the police swooped in and took his place—and he didn't even get the chance to fight back. And then he died mysteriously, and no one cared. I had gotten him a lawyer, you know."

The detective was surprised.

"Yep. Ted Gottlieb, some hotshot criminal defense lawyer. And he was going to tear the government's case apart. But now," she lowered her voice, suddenly aware that she was talking about drugs and murder in public, "Ali's dead, his best friend is dead, and their place belongs to some idiot little girl!"

"What?"

Abby smiled with embarrassment. It was a strange comment. "When I went to the auction, there were only two bidders: a man, Middle Eastern, like Ali, and some girl. Honestly, she couldn't have been older than twenty-five. White, well dressed, but really trendy clothes—young. I couldn't imagine what she was doing there or why she'd want that building."

The detective put down his drink and sat back. "Why do you say that he died mysteriously?"

"They're calling it a murder-suicide. I'm sorry—I just don't believe it. I don't know what kind of evidence they have, but he was not suicidal. We'd just had lunch. And he spoke with such affection for his friend. I don't believe that he'd kill him. I just don't."

"I'm sorry. I'm confused. I thought you barely knew Mr. Rashid."

"Well, I kind of knew him. He drove me home that night. We talked the whole time; he met me for lunch to return my glasses; he called me for help. I saw the fear in his eyes, Detective. I got a sense of him. He was a good man." She needed him to see.

He leaned in and lowered his voice. "Please, call me Marcus," he asked with a smile. "It's safer." He had a great smile.

"Oh, right." Abby looked around. What a strange world she was in.

Marcus continued. "I think Mr. Rashid's case is questionable, as well. Not uncommon, but worth looking into. And because I have connected Officer Reilly to the Reggie's

Bar incident, where drugs were also found, I am looking into it. I don't know about your friend, but when I figure this out, I'll let you know." He sat back and sipped his coffee.

"Really? Because I know I'm not family, and no one needs to tell me anything, but I would so appreciate it if you kept me updated on this case."

"You got it."

Abby could see that he was telling the truth. She'd met cops at her townhouse—and Officers Reilly and Trask—but the only cop she felt like she could trust was the one she'd thought was trying to kill her two weeks ago.

She half expected him to rise with that comment, like the meeting would end. But he continued to sip his coffee. She had no interest in work now, so she figured she'd press for more. "So, has anyone figured out who killed that woman, the prostitute?"

"Police report describes it as a 'john gone wrong' situation. Other than you seeing that man leaving Reggie's, there's nothing."

"Well, if they had sex, there should be some evidence on her body, right?"

Marcus smiled. "Actually, I don't know what kind of forensic testing has happened at this point. Until you called last Friday with that description, that matter was not really on my radar. I'm focused on cops. I can't worry about every crime that happens in that neighborhood. There were six hundred murders last year in Chicago. A huge number of those murders happened within that two-mile radius."

"Do you know what's happening in the case?"

"Well, I know the bartender was arrested for drug trafficking. I don't think they've linked him to murder. The property has been seized."

Abby immediately put her cup down in exasperation. "What? Why?"

"Abby, when drug activity occurs at a specific location on a repeated basis, the property is considered an instrument of the crime. Getting that property out of the hands of the drug dealers is one way police combat the problem."

"Did the bartender own the property?"

"I don't know. I haven't really looked into it." He obviously saw no problem with this.

"You know, I read a lot of cases about this stuff back in law school. A lot of innocent people get pounded by those laws."

"Well, a lot of gangbangers lose their BMWs and crack houses with those laws too. And property owners are held accountable for illegal activity on their property."

The advocate in her was rising. She was getting worked up. "I've read of police departments intentionally busting drug activities in valuable buildings so they can seize the properties, and innocent owners get no rights to counsel and bear the burden of proving their property's innocence, all so the cops can profit."

Marcus tried to respond, but she cut him off. "And I've read of a woman whose eighteen-thousand-dollar car was seized as the 'getaway car' after she stole a twenty-five-dollar sweater. If that's not about police profit, what is?"

"Listen, Abby, I don't know about any of that. From what I've been told, seizure is a valuable tool in combating drug pushers."

Abby stopped. Marcus was not the person to have this argument with. She was sure he'd see the matter differently.

She thought about Ali. "So, is it just a matter of course these days? Go after the property wherever an arrest takes place?"

"Of course not. It really just depends."

Maybe it was justified in the Reggie's Bar case. She wouldn't be surprised if that run-down bar was some haven for drug dealing. She didn't know all the facts.

"So, what happened after I ran out of Reggie's that night, and you chased me?"

Marcus put up his hand to stop her and put down his coffee. "I'm a good guy, remember?"

Abby smiled. "Yeah, I just wondered what those thugs did. I wouldn't expect that they went into the ladies' room and found that dead woman, and if they found the drugs, I'd be surprised if they called the cops. I just wondered how it all went down."

"Actually, I don't know. That's one of the reasons I'm now looking into Reilly. I find his report a bit odd."

"What do you mean?"

"When I came to meet you last week, you said you had told Reilly you saw a white man with wavy blond hair leave the building. He only wrote that you saw a man. The file said 'no further description provided.' And I heard sirens moments after I followed you, but I'm not sure what would have prompted the cops to come. When I got back, the place was surrounded."

Abby nodded in agreement. "Yeah, I was trying to call 911 when those boys came in, but I never got past the '9'. We need to look into this more."

"We?"

She smiled, embarrassed. "You, whatever. I just mean it sounds weird. And if I can help you, I'd really like to. You're essentially doing this alone, right?"

"I am working alone. But I keep my boss in the loop."

"Well, if you need a lawyer or maybe a little research, or just someone to bounce ideas off of, I'm a good listener."

She hoped he'd let her in. If nothing else, it was nice to have someone to talk to about all of this.

AFTER Abby left, Marcus walked over to the Chicago Public Library on Congress. He went up to the computer lab, got online, and pulled out the codes for the department's Intranet from his wallet. Within a couple of minutes he had internal police files at his fingertips. He looked up Michael Reilly's record again. On the force eight years. Last four years, Asset Forfeiture Unit; before that, Gang Task Force. Six complaints of excessive force during arrest, but no disciplinary action taken. Typical stuff. Three requests for promotion. Passed over each time. Only notation: "budgetary." One request for short-term disability leave. Denied. File said the request was so Reilly could take care of his ailing mother. It didn't look like much. He closed the human resources files and went into the active crime file database.

A search on *Rashid, Ali* and he was able to review the police report from the crime scene:

Neighbor reported "arguing and screaming." Police entered apartment with force when no one answered door. One man found with bullet wound in chest. Second man had bullet wound in head. Both dead. Gun, .38 caliber, recovered at scene, next to the hand of the man with the head trauma.

He read the corresponding forensics report:

Chest wound was created from .38 caliber weapon fired approximately six feet away. Head wound came from .38 caliber fired at close range. Conclusion: Head wound was self-inflicted.

Marcus continued to scan the document for a weapons report. There should have been a report on the test results from the gun, showing that it was recently fired, that prints or gunpowder residue confirmed its use. He didn't see any report. He couldn't imagine the testing hadn't been done. He made a note of the name of the physician who'd signed off on the forensics report: Dr. Roberts. And he wanted to talk to the neighbor who'd made the police report. He rechecked the report for the name. No name listed. Strange.

Marcus closed the document and searched for *Reggie's Bar & Grill,* then read the police report from the scene on January 26:

> *Neighbor reported woman's scream from inside bar. Arrived at scene at 12:40 a.m. No one on premises. Woman found in bathroom. Dead. No wounds. Wearing plaid skirt, one fishnet stocking, no undergarment, red shirt, all buttons open, red bra. Red spiked heels. Large mark on neck. Two kilos of cocaine found on bar.*

The corresponding forensic report indicated death by asphyxiation. Time of death was between eleven thirty and twelve thirty. No evidence found under nails. No foreign body fluids recovered. Marcus read the report again. *One fishnet stocking.* So where's the other one? Sounded like a good way to strangle someone. *Neighbor reported woman's scream.* He hadn't heard Abby scream when he walked into the bar. He made a note to ask her if she remembered screaming when she found the body or when the boys grabbed her. The police were already en route when he left the building. That woman must have already been dead.

He wanted to talk to whoever called in the scream. He searched the document for a name. But again, there was no name listed on the report. How could the police not have that name? They would have wanted to interview the neighbors. To find out what was seen or heard. The reports were thin. Too thin. There must have been a 911 call, he thought.

He closed the file and searched the emergency phone records. He had to hand it to Chicago. The electronic organization of the city's files and records was certainly improving his ability to investigate outside the station. He searched January 26 first, the night of the Reggie's Bar murder. He pulled the list of calls made between midnight and 12:40 a.m., the time the police had arrived. There were thirteen calls made throughout the city. Even though he'd only been in Chicago for under a year, he was able to quickly dismiss several calls based on the corresponding addresses listed. He made notes of the eight remaining addresses and did a quick MapQuest search to see where they came from. He found two calls from that neighborhood, but neither address was within four blocks of Reggie's. There was no way a call made from those addresses could have reported a woman's scream inside of Reggie's. There was no 911 call.

He did the same thing for the Quick Mart incident. The day was February 2. The report stated that neighbors heard screaming and fighting. No reference to time. Police arrived at six o'clock in the morning. Marcus checked the 911 records between five and six o'clock on that day. Twenty-two calls made during that time. But again, the addresses didn't match. Not a single call from within four blocks of the building. And Reilly had been the first cop on the scene, again.

ABBY spent the afternoon finding associates to help ease her workload. She couldn't continue to ignore what was in front of her, but she couldn't seem to do it all either. She found two second-years, Kevin and Eileen, chatting by the copier, and recruited them to come with her to Milwaukee the next day to gather the Dalcon Laboratories documents. She then delegated several tasks for the Amro case to a third-year associate. She'd review and revise later.

These disputes—million-dollar claims in many cases—felt so trivial. Ali was dead. That woman was dead. She felt connected to them. She picked up Marcus's card and stared at his name. She was glad she had called. There was something about him, like an emptiness, a sadness. It was familiar. They'd only met two days ago, and he was now the only person in the world she wanted to talk to. She wanted to ask him about that scar—it didn't look that old. She wondered if she'd ever have the nerve to bring it up.

She headed home at eight o'clock, with a craving for chicken pad thai.

The doorbell rang just twenty minutes after she'd ordered, and she ran down with her money. But instead of the deliveryman, she found Mrs. Tanor in her robe and slippers, standing at the front door.

"Hey, Mrs. Tanor. I thought you were my Thai food. What's up?"

"Sorry, dear. I just wanted to ask you something. Do you have a cousin?"

"No." Kind of an odd question. But it was now freezing outside. Abby ushered her in and shut the door. "What's up?"

Mrs. Tanor paused. She looked around like she was searching for something. Maybe the right words.

"You know, I'm not totally surprised. I thought he seemed suspicious, but I didn't want to assume."

"Mrs. Tanor. I'm confused. What are you talking about?"

"Well, a young man came to the gate and rang your buzzer several times earlier today around three o'clock."

"I was at work."

"Of course, dear. I knew you wouldn't be home. I was outside, taking down my Christmas decorations. He looked about twenty-two. He looked tired."

"Twenty-two? Are you sure that was for me?"

"Oh, yes."

"What did he look like?"

"He had brown hair. It was kind of matted, he was unshaven, and his clothes were dirty."

"That's weird."

"Well, I ignored him at first. But he buzzed several times and finally called over to me. I asked if he was a friend of yours."

"What did he say?"

"He said that you were expecting him. Then he said he was your cousin and asked if I could let him in. Something about him made me uneasy. He seemed too…jittery. I told him that I couldn't do that, and I went back inside."

"That's weird. Well, I'm glad you didn't let him in. Let's hope that was a fluke. Please let me know if you see him come back."

"Okay, dear. Good night."

FIFTEEN

O N Thursday, Abby and the second-year associates went to Milwaukee to gather documents and drug parapher- nalia in the Dalcon Laboratories warehouse. After seven hours, they called it a day. It was not exactly fun, but it was nice to be out of the office, and Abby enjoyed the break from her own internal dialogue by listening to Kevin and Eileen tell stories of dates and restaurants and wild nights out as they sat at dinner.

On Friday morning, they finished up, packed up the rental car with boxes of documents and sample instruments for her products liability case, and headed back to the office. It was around noon when Abby sat at her desk to review mail and voice messages. She smiled at the last one. It was Nate. As much as she resisted remembering, it felt so good to have him in her life again. It felt like home.

• • •

WITH the sun shining and snow blanketing most of Millennium Park, Abby shielded her eyes from the intense light. At least thirty people were ice-skating as Abby walked toward the Park Café. The massive park, restaurant, and amphitheater, just completed last summer, were already attracting throngs of tourists and locals as a beautiful new gathering spot on South Michigan Avenue. The skaters' laughter and squeals made her wince. God, what had happened to her? When had she last had a good laugh? Or a good time?

She knew when. She still missed David so much.

Nate was already at the table and waved her over. His warm embrace lifted her spirits, and she thanked him for suggesting lunch.

"Abby, this is actually a business meeting. I've got a case that I really want you to work on with me."

"Nate, I'm just swamped. I can't seem to get out in front of everything. I just got back in town. Just Wednesday, I had to pawn off a bunch of stuff to some junior associates."

"But that's what you're supposed to do. Listen, this is a good case. Interesting stuff and you'll get some good experience."

She'd let him try to sell it, even though there was no way. They ordered their salads and iced teas.

"Well, what is it?"

Nate put down his drink and leaned in, like he was about to share a juicy story. "My client is a woman from the projects on the south side. She has been repeatedly terror-ized by some Chicago cops."

The mention of dirty cops got her attention.

"Abby, the stories she tells are so disturbing. There's quite a drug trade in her neighborhood, and it's like the cops have gone rogue. Stomping over civil rights and breaking laws left and right. She filed complaints with the police, and nothing came of it. We're suing the cops, the Chicago Police Department, and the city. Civil rights violations, wrongful imprisonment, assault and battery, intentional infliction of emotional distress—every claim I can come up with."

"Well, I must say, I'm intrigued." It sounded like work she could focus on, given the last three weeks.

"Abby, to be honest, I want you to work with me for a couple of reasons." He took a sip of his drink, and Abby tried to finish the chunk of bread she'd just grabbed.

"Oh, yeah?"

"Well, first. I'm glad to see you again after all these years, and I'd love an excuse to be able to catch up more."

With hand to heart and a grin, she acknowledged the sweet sentiment. His expression changed then, and she could sense there was another reason. She wasn't so sure she wanted to hear it. "And?"

"And you don't seem happy to me, Abby. I get the sense that you're not enjoying your job. Maybe you're not enjoying your life."

His bluntness took her off guard. He couldn't have been more right, but she couldn't bear to go there. She looked down.

"Listen, I'm not telling you what to do. I just want to spend some time together. The work is not glamorous or high profile, but it's interesting. It's sometimes sad, but it always feels important. And it gives me purpose. I think you would find that too."

She felt exposed. Like Nate had taken one look at her and seen the charade. "I don't know." He had no idea what he was asking of her. She wanted to do this. At least this one assignment, but she couldn't just change her life plan. She was on a path, and she had to honor that. He had no idea.

Nate put his hand on hers. "Abby, just think about it. I'll be at Dirksen in front of Judge Coreus on Monday at nine o'clock on the matter. I'm going to meet with my client afterward. If you can make it, come. You can meet her. I'll give you a copy of her statement, and then you can decide."

Abby opened her mouth to respond, but Nate interjected.

"Just think about it." Right on cue, the salads arrived. "Now come on—let's eat!"

Abby walked through the park before going back to the office. She tried to let the skaters' laughter and happiness fill her head. Nate knew her so well. She almost felt like she had Denny back. He had always looked out for her too. She could still picture his face and the look he gave her when she was screwing up. The look he gave her that night. His irritation at her stupidity.

She walked up the steps toward the massive reflective structure that everyone in town had affectionately named "the bean" because it looked like a giant kidney bean that mirrored the light and the sky and the Michigan Avenue buildings and the children who ran up and under and around it with glee. She walked toward it, closer and closer, searching for her own image, staring at the distortion in front of her. Just like a circus mirror. Her grand plan was falling apart. It was as if all the fear and trauma and sadness of the last few weeks had forced her to stop spinning on the hamster wheel. Her plan was beginning to seem fruitless, even stupid.

BACK at the office, Abby got some coffee and began sorting through her stacks of work. There was a knock at the door, and before she even looked up, Peter and Neil came in and sat in the chairs in front of her.

"Hi, guys. What's up?"

Peter started. "Abby, you look engrossed. Can you spare a minute?"

She sat back and dropped her pen. "Of course, I have a minute. What can I do for you?"

"Well, Neil and I were just going over the ADP case, and I think our response to the defendant's motion to dismiss looks pretty good. Neil said you helped out with this."

"Yes." I only wrote the whole damn thing, she thought.

"I thought it would be best to have you take a look at some of the changes I've suggested. I want more case support. We figured that since you probably still had the research, you could find support faster than Neil. And he's pretty swamped right now."

Neil sat there, smiling at his seamless ability to pass off more of the grunt work. There was no way he was busier than she was.

"Sure. I've still got the research. When do you need it?"

"Monday."

"Okay, then," she responded casually, "I better get going." It was a test. She could feel it. Peter wanted to see if her screw-up had been a fluke.

Peter rose. "Great. Just get it back to Neil by nine o'clock Monday, so we can all discuss and tweak."

This all felt so déjà vu. She couldn't bear it. "Oh, Peter, wait. I just took on a new case. I have to be in court Monday morning. So I'll leave the research on Neil's desk by the end of the day, Saturday." She looked at Neil. His satisfied grin was wiped clean. Good timing, Nate.

Peter didn't seem to care. "Okay." And then he turned to Neil. "You just be sure to get in here on Sunday, so you can take over if there's any more that Abby needs you to do." Abby tried to hide her smile.

After they left, she sat with head in hands, reading through the changes Peter had made to the brief. The cases she had researched would not support what he was now asserting. These were arguments, not law. She was starting from scratch, and Neil knew it.

At five thirty, Abby went to the kitchen for some dinner. It was bound to be another long night, and she thought one of those giant chocolate chip cookies the caterers brought on Fridays might help pep her up. Neil was in line, putting one of the turkey wraps on his plate.

"Hey, thanks for the help today, babe."

"No problem." Asshole.

"I like having you under me," he added with a smile.

"I think I did a favor for Peter today, Neil."

"I don't know. I really felt like you were doing a job for me." It was his typical banter, the baiting, the dog-like circling, trying to get her to play.

She smiled, took a dinner roll, some salad, and a giant cookie, and sat.

He joined her. "What's up, baby? You look blue."

"I've just got a lot going on."

"Maybe we should go grab a drink at Miller's after work. Unwind a little." She felt a come-on approaching and gave him that knowing look.

"Seriously, you look like you could use a drink." He was playing it straight. She'd rarely seen him shtick-free like this in the last six years.

"Thanks, Neil, but I've got a lot more to do tonight. I don't think so."

More associates joined their table, and Abby ate in silence as the others gossiped and relished the break. She missed Sarah.

At seven thirty, she stacked her research to bring home.

As soon as Abby opened the giant courtyard gate, Mrs. Tanor was outside to greet her. She must have been watching by the window for her arrival.

"Hi, Mrs. Tanor, what's up?"

"Abby, that boy was back again."

"Who?"

"That young man."

"Did you talk to him?"

"I didn't know what to do. He kept buzzing your door, over and over. You obviously weren't home. He started yelling, 'Hey Abby! Abby, you gonna let me in?' I was going to call the police, but by the time I got to the telephone, he'd left."

Abby didn't know any young boys. Certainly, no one of Mrs. Tanor's description came to mind.

"Mrs. Tanor, I'm so sorry this is happening. I have no idea what this is about. I just can't imagine who that could be."

"Well, I don't feel safe. He looks like a criminal."

Abby felt she was being blamed.

"All I can say is, if you see him again, call the police."

"I will. Goodnight." Her door shut and Abby heard the chain lock engage.

"What did I do?" Abby wondered aloud, feeling Mrs. Tanor's anger.

MARCUS gave himself the once-over. He had on his gold medallion, his oversized jeans, and untied boots. It was freezing, and he didn't relish hanging out on the snowy streets, but he knew that's where he'd find the boys. He pulled on the black knit cap, did a little swagger, gave himself a tough-guy "Wassup?" into the mirror by the door, and headed out into the night.

It didn't take long to find the action. There were only a few regular spots, and he'd already passed two of them without seeing much. He got to JJ's, the liquor store on the corner of Cicero and Division, and found Darnel and some of the other neighborhood boys hanging out in front.

"Hey, Marcus!" Darnel was always the first to greet. Marcus had done well in choosing Darnel as a point man. He had spent an entire summer day on Darnel's front stoop, filling his head with fictitious stories of New York gang life and time in prison. It had earned him respect and an instant reputation as a crony and one that could be trusted. And his real life, his real story, though he hadn't told much, had actually allowed him to get away with not saying too much more. The whole world had been traumatized by 9/11, and if Marcus had been there and didn't want to talk about it, and left New York because of it, that was fine by Darnel. Marcus was an elder at thirty-three, worthy of respect, and Darnel had introduced him around the neighborhood like a long-lost relative.

There were fist bumps all around and half hugs with Darnel and Fat D.

"What's going on?" He wasn't sure how he was going to get into it yet.

"Same shit, different day, Marcus."

"Fuckin' cold, ain't it? I still ain't use to this wind."

"Couldn't have been much different in New York though, right?" Darnel asked.

148

"No. It was cold. But it seemed like we had more places to be inside on nights like this. There was this one bar—owner was cool. We just brought in our own shit and hung out. He didn't care."

"Like Reggie's," Fat D said. Several of the boys nodded in agreement.

Perfect. "Yeah, let's go there. I haven't been there in weeks."

Darnel was quick to stop him. "Didn't you hear? They shut it down."

"What the fuck? Just because of that dead bitch?"

Darnel answered. "You know how it works; they just take the buildings when they find drugs. There was a load in there that night."

Marcus continued, faking ignorance. "I only been there a couple times. I never saw anything goin' on."

A big guy with a small black diamond tattoo on the side of his neck chimed in. "That's cuz there wasn't. It's bullshit." Marcus didn't recognize him, but the design told him he was one of the Four Corner Hustlers.

He had them talking now. "Whatchu mean?"

The big guy continued: "Freddy had a deal with Leon, the bartender. He'd keep that shit outta the place, and Leon would be cool 'bout everything else."

Marcus didn't know Freddy, but he got the gist.

He played it through. "So what happened with Leon? He get busted?"

Darnel answered. "Hell, yeah! And the fucker wasn't even there!" Everyone laughed.

Another kid wondered aloud, "How come he wasn't there? It was open. He's the only employee."

Darnel had the scoop. "He says he was sent out for some shit."

"What do you mean?" Marcus asked.

"Some cop come in that night. Leon said he sent him out for olives or some bullshit."

"Olives?" All the boys were laughing.

Darnel continued. "I'm serious. Some cop come in, told him to go get him some shit, and Leon left. He went about four blocks up the road, got pulled over for jaywalkin', was hassled for, like, twenty minutes, and then he was let go. When he got back, the place was surrounded and he was arrested."

Fat D had the same thought as Marcus. "Why'd he leave his bar with that cop inside?"

"Cuz the fucker was a repeat customer. Leon said it was the same fucker who come in a few weeks back."

The gossip was passing the time well, and Marcus and the others were huddled in a circle, keeping out the chill.

"How'd you hear all this?" Marcus asked Darnel.

"Leon's out on bond. Stayin' at Rickie's. Waitin' for his grand jury hearing. I smoked a J with him yesterday."

Marcus wanted to talk to Leon.

"Yeah, he's screwed. Arrested two times in the last six weeks for drug trafficking. He got no chance."

"Twice?" Maybe Leon was a dealer, and these arrests were legitimate.

Fat D broke in. "Yeah, my bro was with him the first time. Fuckin' psycho cops come into Reggie's. No uniforms, but wearin' all their bulletproof vests. 'Cept one of 'em. Anyways, they was throwin' shit, broke some chairs, beer bottles, tossed the picture of Malcolm X 'cross the room. Put guns to their heads. Had 'em on the floor and wailed on 'em 'bout wantin' to find drugs."

"Did they?"

"One of 'em went in the back and came back with a big bag a' shit in one hand. Then they arrest Leon for dealin'."

Another kid broke in: "I known Leon a long time. That guy smokes weed every day, but he would never deal."

Another one added, "He couldn't handle the math."

Everyone laughed. The jokes continued at Leon's expense, and Marcus processed the information. He wanted to look up the arrest record as soon as possible. He wanted to know who those cops were.

Marcus needed a bit more. "Well, I hope I don't run into those cops anytime soon. What'd they look like?"

"My brother said they was Nazi muthefuckas. White, crew cuts, light hair. 'Cept one. He had kinda wavy blond hair."

It clicked right away. Marcus turned to Fat D and Darnel. "Hey, 'member the other week we was hangin' out at Carter's and that white cop came in and you said he was bad shit. He had wavy hair. Was it him?"

No one could answer. It was all second-hand information, and no one had been with Leon either night.

Several of the boys were finishing their cigarettes. The big one said they were heading to Suga' Ray's on North for some food. Darnel and Fat D agreed to go. Marcus said he needed some beer, said good-bye, and headed home.

SIXTEEN

ABBY spent Saturday and Sunday at the firm. She finished Neil's draft Saturday night, but spent most of Sunday sorting through the Dalcon Laboratories documents. By four o'clock, it was getting dark, and she headed home.

The snow had melted off the sidewalks, leaving just the giant mounds pushed to the curb by the snowplows. Abby stopped at the mini-mart on the corner for some much-needed groceries, and as she rounded the corner at Texas Star Fajita Bar, she noticed a kid outside her front gate. He looked a lot like the kid Mrs. Tanor had described. There were no young twenty-somethings who lived in the building.

"Hey!" Abby shuffled toward the gate, juggling her groceries and briefcase.

The boy looked in Abby's direction and ran the other way.

"Wait! Who are you? What do you want?" She was yelling and running as fast as she could, but the boy was faster. In no time, he was long gone.

Abby stopped at her gate, just in time to catch the milk, now busting out of the bottom of her grocery bag.

Abby rang Mrs. Tanor's, wondering if she'd seen him and called police, but no one answered. She fumbled with her keys, lost the delicate balance of bags, and watched as the eggs splatted onto the concrete.

"Goddammit!" This was not her day. In fact, she thought, 2004 was not feeling like her year.

ON Monday morning, Abby stood in the security line at the Dirksen Federal Building, emptying out her pockets in anticipation of the metal detector.

"Ms. Donovan?"

Abby turned to the voice behind her.

"Yes?" Abby did not recognize the short, graying man in the blue suit, who now stood, smiling, behind her.

He offered his hand. "Hello. I'm Ted Gottlieb. You sent me that forfeiture matter a few weeks back."

"Oh, sure. Hello." Abby extended her hand to shake. "But how did you know who I was?"

"I just caught a glimpse of the ID tag on your briefcase."

"Right," Abby said with a smile and turned back to move forward in line.

Gottlieb continued. "Ms. Donovan, I'm glad that I ran into you."

Abby turned back. "Why's that?"

"I have some personal effects from Mr. Rashid. I know you didn't know him too well, but you knew him better than I. I wonder if there's anyone I should call."

"What do you have?" Gottlieb and Ali had only met the one time, as she recalled.

"Well, Mr. Rashid brought me some videotapes from the surveillance camera in his shop."

"Oh." Abby thought about this. "Did he have footage from the drug-trafficking arrests?"

"Yes."

"I'd really appreciate getting those from you. There are issues about his case that I'm still involved in." It wasn't a total lie.

"Sure." He gave her his business card. "Just call my secretary, and she'll messenger them to your office later today."

"That's fabulous. Well, it was really nice meeting you. And if I ever hear of another person needing a criminal defense lawyer, I'll pass on your name."

"I appreciate that."

They both loaded their briefcases onto the conveyer belt, moved through the security area, and said good-bye at the elevator bank. Abby hit "4" to go to Judge Coreus's courtroom.

There were about fifteen people in the courtroom—attorneys mostly, waiting for their turn to present the judge with their motions. The judge walked in just as Abby was entering, so she took a seat in the back. Fortunately, Nate's case was the first to be called, *Ramirez v. City of Chicago et al.* Nate presented his motion to the judge, and the defense counsel stood, ready to argue. Nate wanted additional time for discovery because he had not received all requested documents from the defense and had been unable to complete his depositions. The defense was quick to assert code provisions regarding time limits, and Nate shot back a claim about stonewalling and the defense's failure to respond.

The judge cut them off quickly and fired questions at both attorneys. He ordered the parties to reset the trial date and continue with discovery for another sixty days, and threw out some vague warnings about abiding by the rules for full disclosure and cooperation.

As Nate returned to his client, he looked pleased. Abby caught his eye and waved. Nate nodded and ushered his client toward the exit. Abby followed them into the hall.

"Abby!" Nate gave her a warm and knowing smile.

"Isabel, this is Abigail Donovan. She's another attorney who's going to be working with us."

Abby shot Nate a look because she hadn't agreed to anything yet, but he just grinned. Abby offered her hand to the woman. The woman, who stood a couple of inches above Abby, offered a tentative smile and shook Abby's hand weakly. She had on an orange parka, a bright white, church-going, polyester dress, and giant boots.

Nate turned his attention to his client. "That went well. Thanks for meeting me here. I'll call you later this week and give you an update. Get some rest."

The woman smiled. "Thank you, Mr. Walters."

He stopped her. "Isabel, come on. If I'm going to call you 'Isabel,' you have to call me 'Nate.'"

"Okay, Nate. And nice to meet you, Ms. Donovan."

Abby smiled. "You too. And please, call me 'Abby.'"

Isabel walked to the elevator with tentative steps and nearly jumped from the movements of others in the hall.

Nate turned to Abby. "You came!"

"Yeah, yeah—so what is this all about?"

"Here." Nate pulled a document from his briefcase. "This is a copy of the testimony she gave me when this first began. Read it over. It'll make your blood boil."

Abby took the paper. "So, why'd she come today?"

"She's not employed right now. She's scared at home. I think it gives her a sense of security to meet me and see that the case is active. Even if we're just in the pre-trial stage."

Abby could understand that. They headed for the elevators.

"Besides, I kind of like reminding the judge and the opposing counsel of the face of this case. Everyone gets caught up in the game and maneuvering. I want them to see this woman's face all the time."

"So, what now?" Abby asked. They were walking back into the sea of bodies on the main floor.

"Now I go over to Judge Moore's chambers on another matter." He checked his watch. "In fact, I better get moving."

"Okay, well, have a good day, Nate. I'll call you later."

"You better." He was already halfway down the hall. "Welcome aboard!"

Abby shook her head in slight disbelief that she was even here. She followed a mass of people leaving the elevator banks toward the exit. The line for the metal detectors now extended to the front doors. Officer Reilly walked in. He was in uniform, walking with another officer. It made her stomach jump. He was probably here to testify in a case, but she felt afraid. He'd been nothing but nice to her, but now she wondered. Was he a crooked cop? She remained behind the other people walking toward the exit and tried to blend in with the crowd. As she got through the revolving door, she looked back. He was chatting casually with another officer.

Stepping out into the sunshine, she grabbed her sunglasses and tried to relax, while a sea of people headed toward her and the courthouse. And then she saw him. It was hard to miss him. He had a swagger and his wavy blond hair almost sparkled in the sunshine. She looked down immediately, wondering if he'd recognize her, wondering why he never called, wondering if he'd seen her naked. What if they'd slept together? Just a sleazy one-night stand. Of course he wouldn't call. He'd probably left as soon as they finished.

What was he doing here? He was heading toward her. Just say hello, she silently commanded. Act confident and ask for a date. She reached to remove her sunglasses and opened her mouth, but froze as a wave of insecurity took over. What if he didn't remember her? What if he blew her off? Her ego couldn't take it. She quickly looked away and bent over, as though she were pulling something out of her bag. She hoped he didn't notice her.

He walked right past her and through the revolving door. "Should I call him?" She tried to remember what she had done with that cocktail napkin.

TRIP removed his coat, readying himself for the detector. Waiting in line with the other civilians, he looked over at the officers and attorneys going through their own shorter, faster security checkpoint. That was really the only thing he missed. He saw a few familiar faces and said hello, then spotted Mike leaning against the wall by the elevators. Trip pushed the button, and they both waited in silence. When the doors opened, several people entered, and Mike pushed the button for the third floor. Trip followed Mike toward the first courtroom. It was empty. They sat in the back row by the door.

Mike turned to Trip. "The judge will be here in fifteen minutes."

Trip pulled the envelope from his back pocket and said, "Two thousand."

The giant courtroom echoed. Mike responded in a hushed voice. "I thought you said it would be four."

"This is just for Quick Mart. I was hoping we'd be done with Reggie's by now. When's the auction?"

Mike looked around and put the money away. "Why are we meeting here, anyway? I don't think we should be seen together."

"First of all, we're here because you needed to be here this morning, right? And I have some properties to see in the neighborhood. And the room's empty. Besides, who cares if people see us? We were friends on the force, we're still friends. No crime in that."

"This has gotten more serious, Trip, and you know it."

"Mike, you didn't do anything. You made some arrests. Moved forward for seizure. It's your job. What's the big deal?"

Mike looked at Trip. He wasn't going to say it out loud. But Trip could tell this was about the murders. The death of some useless hooker and some fucking terrorists. There was no reason to panic.

"What if someone connects these cases?"

"Who? Really, what are you afraid of? You've brought in big scores of drugs and seized some buildings, and the department will get a nice profit. Hardly a cause for investigation."

"But that bartender at Reggie's—I mean, what are the chances that charge is gonna stick? There are no prior convictions. No eyewitness to dealings. We're just talking about possession."

"First of all, who cares if the charges stick? You know it doesn't affect the case. Besides, Leon's got more than possession. It was a lot of coke. That's possession with intent. And we've got three cops that will testify to finding drugs on his person several weeks ago. What better testimony could you ask for?"

"When did that happen?"

"Don't you worry. You didn't really think you were the only cop I was counting on, did you? This is no small gig. I've got friends in all sorts of places. And we both know cops don't make enough money."

Mike continued to look at the door. He wouldn't sit still.

"Mike, come on. Relax. How's it coming with the Madison property? Have you reported any suspicious activity yet?"

"Not yet."

"I want the trail set by March. If I can get in there by summer, it'll be ready to flip in the fall."

He looked at Mike for confirmation and grew impatient as he waited. "Mike, your mother doing better these days?"

"Why?"

"I know you can use the money, that's all. Now focus. Let's clear Reggie's and this next one. I'm sure that will help with her medical bills."

"I don't even know when you'll get Reggie's. Owners filed a claim fighting the forfeiture."

"Leon can't fight this case. We've got him for trafficking."

"Turns out Leon's father is the owner."

Trip slammed his fist against the bench in front of them. "Goddammit! You investigated title! How could you not know that?"

"They have the same name. I didn't realize."

"Jesus fucking Christ."

"Sorry, Trip. It was an honest mistake. The property is still an instrument of the crime. The owner will still have to prove he couldn't have known. He'll lose. It's just going to take a while longer."

Now Trip couldn't sit still. He was talking to himself as much as Mike. "That just fucks with my plans. I was counting on that property. I've invested money and time already." He looked at Mike then. "I better get that property."

Mike looked away. People were starting to pour in.

Trip shook his head in disbelief and stood to leave. "I'll be in touch."

Mike leaned over. "Hey, you sure that Abigail Donovan is nothing to worry about?"

Trip wasn't sure of anything anymore; that's why he'd been moving forward in dealing with her. Just in case. "Why?"

"I saw her a few minutes ago, downstairs. Made me think of it."

Trip sat back down. "Well, she is a lawyer, Mike."

"I know, it's just that…"

"What?"

"She saw me. She looked away. She looked kind of nervous."

"Mike, why wouldn't she look away? Did you expect her to come over and chat? That doesn't sound like a problem." Trip was feeding Mike bullshit because he couldn't take him getting any more nervous. But Trip had felt uneasy about Abigail Donovan ever since he'd heard about her going to the Quick Mart auction. It seemed like she was nosing around. And he wasn't about to let her figure any of this out.

"When I picked her up a few weeks back, she was researching forfeiture laws."

"What? How do you know?"

"She was holding the papers when I got there. Dropped them right in front of me."

"But you were at her office, right? In uniform?"

"Yeah."

"Good." Trip thought some more. "Listen, I want you to call her office a few times this week. If she answers, just say you're checking in to see if she's remembered anything. If she doesn't, leave messages with her secretary. Don't do voicemail."

"Why?"

"Don't worry about the why. Just do it. And I'm going to see what I can find out."

"Well, I just saw her with Nate Walters."

"Who's that?"

"He's the lawyer suing the department and several cops for all sorts of shit. Everyone's up in arms about it."

"What's the basis?"

"Some woman that lives in one of the few remaining projects by Cellular Field. She says she was terrorized by some cops on more than one occasion."

"I don't know about that."

The courtroom was filling quickly now.

Trip got up to leave and leaned in. "Don't worry. I'm taking care of Abigail Donovan. Just in case."

Mike looked up at him and opened his mouth but didn't say anything.

Trip gave him a pat on the head. "See ya."

SEVENTEEN

ABBY sat in the conference room, staring at the frozen television screen. She called Marcus in a panic. He picked up on the third ring and sounded glad to hear from her. "Detective, something's happened."

"What's up, Abby?"

"Something's going on here. I don't know what to make of it."

"Just start at the beginning."

"I just ran into Ali Rashid's attorney. The one I found for him. We were at the courthouse. Anyway, he said Ali had brought him some security tapes from his store. He offered to give them to me, and they just arrived."

"Okay?"

"Officer Reilly is on tape, coming in for coffee, and then finding drugs and arresting this kid."

"Okay."

"I recognize the kid! He's been to my house. Three times now. I don't know who he is or what he wants. He always comes when I'm not home. He yells my name. It's weird. He tried to get my neighbor to let him in, saying he was my cousin. I saw him yesterday as I was walking home, and I yelled out to him, but he ran off."

"Why didn't you call me?"

"I didn't think of it. I mean, it never occurred to me that he could have something to do with Ali. I didn't know what to think. I just thought it was some punk."

"Where are you now?"

"I'm at the firm."

"I want to see those tapes."

"Can you get here now? I've got a monitor and player set up in the conference room. I'm on the fiftieth floor." She had requested the room and equipment to go over video depositions all afternoon. "It's private."

"I'm not exactly dressed to come to your firm right now. I'm in my 'hood wear."

Abby enjoyed the reference. She could picture it. It was quite a transformation, even though it was just a matter of wearing baggy clothes and a lot of gold jewelry.

"Just take off that giant medallion. No one will really see you anyway if you come to this floor. There's no main reception. The conference room is right off the elevator banks. You'll see me."

"Okay. I'm on my way."

MARCUS and Abby watched the footage: it was the same kid. Arrested twice, and he was on the tape moments before drugs were found at the coffee station.

"So if this kid planted drugs at Ali's store, why would he come to your house? How would he know about you?"

163

"I don't know. What if he comes back?"

"You call the cops. I'd say call me, but a local cop could get to you much faster."

"Have you found anything out?"

"Only that the bartender of Reggie's thinks he's being framed. The kids in the neighborhood say he's not a drug dealer. Apparently police officers came in weeks before that night, harassing him and the patrons, allegedly finding drugs. He's now up on two separate charges. He assumes he's screwed. He might be right."

Abby sat with her notepad and pen, sketching her thoughts as they talked. "So we've got three people dead. All bodies found by Reilly. Both crime scenes allegedly connected to drug trafficking. Both properties seized."

"And in both cases, there's reason to doubt that there was actual drug trafficking going on."

"What if this is about property?" Abby asked. "I mean, both places have been seized, both the result of drugs that could have been planted there."

"But what's the motivation? The department might make some money when the properties are sold, but how does that help a cop on the street?"

"Real estate forfeiture brings in a lot of money. According to the law, sixty-five percent of the profit from the property sale goes directly back to the agency that conducted the investigation. Don't you think that creates an incentive to make it happen? I'm not saying the department would suggest planting evidence, but if there are incentives to the officers—even Christmas bonuses, perhaps? People have committed crimes for less."

"I don't know. I'll discuss it with Duvane and see what he can find out. Seems pretty unlikely."

"Well, maybe we should see if Reilly's made any other arrests that resulted in real estate seizures in the last year. And maybe we should find out what's happened to those buildings."

"You're going to keep helping me, aren't you?"

Abby smiled. "And why not?"

"Abby, I'm concerned about this kid showing up at your place. I want to figure out who that is."

"Me too." He had only seemed like an irritation. "But if he was involved in Ali's arrest, and Ali ended up dead ..." The thought was hard to finish. "I wonder if there are any more tapes at the store. Maybe there's a tape from the day of the murder!"

Marcus retrieved the tape from the machine. "I'm going to take this, okay?"

Abby stood, excited by the thought. "Absolutely. Hey, why don't you go to Quick Mart right now? It's probably still as it was. It was just last week that it went up for auction, so the new owners don't close until Friday."

Marcus was putting on his coat. "Just slow down a minute, Abby. I don't know about breaking into the Quick Mart. I have to be pretty careful about not getting myself arrested. Let me talk to Duvane. Maybe he can get an officer in there to check the machine."

Abby thought about this for a second. "You don't have to break in. Go to the back door. There's this loose brick. It's just about a foot above the door handle. Pull the brick out and you might find a key. I know it seems dumb, but when Ali drove me home, he put the key there for his friend. It was pretty inconspicuous. Maybe they always left keys there for each other."

Marcus was still thinking.

"Please, it's worth a try. Now go!" She was pushing him out of the room. He laughed at her forcefulness. It made her smile too.

In only a week, she felt connected to him. It felt good to have someone to talk to again.

MARCUS left Abby and jumped on the Green Line. He pulled his gold medallion out of his pocket and as though touched by a magic wand, blended in perfectly again. He got off at the Pulaski stop and found the Quick Mart on the corner, at the bottom of the stairs. Brown paper now covered the windows of the store, so he couldn't see in, though the sign remained. He walked around to the alley, found the back door, and saw the loose brick. He pulled it out and, sure enough, found a key.

Once inside, Marcus quickly surveyed the space. Just as Abby had said, the shelves were still full of food and convenience store items, though all of the refrigerators along the back wall were empty and turned off. He went to the front by the cash register. A tape machine and a monitor were on the shelf just below the counter. But the machine was empty. He began searching the cabinets and boxes in the area for any tapes.

Bell chimes rattled and startled him. He looked up and saw the shadow of someone just outside the front door. Someone had obviously tried the door. Marcus froze and watched. He could hear someone outside. It was a woman's voice. She was on the phone. He reached over the counter to the window by the door and pulled back a bit of the brown paper. He could see long hair and part of a big, fluffy, white coat.

"Yeah, it's locked. Don't worry." It wasn't hard to hear her. They were only about two feet apart, and the glass couldn't have been too thick because Marcus could feel the cold air as he leaned toward it. "I put up the sign. Okay, will do." The woman closed the phone and headed toward the street. Abby had said a young woman at the auction bought the building. This must be her, though it sounded like she was working for someone.

She got into a red Porsche that was pulled up front. He grabbed a pen by the register and noted the license plate on his palm as she drove off.

He pulled out his cell, called Duvane, and left a message. "It's Henton. I need someone to run this Illinois plate for me: C V R 1 9 0. Could you ask your assistant to do that and fax me the registration at my place? Thanks. I'll keep you posted."

TRIP left Mike at the courthouse and called Jason from his car. The Walters lawsuit Mike had mentioned sounded a little too familiar. Jason answered on the third ring.

"Hey Jason, it's T. Listen, I've got a present for ya. Where are you?"

"I'm at home."

"Why?" Jason always worked the day shift on Mondays.

"Because I've been put on leave."

"What happened?" He feared he already knew.

"Remember those little house calls we made back in November?"

"You'll have to be more specific."

"That woman at the Gardens."

"Seventh floor?"

"That's the one. She got a lawyer. She's suing the department and named me, Darrel, and Joe. We've all been put on leave. Of course, the city's fighting back hard, but she's not rolling over. Shit is hittin' the fan."

"Shit."

"You're tellin' me. You're one lucky fuck too. I guess no one has figured out who you were. You're described in the complaint, but never named."

"You gonna name me?"

"T, come on. You know us better than that. All three of us are denying ever going there. Our lawyer is pulling up her background, calling her delusional, drug addicted—whatever. We can't name you, or we'd admit to being there. You're fine."

Trip took a deep sigh. He'd been pushing it. Two years off the force. No problems. He was finally getting everything he'd wanted. He couldn't take any more chances. This was all getting too close. "Dude, I'm really sorry. Hey, who's the lawyer for the woman?"

"Nathan Walters."

So Abigail Donovan was working with Nathan Walters. "Who is this fucking bitch, Abigail Donovan, and why does she keep getting in my business?" Trip thought. "Listen, I just wanted to give you your cut," he said.

"Fed Ex me a check. Cashier's check."

"Will do. Tell Darrel and Joe I'll do the same for them. And listen, I hope this goes away. Let me know if you need anything."

"Sure."

That settled it. "All good things must come to an end," Trip said out loud. Now he just needed to be sure no one could take him down. He felt pretty good about everything that had gone on during the last few months. And most of his deals were years old by now, too far to trace back or worry about. This lawsuit was a little too close for comfort, but it looked like he was clear. But if Leon or any of those fucks from Reggie's fingered him with Jason, Darrel and Joe, that would be a problem. He couldn't just sit and wait to find out. He'd get rid of the loose ends and move on.

ABBY went home at five that night, anxious to escape the office and feel the warmth of a fire at home. Her mind had wandered all day from the work in front of her to Ali, the kid on the tape, and now Isabel Ramirez.

She sat in her overstuffed chair by the fire, with her hot chocolate in hand, and reviewed Ramirez's testimony about the events that led to the suit.

On November 6, 2003, at about 3:30 p.m., I was grabbed by four men as I was leaving my building. They was all wearing bulletproof vests. They didn't identify themselves as officers, but I knew they was. An unmarked car, blue Ford, was parked twenty feet in front of us. They was armed. One grabbed me hard by the arm, put a gun to my head, and took my keys. [Ms. Ramirez later identified this man as Officer Jason O'Brien.] They led me back into the building, demanding that I take them to my apartment. Once inside, they started yelling about wanting to find drugs. I had no drugs and didn't know why they was picking on me. They threw things around the apartment, looking for drugs. They tossed my framed picture of Jesus Christ across the room and shattered the glass. They called me names. I was crying and begged them to go. Another officer [who Ms. Ramirez later identified as Officer Joe Mackenzie], pulled me into a bedroom, told me to open my clothes and show him the drugs. I cried and pleaded for mercy as I opened my blouse and pants. The officer pushed me aside afterward. They all continued to search through the apartment. They kept calling me names—nigger, bitch, whore—and threatened to come back and shoot me if they found out I was hiding anything. A couple a' my neighbors heard the commotion and so they came over to check on me. The officers pulled them into the room with guns drawn, threw them to the ground and told them not to move. After about ten more minutes, the officers had trashed my house and were ready to give up. One of them [Ms. Ramirez later identified as Officer Darrel Miller] told those boys on the floor to beat each other up or they'd do it for them. I just cried and cried. The boys looked up at them like they was crazy. But one of the officers kicked at them in the back, like they was animals in a show. The boys began to punch each other. The officers clapped and cheered. I reported them to OPS [Office of Professional Standards]. I found out who three of the four officers was. The fourth was white with blond hair. The other officers called him "T." The OPS didn't help me none. Those cops returned two weeks later and did more of the same. I have not slept through the night since it happened.

Abby wiped her tears, thinking of the woman she had met this morning. She closed the document and picked up the phone. Nate's phone went to voicemail.

"Nate, it's Abby. I just read through the papers you gave me. I'm in."

EIGHTEEN

THE week flew by. There had been no sign of the boy all week, and work had consumed Abby's every thought. It was a welcome break from her latest stresses. She spent several fourteen-hour days at the office, and by Friday she felt some sense of relief, calm, and exhaustion. There was more to do, always, but work had taken enough of her energy this week. She had caught up on her major cases, and so she lay in her bed and tried to relish the peace of the moment. Her stomach had been in knots for weeks now. Months, really. She started thinking about the last time she'd had fun. It had been at least six months. Other than Sarah's wedding, she hadn't even really gone out socially since the breakup. She missed laughing.

David had made her laugh. He was the only person who could bring her out of her intense locomotion. But even he was only successful for brief periods. Something always pulled her back, pushing her to regain focus, to keep her eye on the goal. And now, on top of work, she had murders and drugs and dirty cops on the brain.

She watched *The Today Show* and read the *Tribune*, taking time to review the Friday section to see who was playing at the Green Mill. She and David had loved going there to see all the different bands. She watched *Oprah*, then put on some music. Finally, by ten thirty, she figured she needed to get into the office.

Abby was showering, singing along with Sheryl Crow, who was blasting from the bedroom, when she heard a faint buzz. She stopped singing and heard it again. She turned off the water, wrapped herself up in a towel, and ran over to her bedroom window to look out into the courtyard. A young guy was standing on the sidewalk on the other side of the gate. It was that kid again, and again she heard the buzzer. He was ringing her unit, pacing in front of the gate, and clapping his hands together. She could see his breath. It was about fifteen degrees outside. She watched, not sure what to do. He looked around and then grabbed the gate and started shaking it, like a monkey in a cage. He began screaming, "Hey, Abby. Get out here. Where are you? I gotta see you!" She hid behind the curtain. Who the hell was that guy?

She grabbed the phone by her bed and went back to the window. There was a flashing light. Through the trees she could see a man handcuffing the boy. He stuck the kid in the back of his car—a plain blue car with a blue flashing strobe light stuck near the edge of the roof, just over the driver's door. Abby quickly searched through the pile of unfolded laundry on the floor for some underwear, grabbed her glasses from beside her bed, and peeked out the window. Mrs. Tanor was walking over to talk to the man. Of course.

Mrs. Tanor had probably been watching from her window too, frightened and worried by the repeat visitor. Mrs. Tanor and the officer were now on the other side of the front gate, and the trees blocked Abby's view. She got down on her knees, so she could see what was happening. She should get down there. She dropped the phone, fumbled for a T-shirt and pants, and took another look out the window before heading for the first floor. Mrs. Tanor and the officer came through the gate into the courtyard.

She saw that hair. He looked up at Abby's window. She gasped and hid behind her curtain. She sat, dumb-struck, staring into space, with her hand clutching her open mouth. A sickness welled up in her belly. She saw her digital camera on the dresser, grabbed it, and crawled back to the window. From behind the curtain, she zoomed in on his face and took the shot. She then watched as the man shook Mrs. Tanor's hand and left.

Mrs. Tanor walked back to her apartment and paused to look up at Abby's window. Abby ducked out of sight. Mrs. Tanor looked baffled. She was shaking her head as she went inside. Abby felt like she had done something wrong. She couldn't imagine what.

MARCUS arrived twenty minutes later. He had on his gang look, though it no longer fazed Abby. She had called him as soon as Mrs. Tanor went inside and he had told her to stay put. She hadn't moved an inch since she dropped the phone.

He was just inside the front door when Abby shoved the camera at him. "I know this guy. His name is Trip." She started up the stairs. The kitchen and living room were on the second floor. She kept going up. "Let's put it up on the computer so you can see it better. I've got an office in the spare bedroom." They headed up to the third floor and began downloading the pictures. Within a minute, Abby had the image on the big screen.

"I'm telling you, that's him." The picture was now as big as the screen.

Marcus stared at the photo. "So tell me how you know him."

"Two weeks ago I went to a wedding at the Drake. It was that Saturday before I met you. I met him at the bar in the lobby. He bought me a drink. He was friendly, a bit forward. He said he was a businessman."

"What kind of business?"

"Didn't say. I don't remember. He didn't tell me much. He wanted me to leave with him. He said his name was Trip." Should she add that she might have even slept with him, but couldn't remember? "That's him. I'm sure of it. In fact, I just saw him again on Monday. He was walking into the courthouse as I was walking out."

"Did you speak with him?"

"No. He didn't see me. But Mrs. Tanor just talked to him. Come here." Abby jumped up from the computer and pulled Marcus down the hall and into her bedroom. "Look out my window. I have a good view of the courtyard. Maybe we should go ask Mrs. Tanor what he said."

"Wait."

"What? She talked to him!" Abby began toward the door, and Marcus grabbed her arm to stop her.

"Abby, wait. This kid has been coming to your house. This same kid may have planted drugs at Quick Mart. The man that came here and arrested him found you at the Drake."

"So? What do you think?"

He released her arm and went to the edge of the bed and sat as if to work it out first. "I think I know who it is."

174

"Who?"

"A couple of weeks back, he was pointed out to me by some kids as a dirty cop. Someone to avoid."

"Why would he be after me? What's going on?" She paced the room, fell against the wall, and slid to the floor. "He didn't seem like a cop."

Marcus crouched in front of Abby and put his hand on her head, now resting on her knees. "Abby, that was the Saturday night before we met, right?"

"Yes."

"You called Officer Reilly on that Friday night with a description of a man leaving Reggie's."

Abby finished his thought. "A white guy. Light hair." And then it came to her. "He's a blond, white guy." She clamped her own mouth, afraid of the revelation. "So, maybe this is the man I saw coming out of Reggie's?"

"All right, let's just think about this." Marcus began pacing the room.

"Do you think he's after me?"

"Well, hold on." He went to the window then and searched the courtyard as if for answers. "If this is the man you saw coming out of Reggie's, and he showed up at the Drake after you called in that ID—"

"Was he going to kill me?"

"Maybe he just wanted to see if you would even recognize him, see if he had anything to worry about."

"Well, obviously I didn't. But here he is. So what does it mean?"

"It means I need to find out who this guy is and what he's up to. I'd rather not go to Mrs. Tanor. I'd like to see what she says to you about all of this. Let's not let her know about me or any of this if possible."

"Why?"

Marcus didn't answer right away.

"She'd be in danger?"

Marcus's eyes met Abby's, but then he looked away.

"What?"

"Abby, it's just that, in my experience, if a cop is dirty..."

"He's dangerous."

Marcus crouched down in front of her again. "Now, don't look so panicked." He patted her knees, stood, and offered her his hands to help her stand. She took them. He led her out of the bedroom and back into the hall. "Let's just see what Mrs. Tanor says to you. Without me here confusing things. Let her make contact. She does that, right?"

"Well, she certainly has a thousand times before. And she's been disturbed by this boy showing up here. She thinks I'm at work right now. I'd guess that she'll be stopping by tonight to tell me all about it."

"Okay, then."

Abby stopped walking. She felt frozen.

Marcus pulled her in for a hug, and she buried her head in his big leather coat.

"I'm here, Abby. And this cop, I should be able to figure out who he is pretty quickly. If he just arrested that kid, then within the hour I should be able to look up the booking records and get a name for the kid and the officer. He doesn't know anything about me or my investigation. We'll get to the bottom of this."

Abby pulled back and looked up at Marcus. "But if this is the guy from Reggie's, then I've had drinks with a murderer. And he knows where I live, and...," She wanted to say the rest but it stuck in her throat.

Marcus stopped her. "Okay, okay. We're going to figure this out, Abby." And then a smile emerged. "You've got one bad-ass cop on your side," he offered with a nudge. Abby smiled and took a deep breath. "You are pretty beefy, aren't you?" she offered with a faint smile, grabbing his biceps. They both chuckled. He was massive and he really did make her feel safe.

"Now where's that camera?"

Abby headed back into the spare bedroom and Marcus followed. He pulled the storage disc from its side. "I'm going to take this, okay?"

Abby nodded in agreement.

They walked back into the hall to go downstairs and Marcus paused, looking up at the slotted steps above him. "Hey, what's this?"

"Those go to our roof deck."

"Our?"

"My. I mean my roof deck."

"Wow, nice place."

"Yeah." She didn't see the point of sharing all the details. "I think I'm going to sell it, though." She didn't think she could continue living here with all the memories. "And those stairs are terrifying. They're so steep and really scary when you're on the roof and you want to come down. It's just like climbing a ladder—not exactly the best when you're trying to carry food up and down to barbeque." Actually, she and David used to love the climb up to the roof. It felt like they were going up to their tree house. And they would sit up there and look down at everyone on Clark Street and make up stories about their lives and what they were doing and laugh. When the Cubs were playing they would sit up there and listen to the roar of the fans in the bleachers.

He continued down the steps. "Still, pretty cool to have a roof deck."

"Yeah," she agreed without much conviction.

"Abby, I'm going to check the records and meet with Duvane about all of it."

They were back on the first floor at the door. Abby grabbed for the door but stopped. "Well, what now? How do I go to work and act like everything's okay?"

"Why aren't you at work, anyway?"

"It's been a long week. I took the morning off. But I was getting ready to leave when all this happened."

"So maybe you should go."

"Are you kidding me? A dirty cop—a murderer according to you—just showed up at my house. He knows where I live. I can't go to work."

"Abby, I'd rather you go to work. What kind of security do you have anyway?"

"The gate is impossible to climb, you need a key for that, and I've got an alarm system."

"Good." He put on his hat.

As soon as she mentioned the alarm system, she knew she had to tell him. "Marcus."

"What?"

"I drank with him. I danced with him, I ..." She looked away. "I kissed him."

Marcus took a seat on the back of the sofa, like he knew there was more.

"I got so drunk at that wedding. I saw my ex-boyfriend. I was depressed, and this guy was so flirtatious and good-looking, and—"

"And?"

She was practically whispering. "I can't remember." She looked up at him. "I know we were together for most of the evening. I remember leaning against him outside. We were in front of the hotel. But it's just a flash. I woke up in the morning here. Alone." She wondered if it was really necessary to add that she had been naked. Maybe she had just drunkenly stripped down and crawled into bed.

"Do you think he might have been here with you?"

She winced at the thought. "I don't know. There was no sign of him when I woke. But he's never called me. Jesus. Marcus, I don't do things like that. I don't bring strangers home and sleep with them. I just..." She didn't finish. Her hands now covered her face.

He stood and took her by the shoulders and made her look at him. "Abby, I'm not judging you."

She took a breath. "But he never called. I kind of assumed that maybe I did. Sleep with him, I mean. Like some one-night stand. And maybe that's why I've never heard from him."

"Maybe. Or maybe you rejected him, and that's why he's never called. Here's what I'm thinking. This guy Trip wanted to see if you'd recognize him when he went to the Drake. You didn't. You're an attractive woman. You had a good time together. If he was gonna hurt you, it would have already happened. Sounds like he had the opportunity."

Abby held out Marcus's gloves. This wasn't helping either of them. "Have you figured out anything since we last spoke? You didn't call me after you left Monday. I guess you didn't get into Quick Mart?"

"Actually, I did. The key was there, just as you said. But there weren't any tapes."

"Damn."

"I did find out who bought the building, though. It's a company called Weber Properties."

"Does that mean anything to you?"

"Not yet, but I looked up its property records. It has several buildings in the south and west area of the city. It's not a corporation, so my check on the secretary of state filings came up empty. I haven't been able to find out anymore yet, other than the fact that six of the company's ten current properties were bought at auction. There's an office address. I was going to check into that today, but I think I better worry about this guy first. Listen Abby, I want that alarm on at all times. And change the code."

She knew what he was thinking. If Trip had been here, he might have watched her disarm it.

"I should get going."

"You know, I'd never have guessed in a million years that he was a cop."

"Why's that?"

"It was just the way he was dressed and his manner. He was wearing pretty expensive, tailored clothes. No offense, it's just not the stereotype I have in my head."

Marcus smiled. "Well, look at me," he said, displaying his badass thug wear. "You didn't think I was a cop either."

Abby turned suddenly as she remembered. "Wait!"

Marcus stopped.

"I have his phone number." She ran to her coat closet and pulled out the cocktail napkin, still folded inside her long dress coat. "He wrote this."

"Perfect. Thanks, Abby. I'll be in touch later. Now go to work."

• • •

MARCUS sat in his apartment, staring at the laptop. His eyes were stinging. He was on the phone with Duvane.

"There's no arrest record for this kid in the first or the nineteenth or twenty-third districts in the last two hours. If he took a kid in, it would be in one of those districts. It should be in the system by now."

"Did you check the thirteenth district, where you saw this cop for the first time?"

"Nothing."

"Well, what about the internal docs? Did you go through all the cop photos yet?"

"I've searched first name *Trip* in every district. I've checked the pictures of all the cops in the two districts where we've seen him and the surrounding districts. This guy is a ghost. He's either not a cop, or his name's not Trip."

"Or both. I don't like it. Marcus, I know there are twelve thousand cops on the force, but I want to find this guy."

Marcus had already checked hundreds of internal photos. He couldn't imagine how long it would take to get through them all.

Duvane must have sensed it. "Marcus, don't worry. I'm not expecting you to do it alone. I'm going to get some staff on this."

"Okay. I also think I should tail Reilly. He's connected to this. He arrested that kid at the Quick Mart twice in the last year. We saw the store's surveillance tape."

"So, are there charges pending against this kid?"

"No. Charges dropped. Insufficient evidence."

"This doesn't make sense. Reilly's on duty right now." Duvane was obviously on the system as well. "Gets off at five. Keep your phone on. I'll check with dispatch and see if they can track his location."

"Great, thanks."

"And Marcus—"

"Yeah?"

"Keep your eye on Ms. Donovan. If we're talking about a murder rap, I don't want anything happening to our witness."

"Got it." Duvane didn't even have to say it. Abby had gotten to him. He wasn't about to lose anyone else he cared about.

"And Marcus: Find that kid."

ABBY had just settled down at her desk and was trying to get through thirty new e-mails when her secretary, Mary, popped in.

"Hey, Abby, where've you been?" It was now two o'clock in the afternoon. Marcus had left Abby's by eleven thirty, but she had taken her time getting here.

"It's just been a long week, Mary. I took the morning off."

She could see the surprise on Mary's face.

"Well, Jerry came by looking for you."

Not again. "What did you tell him?"

"I said you were at a dentist appointment. He left this for you." Mary was holding a large envelope.

Abby took it. "Thanks, Mary. You're so good to me."

Abby waited for Mary to leave to open the envelope. She half expected some sort of written warning that she was slipping. She knew it was true. She had done a lot this week, but the last two weeks had been ridiculous. She had been leaving by five whenever possible, showing up after nine, and turning down new assignments. She'd delegated as much as possible, so the clients were covered. She just couldn't seem to do much work herself. And it was just a matter of time before some new screw-up would expose her lack of attentiveness.

But it wasn't a warning from Jerry. It was a confidential memo sent to the seven associates up for partnership consideration. The memo asked the associates to spend some time outlining their work history at the firm, the major cases they were involved in, the partners they worked for, the procedures they had mastered, and the skills they had acquired. Then they were to create a summary of how they had developed as attorneys during the last seven years, and the clients and prospective clients they had strong relationships with. For Abby, of course, it had only been six years, but Jerry had always said she was on the fast track. It was assumed the associates would spend considerable time evaluating themselves, thereby making the process easier for the partnership committee. The report was due Monday morning.

This was it. It was time to shine. This was all she had focused on for the last six years—longer, really. Nothing else, no one else, had ever been as important as achieving this goal, and yet now, today, reading the memo made her feel emptier. She wondered if becoming partner was really going to make everything okay. It seemed like a stupid idea all of a sudden. And yet, for years she'd been sure this was what she had to do.

She brushed aside her introspection after a minute. It was too late to second-guess her whole life now. It was going to take a long time to go through her files and memory about everything she had done for the last six years, so she would spend time this weekend on it. She put the memo in her briefcase and got back to work.

• • •

MARCUS walked down Cicero toward Lake. The late-afternoon sky was darkening, and the temperature was dropping. If he was lucky, he could hook up with Darnel and the boys, who should be out in force on a Friday. Maybe the neighborhood boys had an opinion about Reilly.

His cell rang. It was Duvane. "Reilly's at the corner of Lake and Kildare."

"Got it." Marcus headed that way.

ABBY pushed aside her work and called Marcus. He should have called her with news by now. He answered in a hushed voice.

"Marcus? It's Abby."

"Oh, hi, Abby. What's up?"

"Did you find that cop and that kid? Please tell me this is over."

"Well, actually, no, I didn't."

"But I gave you a name, a picture, a phone number."

"Abby, the name must be bogus. No 'Trip' in the system. I went through hundreds of officer photos. I can't find him. I'm looking into the phone number, but because it's not a landline, it's harder to trace. It may take a few days to get a name."

"But he made an arrest, right? What about that?"

"Well, there are no arrest records matching up to a kid being arrested at your address. I'm thinking it was staged."

"What? Why?"

"I don't have all the answers yet, Abby. But I'm working on it. I've been chatting up the neighborhood and found out a little more scoop on that Trip character. I think I might be able to place him at Reggie's."

"The night I was there?"

184

"Maybe. I met Leon, the bartender. He was arrested for trafficking that night, and he's out on bond. He describes a cop that came in the night you were there. It matches our guy."

"So isn't that enough? I saw a white guy with blond hair leaving the scene. The bartender tells you of the same man. A woman was found dead!"

"Well, first, we have to find him. Everyone seems to think he's a cop, but I'm not so sure. And second, Leon's not a reliable witness. He's up on drug-trafficking charges. His testimony's almost useless. Abby, there's something going on here. More than that murder, and I need to figure it out."

"But, he's—"

"Oh, hold on. I gotta call you back."

The phone went dead and Abby listened to the silence, unable to hang up.

NINETEEN

MARCUS was standing in the side yard of a beaten-down two-flat with boarded-up windows, watching the activity across the street at Kildare's, a cop bar frequented by the eleventh district, Officer Reilly's district. He felt bad hanging up on Abby, but when the headlights caught his eye, he had to move.

A black Mercedes with tinted windows pulled into the gravel lot in front of the building, and a man got out and hit the button on his key chain. The locks engaged. Marcus stood back, hidden from view by a shrub, and watched. The driver—white, wavy blond hair, just as he'd remembered from that day at Carter's—got out of the car and headed into the bar. Marcus snapped a picture. It flashed, but the man didn't notice. As soon as the man was inside, Marcus jogged across the street, zoomed in on the license plate, and snapped another.

Just a moment later, he could hear the sounds from inside the bar as the door began to open. He ran over to the side of the building, out of sight, and watched Reilly and Trip get in the Mercedes and drive off. He rushed to his car and followed.

ABBY had been unable to get back to work after Marcus hung up. It was now almost five thirty. Dinner. She couldn't concentrate on work at this point, but she did not want to go home. She walked toward the cafeteria.

A group of about eight associates, mostly first- and second-years, were standing by the elevator banks, with coats in hand.

"Hey, Abby!" Josh called out. Josh was the first-year she was supposed to be mentoring. He was a good kid. Eager, excited, smart enough, and Abby felt bad she hadn't given him more time this year. Her mentor had often taken her out for drinks and showed her (or pretended, anyway) that working at the firm could be fun.

Abby smiled and stopped to chat. "What are you all up to?"

"Happy hour! Timothy O'Toole's on Clark. Join us, Abby. Come on—you haven't been out with me since September."

Abby opened her mouth to say she was too busy. "I'm...okay, sure." The words surprised her.

"Really? That's great!" Josh and the other associates were pleased to have captured another attorney for the adventure. Abby couldn't help but laugh. Nothing sounded better right now than trying to forget all this madness.

• • •

THE first three pitchers went down quickly. One of the guys said he was going to order a yard of black and tan—Bass Ale first, topped off with Guinness. Others hopped on the bandwagon and within minutes a group decision was made for yards all around, though Abby pleaded for a weiss beer instead. Before long, she was squeezing a lemon into her yard-high glass and standing to carefully tilt the tall glass to her lips. The young associates told animated stories of firm life so far. It was a great distraction. When they asked about certain partners, wondering if the reputations were accurate, Abby chimed in. They looked to her for some great stories to tell, and she tried not to disappoint.

After another hour, loud music could be heard every time the front door opened. It was obviously coming from across the street—the Blue Note. Abby looked out the window and watched the front door of the bar, wondering if she'd see him. Both of them, maybe. He used to play a late set there on Fridays. She silently drank her beer, tuning out the chatter around her and enjoying the memory of watching David and his band play there so many times over the years. She had been his personal groupie, happy to sit and watch and soak in the music. It was as close as she'd ever come to being on stage again. Now, she realized, someone else was watching him, admiring him, loving him. Her heart ached, still.

Someone in the group suggested heading over for the music. Josh nudged her.

"What do you think? Up for it?"

Abby checked her watch. It was just after eight o'clock. She had no intention of leaving the group and going home. "Sure."

Once inside, the group maneuvered a few tables to create a giant table by the empty stage. Maybe a band would go on later, but for now, the loud music came from the speakers on the ceiling. They ordered more beer and some nachos, cheese sticks, and wings for the table. When the food arrived, the group lunged forward with speed and excitement, and Abby, feeling somewhat like the old lady of the group, sat back to let the children go first. A sad, cheese-soaked chip and a lone wing remained, and she ate the scraps. After another hour, after the table games had begun and the cocktail waitress had delivered several rounds of shots, the dares began. A karaoke machine was on the stage, and the patrons were beginning to take turns making fools of themselves. Susan, another first-year, dared Josh to take the stage, and he said he'd do it if Abby joined him. "A duet, m'lady!" he suggested.

Abby laughed and shook her head in protest. But the group was not going to have it. The chanting began. Before she could say more, she was being pulled by the arm toward the stage. Once in front of the crowd, Josh headed for the machine to program their song.

Abby assumed this would be the typical Sonny and Cher "I've Got You Babe" routine. When the music started, she looked at Josh, confused by the choice. He smiled and whispered in her ear, "I can't sing. But I heard that maybe you can." He handed her the microphone, jumped off the stage, and went back to the table to join their friends.

Abby didn't even have time to protest. The crowd was already clapping in anticipation of the familiar song— Melissa Etheridge's "I'm the Only One." She knew it well. She wanted to be mad. She felt silly to be so vulnerable in front of the associates. Sarah had such a big mouth. She stood on the stage, frozen, in her business suit, her glasses, looking like the polar opposite of a girl who would belt out a Melissa Etheridge song. But the crowd was cheering, awaiting her performance. She held the microphone tightly, laughed with embarrassment, closed her eyes, which caused a momentary stumble, and tentatively began. She looked down at the floor and off to the sides—everywhere but at her friends—and got through the first verse.

The clapping and hollering from her group's table made her laugh. She pointed at Josh with a smile as she began the second verse with more confidence.

Josh stood and whistled. Everyone in the place began to cheer. The crowd was clapping along. Being on stage, feeling the crowd, the rush that she once knew so well, Abby gave in to it. With an exaggerated and dramatic gesture, she pulled off her glasses, took the clip out of her hair, and shook it loose. It was hilarious and she loved it. And the crowd loved her.

She belted through the chorus, letting her voice get rough and full. The words poured out of her. She never even looked at the screen. It was beautiful. Great tone, great vibrato. The crowd was on their feet. And she moved on the stage like she owned it.

When she finished, the room shook with applause. Abby slipped the glasses back on and made her way back to the group.

"Holy shit, Abby!" Josh was clearly impressed.

Everyone offered praise: "That was amazing! You look like you've been doing that your whole life!"

She smiled at the kind words and offered, "Not anymore."

The table banter continued, and they all joked about who would go next. No one wanted to follow her. Abby sat back, drank her beer, and laughed. She couldn't stop smiling. She had put all that behind her so long ago, and she never let loose with firm people, ever. And here she had just done both. It was like she'd just gotten off the most thrilling roller-coaster ride. She was almost giddy. And a bit queasy.

Abby dropped her keys three times while trying to unlock the front door. She finally got it open and stumbled inside. She plopped onto the love seat by the door, closed her eyes, and pictured herself on that stage, working the crowd. Feeling the lyrics. Finally, something good to think about. The room began to spin. She sat up. She needed some fresh air.

Abby lay on a lounge chair on her roof deck, under a thick blanket, staring at the stars and munching on pretzels. It was after ten. She had to work on that partner memo in the morning, and she could already feel the beginning of an intense hangover. But it felt good to breathe in the cold air. It was a balmy thirty-five degrees now. A warm front was coming through.

She hadn't been up here since that night with David. A perfect August night. It was just starting to get cooler. No mosquitoes. A slight breeze. But he'd been up there for two hours before she got home. He was surrounded by burned-out candles and cold food and more wasted effort. And he was sick of it. Sick of waiting. Sick of playing second. And he was sure it meant she didn't love him. His voice was full of anger, but his face just looked sad. Tears had streamed down his cheeks. "Who remains engaged for two years!" he had yelled. "Why can't we move forward?"

She'd had no doubt Mrs. Tanor and the other neighbors had heard all the details. But she didn't have an answer for him. She'd felt paralyzed. So she just let him go. And then she'd spent hours up there, looking up at the stars and crying. Tears that started because of David but continued because of Denny. The next day David had moved out.

And now the tears came again. "I'm so sorry," she muttered. She wanted to take it all back. To set a date, to do everything David wanted. But she knew that she couldn't. She didn't have the right. She cried softly as she relived the night that had started it all.

She heard a buzz, sat up, and listened. There. Again. *Bzzz. Bzzz. Bzzz.* It was her doorbell. The hatch was open, and she quickly climbed down the ladder stairs and pushed the button on the third-floor speaker. "Who is it?"

"It's Marcus. Henton."

Abby buzzed him in and ran down the stairs.

He was dressed in his gangbanger-style clothes. Abby scanned the courtyard and pulled him inside.

Marcus had an urgent look on his face. "Where have you been? I've been calling."

Abby was confused. "You hung up on me!"

"Yeah, sorry about that. But I've been trying to reach you all night. You never picked up your cell."

"Oh, I must not have heard it. I was in a bar all night. Come on." She headed up the stairs to the kitchen. "You want anything to drink? I need some water."

Marcus followed her upstairs.

She stumbled on a couple of treads.

"You okay?"

"Oh, yeah," Abby offered. "Just some beer."

"I see."

He had that brotherly tone she remembered well.

"Okay, maybe a lot. But I'm freaking out over here!"

They were in the kitchen.

She leaned across the island, munching on a chip. "Why are you here, anyway?"

Marcus took off his coat and threw it onto the chair. "I hope it's not too late."

"No. I just got home a little while ago."

"Abby, I'd like to stay here tonight if it's okay with you."

"What? Why?" Now she was scared.

"I saw Reilly and that Trip character together tonight. That's why I hung up on you. I had to follow them."

"So, what happened? Where did they go?"

"Down to the Loop to a bar on Chicago and Racine. Met another man there. Had drinks for a while. They all split up and I followed Trip. He headed north to Rogers Park, but there was an accident on the street, and I lost him in the traffic."

"So what about this third guy? Any ideas?"

"Well, I snapped his picture so I can run it through the system and see if he's a cop too."

"Can I see?" She took the camera and zoomed in on the shot. "Wow. He looks really familiar. I just can't place the face."

"Are you sure?"

"Wait—I remember. Oh, he's an asshole! Hard to forget."

"How do you know him?"

"I met him once at a party with David. It was David's Christmas party."

"So this guy works with your ex-boyfriend?"

Abby nodded. "He's a prosecutor in the state's attorney's office like David, but they're in different departments. David didn't know him. There are hundreds of attorneys.

But this guy was drunk, obnoxious, a total creep. He introduced himself. I just can't remember the name."

"Interesting." Marcus made a note. "Well, I also got a picture of the license plate on the black Mercedes Trip was driving. It's registered to TWC Industries. And guess who owned the title before TWC Industries?"

"Who?"

"The Chicago Police Department."

"What?"

"Something's going on, and you're obviously mixed up in it. But that guy's not a cop. We've checked the file of every officer on the force. He's not there. I'll just stay on your couch, if that's okay."

Abby stood up and took a deep breath. Her beer buzz was gone. "Of course. I'm happy to have you here."

They walked into the living room.

"Good. Me too."

She pulled a blanket and pillow from the cabinet under the television, hit the switch for the gas fireplace, and brought Marcus the remote control for the TV. "Make yourself comfortable. Help yourself to anything in the kitchen."

Marcus sat on the couch and put his gun on the coffee table.

"Thanks, Abby." And then he gave her that big brother look. "Now, you go get some sleep, young lady. I'll be right here."

Abby smiled. "Will do. Goodnight."

Abby lay in bed thinking about Reilly and Trip. She couldn't imagine why anyone cared about her.

MARCUS slept for a couple of hours but woke to the sounds of a scream. He jumped up and grabbed his gun. The television was still on. It was some old horror movie. He got up, turned it off, and headed to the kitchen for some water.

It felt nice to be here. It felt like a home. Not like the apartment he was living in. Though he had nothing to complain about. He had agreed to all this. And it was better than being in New York.

He went back to the couch and stared out the window into the darkness. He never slept well. He hadn't made it through the night in years. He heard the creak of the stairs and turned. First, he could just see her feet, then her knees as she crouched down, and then her face as she leaned forward trying to get a look.

"Hello, Abby."

"Oh, sorry. I thought you'd be sleeping."

"No. But why aren't you?"

She came into the room and sat by the fireplace on the floor, facing him. "I don't sleep all that well anymore."

"Usually someone with a lot of alcohol in them will fall asleep hard," he noted with a grin.

"You'd think, right?" They both sat in the silence, listening to the hiss of the gas fireplace.

After a minute, she broke the silence. "Marcus, how'd you get that scar?"

His eyebrows rose, as he was a bit surprised by the question.

"I'm sorry. If you don't want to tell me—"

"No, it's okay." He felt like he could tell Abby anything. But he didn't answer right away, unsure where to begin. He sat forward.

Abby pressed again. "Why'd you come here from New York, anyway?"

"I was working on 9/11. Called to the scene. One of the first up the north tower, actually." Her surprise was apparent. He continued, staring down at the glass coffee table. "Anyway, there were several of us. Guiding people down the stairs. We were just getting down to the ground floor when we heard the crack. And then the rumbling. We could feel the vibrations. There were about ten of us together. And we ran. We got out the front door and ran and ran and felt the collapse happening around us. The soot, the papers flying, the debris." He put his hands up to the scar and turned to her. "I guess that's how I got this."

"You don't know?"

"I don't think I could even feel anything. There was such adrenaline. I've never been through anything like it. It wasn't until a few minutes later when I started walking back toward the building to find my guys. Someone told me I was bleeding." He leaned back and relaxed. He'd done it. Without crying.

"You're so lucky."

But then he could barely speak. "I don't know if I'd say that."

"You survived the worst thing I can even imagine."

He took a sip of water and looked into Abby's sleepy eyes. He hadn't talked to anyone about that day in such a long time. He could remember the counselors and his parents trying to talk to him. He could never do it. But he could feel a kinship with Abby. She was another lonely soul.

"Is that why you left New York?"

He ignored the question and continued, holding his gaze at the table, trying not to blink. To hold it together. "I tried to call home. I knew my wife would have seen the news and been nervous."

"You're married?"

He looked at Abby. The tears pooled in his eyes. He turned to face the window and continued. "But no one answered. I called six times. I ran home once my chief told me to get out of there. But they weren't there."

"They?"

"My wife. My baby girl. Just six weeks old." A single tear escaped and streamed down over the rough terrain of the pink scar.

"Oh, my God, Marcus."

He didn't answer.

"You don't have to talk about it. It's not my business."

He wiped his face. "I never found them. I searched and put out missing persons reports. I posted pictures like everyone else all over the city."

"They were in the buildings?"

He turned to her. "I think so." He could see her confusion. "I'll never know for sure. I kissed them both good-bye that morning. I was running late. I didn't ask my wife what she was doing that day. She was on maternity leave. But those buildings collapsed and thousands died, and I never found them."

He got up and moved over to the bookshelf, checking out her photographs. "She had a good friend who worked on the hundredth floor. My guess is that she wanted her friend to meet Madeleine."

"And the friend?"

He remained fixed on her pictures. "She's dead."

"Haven't they been recovering…" She paused, obviously not sure how to phrase it.

He looked at her then. At her trepidation. "Body parts?"

She answered quietly. "Yes."

He went back to the couch, took another sip, and sat down. "It's been two and a half years, Abby. Two and a half years. They've only been able to identify twelve hundred people. They think almost twenty-eight hundred people died. All that soot that was flying around that day? It was not just buildings. It was people. Turned to dust."

"Oh my God."

"Yeah." Marcus wiped his face and looked back out the window. "I tried to stay. I tried to do the job. They needed cops—we had lost half my unit. But I couldn't be there. I couldn't go home. Ceelie's parents wanted to have a funeral. I didn't want to declare them dead. To me, they were still missing."

"I'm so sorry."

"Yeah. Anyway, after about a year and a half of being a zombie, waiting for the call, for an examiner to say he'd found them, I gave up." He looked at her. "I went to my chief and quit. I figured I'd just take off. Go to the Bahamas or something. Bartend. Just get away from everything. But then a couple of days later he called me and told me about his buddy, Duvane. Told me about their conversation. About me doing some undercover work for the Chicago police."

"And that brought you to me." Abby smiled.

"Yep." He sat back and took a deep breath. It felt good to tell her. To feel some connection to someone again. "So, what's your story, Abby? I bet you've got a story."

She turned away from his glance. "Not really."

He sat back and put his feet up, and tried to lighten the moment. "Come on. Why are you living here all by yourself? You ever been married?"

She smiled. "Nope."

"Do you want to get married someday?"

"Oh, I don't know." She started getting up. "We should both get some sleep."

She was a tough nut to crack, but he wouldn't give up. Though maybe it wasn't the time. They did need some sleep.

Abby reached out for his hand. He gave it to her and looked into her eyes. He recognized the sadness. She said good night. He did the same.

TWENTY

ABBY woke in a haze. Her head pounded. Her bladder ached for relief. She checked the clock—8:20 a.m.

Down the hall, Marcus was in the second bedroom, sitting at the computer.

"Hey."

He turned to the door. "Good morning, Abby. I hope you don't mind. I've got some work to do."

"No problem." She yawned. "I need some coffee. You want some?"

"That would be great."

She started down the stairs.

Marcus called out. "How're you feeling?"

"Ugh."

She took each step carefully, hoping to minimize the pounding in her head. Her mission was simple: a giant glass of water, several Advil, coffee. She sat at the table, held her head, and waited for the pain to subside. She needed to focus on the partnership memo, but it didn't seem possible.

She brought Marcus some coffee, curled up in the big chair in the corner of the bedroom, and watched him work.

"Marcus, have you looked up the circumstances of the forfeitures?"

"Which ones?"

"I was thinking about this last night. You said that Weber Properties has many properties that were bought at auction. We know it bought Quick Mart, and we know the crime that led to that building's seizure is suspect. And we know Reilly did the busts at Ali's, and this kid that was here yesterday may have been involved in setting up Ali. So, I'm thinking, what if Reilly was involved in some of those cases too? That would seem more than coincidental, right?"

Marcus stopped and thought about it. She had his attention.

"And you said Reilly and this Trip guy know each other. What if this guy is behind Weber Properties? He told me he was 'in business.' What if his business is real estate?"

She could tell that Marcus's wheels were turning.

"Okay, I'll let you work." She needed to do some work too.

ABBY came back into the room a few hours later and plopped onto the chair again. She had been in the living room trying to piece together her life history at the firm for the evaluation. Marcus was still staring at the computer with a legal pad full of notes to the side.

"So, what do you have?"

Marcus turned to her. "Well, this is interesting. Weber Properties has six properties that it bought at auction over the last year. It's also listed as the seller of another fifteen properties that were sold over the last few years."

Abby pulled her knees up to get comfortable and waited for the stories.

"So far, I've only gone through its current properties. We know about Quick Mart, but as far as the others…" Marcus turned back to the monitor and read aloud. "Well, here: a building on the corner of Cicero and Madison. Looks like there was a store front on the first floor and an apartment above."

"Just like Ali's building."

"Yeah. The owner, Gloria Washington and son, both arrested."

"By Officer Reilly?"

"Yes." He paused dramatically. "Alleged drug trafficking. The building was seized."

"When was this?"

"May 2003."

"And?"

"Both convicted, two months ago."

"That doesn't sound bad, does it?"

"Not really. But Weber Properties bought it at auction for eighty-two thousand. The sales disclosure stated structural damage."

"So?"

"So, it was bought at auction in November and it's on the market right now for two hundred and fifty thousand. I don't know what they did in just three months, but that's quite a profit.

"Here's another one. A three-flat on Davis Boulevard. That's by Cellular Field. Last spring the building was seized as part of a drug bust. Cash and a large quantity of drugs recovered in one of the apartments. Tenants arrested."

"Who was the arresting officer?"

"J. O'Brien and D. Miller."

"Oh. Okay, what about the owner? You said 'tenants' were arrested?"

"Yeah. Owner was Juan Domenz."

"Did he fight for the building's return?"

"No."

"Why?"

"He's missing. There was a missing persons report filed for him on June first. Case is still open."

Abby didn't know what to make of it.

"So no one stopped that building from going up for auction?"

"That's right. It just took a few months. Building sold at auction for a hundred and seventy thousand. It's on the market now as condos, each listed for two hundred fifty thousand."

"That's incredible."

"Here's another one. A liquor store on California Avenue. That's by the United Center. Owner of the store, Jimmy Robinson, was arrested for drug trafficking in August. He was convicted last month. He's serving a fifteen-year sentence."

"Well, that doesn't sound too suspect. Who was the arresting officer?"

"M. Reilly."

"Officer Reilly."

"Yeah. The fourth property has a similar story. Drug bust. Arrests, convictions. And the arresting officer was J. Mackenzie."

"And the last one?"

"Another Reilly arrest."

"So Reilly is not the only officer behind these buildings."

"No, but I know about these other officers. They're not to be trusted."

"Who?"

"J. O'Brien, D. Miller, J. Mackenzie. They're all on leave right now. There's a lawsuit pending."

"Wait, I know those names too." Abby jumped from her chair, ran down the stairs to the living room, and came back moments later with the Ramirez testimony in hand. "I just took on this new pro bono case." She quickly reviewed the document. "Those are the names of the three officers that apparently assaulted and terrorized this woman down at Stateway Gardens."

"Yeah, Duvane told me about the case. Wanted me to look into it, see if I could come up with the fourth cop, the only one unnamed in the complaint."

Abby was still reading from the papers. "The named officers all had crew cuts. The fourth had blond hair."

"And you know who else described three cops with crew cuts and a fourth with blond hair?"

"Who?"

"Leon. The bartender from Reggie's. And he swears he's been set up to go down for trafficking."

"And the building's been seized."

"Yep."

Abby continued. "We need to figure out who's behind Weber Properties. And maybe we should look into that missing person case—what did you say his name was?"

Marcus reviewed the notes again. "Juan Domenz." He looked back up at Abby. "But listen, I'll handle the investigating. I'm here to protect you."

"I know. I'm not suggesting I become your gun-totin' sidekick." She stood to leave. "You keep working. I've got stuff to do anyway." Abby went to her room, changed into jeans, and headed down to the living room. She opened her laptop, got on Google, and typed "Juan Domenz Chicago missing 2003" and waited.

MARCUS pulled up the Weber Properties address and called Duvane.

"Hey, Henton here. Listen, this Trip character, the mystery cop, he's connected to Reilly. And I think there's something to this Weber Properties that now owns the Quick Mart."

Duvane cut him off. "I know who he is. I was just going to call you, Marcus."

"Well?"

"His name is Thomas A. Callahan, the third. After you left me that message last night that he didn't match any of the records, it occurred to me to check officers who aren't on the force anymore. Thomas Callahan was an officer from 1994 to 2002. His file is clean. He was well-liked. Out of the twenty-fourth district. That's Rogers Park. He was on different task forces during his tenure. First the neighborhood outreach, a little SWAT, and then the Asset Forfeiture Unit. No problems."

Marcus was taking notes. "A career cop that leaves his job at what, thirty-four? Who does that?" Of course that's what Marcus had tried to do, but he knew it was unheard of.

"Exactly."

Marcus looked at his notes and circled Callahan's name, Reilly's, Mackenzie's, and the others' too. "We're thinking maybe this has something to do with property. All the Weber Properties I've looked up were seized by one of the cops we're investigating. And Callahan seems connected to at least a couple of the properties, and he's connected to all these cops. What if this is a forfeiture scam?"

"How do you figure?"

"Weber Properties is buying bargain properties and selling them for fantastic profits."

"Look at the market. That's the way it is now."

"Callahan is driving around in a Mercedes owned by a TWC Industries, and title was transferred from the Chicago Police Department."

"Another auction purchase?"

"I don't think so. Looks like the Illinois State Police auctions off forfeited vehicles. Chicago Police would own the car if they kept it after forfeiture for 'official business.' Title transferred to TWC Industries in December 2002. And didn't you just say Callahan left the force in 2002. When?"

"Let's see. December."

"And he's got friends on the force. He knows the system. He was with the Asset Forfeiture Unit. Reilly's still in that unit."

"Interesting."

"You gonna bring him in?"

"Not yet."

"He may have murdered that woman at Reggie's. I think the bartender can place him at the scene."

"But Ms. Donovan can't. And the bartender is up on charges."

"Well, we've got him on impersonating an officer, then."

"That's nothing, Marcus. I want to get to the bottom of this bullshit. If this involves the Chicago Police in any way, we better be very careful here. The asset forfeiture group brings in major money for the department. If we start making allegations without solid evidence, shit will hit the fan. I want Reilly if he's doing something, and if there are more cops involved in what Callahan's up to, I want them all."

"Okay. There could be a connection to the prosecutor's office too. I spotted Reilly and Callahan with a guy last night who Abby recognizes as a prosecutor from the state's attorney's office."

"Shit. Marcus, we gotta get to the bottom of this."

Abby came back into the room in jeans and a sweatshirt. Not an ounce of makeup on her face, and she looked like an angel. A really tired angel.

Marcus hung up with Duvane and stood. "Abby, I gotta go."

"Where are you going?"

"I need to go check out the Weber Properties office and then I'm going to see some of its properties."

"I want to come."

"No way, Abby."

"Didn't you say you wanted to protect me?" She didn't wait for an answer. "This guy may have murdered a woman, and he's after me. If you felt you needed to sleep here last night, then you shouldn't leave me alone now."

"Abby—"

She cut him off again. "Didn't you tell me the address for Weber Properties was in River North? That's not exactly the west side. I just want to ride along. I'll sit in the car. I don't want to be here, Marcus."

Marcus wasn't sure about this, but then again, he wanted to keep her close. It was the only way he knew to protect her. "Okay, let's go."

• • •

ONCE Marcus pulled out onto Lake Shore Drive, Abby stared out the window at the icy lake. Much to her amazement, people were running along the lakefront. It was about thirty-five degrees. Everyone in the city obviously appreciated the break from freezing temperatures. Chunks of ice were floating along the shoreline. Marcus was heading south, giving her a great view of the skyline and the Drake Hotel perched near the water's edge. Sarah's wedding. It seemed like years ago now. She missed Sarah.

Abby leaned back against the headrest and turned to Marcus. "I did a little more research on the Internet."

"Abby, I thought you'd leave the investigating to me."

She didn't respond.

"What did you find?"

"Two things. First, I looked up Juan Domenz. Found a *Sun-Times* article from the time of his disappearance. Neighbors and relatives were interviewed. I didn't really learn anything. It was a brief article. And no other stories out there."

"But something's on your mind, I can tell."

"Yeah." She turned to face him. "We've got at least three crooked cops—maybe four, if Reilly turns out to be crooked too—connected to the forfeitures of buildings that end up in the hands of Weber Properties. And the man I met, who showed up at my townhouse yesterday—"

"Thomas Callahan."

"What?"

"Duvane just told me. He's an ex-cop and his name is Thomas A. Callahan the Third."

Abby nodded. "Well, that makes sense. I was going to say that I looked up the name 'Trip' on the Internet because I remembered joking with him about that name. He gave me the sense that it was a nickname. Turns out 'Trip' is short for 'triple' and often used as a nickname for boys who are the third. I was going to say you should search for cops with those kinds of names.

"Anyway, Trip," she corrected herself, "Callahan, is connected to all these guys, and I probably saw him leaving Reggie's Bar."

"Yeah."

"Seems like anyone who could fight those forfeiture proceedings was eliminated. And he's coming for me."

Marcus put his hand on Abby's and squeezed it. She looked at him.

"Hey. Don't go there. Callahan doesn't think you saw him at Reggie's."

"But then why—"

Marcus cut her off. "Come on. Let's stop the speculating. One step at a time." They were exiting onto Wacker. "Let's just get to Weber Properties." He followed it west and took a right on Lake Street.

The rattle and swoosh of the L train passing overhead brought Abby back to that night, just weeks ago when this all started. She looked over at Marcus, at his scar, at the face and those clothes that had once terrified her. What a nice surprise he had been. She turned back to the scenery and asked what they were looking for.

Marcus checked his note. "The address is 452 Fulton. We need to take this west to Union. And then I think it'll be down a couple of blocks on the right."

Abby pointed out the sign for Union and they took a right, just past Einstein Bagels.

It was an old street with patches of hundred-year-old brick exposed beneath the asphalt road. There were a lot of industrial properties, some run-down buildings, and some new construction. They found the address: an old warehouse. The brick looked centuries old, faded and slightly chipped, but the windows were new, and a giant black steel and glass door graced the front. Brittle, thick ivy vines clung to the south wall. Marcus pulled over to the curb, just south of the driveway that led to the back of the building. He jumped out and jogged up to the small marquee by the door and read through the office names inside.

"It's in there. Suite 404." He was back in the driver's seat, looking up at the building, counting the levels. "That's the top floor. I'm going in."

Abby stopped him. "Do you think it's open? It's Saturday."

"Well, there are several cars in the lot back there." He nodded toward the back of the building. "And this is real estate. Weekends are workdays as far as I know."

"Wait." Abby grabbed his coat. "What's your plan here?"

"I'm just going to see if anyone's there. If it's Callahan, he doesn't know who I am. I'll just act like an interested buyer, see if I can get a look around. And if he's not there, I can charm the receptionist," he said, with raised eyebrows.

"Marcus, look at yourself. You look like a gangbanger. If I were working reception, you would scare the shit out of me."

"Right." He removed the big medallion and grabbed a sweater from the backseat.

Abby pulled her phone out and dialed. "Let's see who's up there first." Then she spoke into the phone. "Chicago, Illinois. Weber Properties on Fulton."

She looked over at Marcus. "It's ringing." A woman's voice answered the phone. "Hello. I was just driving by one of your properties. The one on Lake Street. And I was wondering if there would be anyone available to discuss the details of that property?"

"Actually, my boss would be the only one to speak to, and he's out visiting our properties right now. Could I take your name and number to pass on?"

"Oh, I'll just call back. Thank you." Abby quickly hung up.

"Well?" Marcus had adequately transformed himself.

"Whoever is in charge is out viewing properties right now." He grabbed the door handle. "Okay, I'm going in."

"Wait!"

"Abby, lock the doors. The windows are tinted. No one will even see you in here." He sounded impatient now.

"Hold on." She was looking at the building and motioned for him to do the same. A twenty-something woman with long hair and a fluffy white coat was leaving the building. The girl from the auction. "That's her."

He checked his watch. It was twelve forty-five. "Must be going to lunch. Stay put, I'm just going to check it out."

Before she could even protest, he was out of the car and running for the door.

Abby studied the street, observing its diversity. It was definitely in the throes of urban renewal, that term she often read about in the real estate section. She sat for what seemed like hours, though it was only about fifteen minutes. Her stomach was growling. She hadn't eaten a thing yet today. Neither had Marcus. The Einstein's was just a block back. She did a quick check in her wallet, found a twenty, a pen, and an old receipt. For all she knew, he'd be in there another ten minutes. She wrote a note: *Went to Einstein's to grab us some sandwiches. Come pick me up!* She grabbed the door handle. A car was pulling into the lot in front of her. She couldn't see through its tinted windows. A red Porsche

211

with spinning hubcaps. As it passed, she noticed the rhine-stone license plate holder. It seemed so ridiculous. Like driving around in a giant gold chain. It pulled around to the back of the building and out of sight. Abby jumped out and jogged toward the bagel shop.

THE fourth floor of the building housed several businesses. Marcus quickly found the door to Weber Properties, but the lock was new and it took a while to get in. He entered quietly and slowly, waiting for any sound, any evidence that someone was inside. It was a large space, maybe fifteen hundred square feet. The ceilings were at least twenty feet high with exposed ductwork and beams and giant skylights. In fact, there were no windows on the walls, but the light from above flooded the space. He spotted another door straight ahead, at the other end of the space. Looked like another exit. To his left, the exposed brick wall was lined with black-framed photographs of various buildings in the city. There must have been twenty of them. He stepped into the room, studying each photograph. All nicely rehabilitated structures. Several three-flats and several old buildings with commercial space on the ground floor and what he assumed were apartments above. No addresses were shown.

After studying the photographs, he turned back toward the front door. A glass-topped desk was just a few feet to the right of it. The secretary's desk, he guessed. A giant oriental rug covered the dark wood floors. A frosted glass partition created a T in the middle of the space, and another parti-tion extended from the west wall toward the center. Marcus surveyed the space. Behind the center partition was a coffee station and a restroom, and on the other side there was a large, dark wood table with architectural drawings strewn about. Moving toward the right partition, he found a bigger, glass-topped desk on the other side. A huge map of the west and southern parts of the city hung on the brick wall behind the desk. He noticed the United Center and Cellular Field right away. There were little pins stuck all over it. Flags and circles. There had to have been thirty of them. Mostly flags. He got in close and found Lake and Pulaski—the Quick Mart location. There was a flag pin marking the spot.

The desk was covered in papers, notes, files. And then he saw it: a file labeled "Reggie's." The bar had been seized. But the legal proceeding to forfeit the building had barely begun. He looked back at the giant map and found the cross streets for Reggie's—it had a circle pin marking the location. He pulled out his camera and snapped shots of the map and zoomed in on the other circle pin location. He needed to find out more about what was there.

The front door opened.

Marcus turned quickly toward the door. It was him. Callahan.

He ducked, but the table, being glass, provided no retreat. Callahan was looking down, reading something, maybe mail, and heading toward the center partition. Marcus heard papers drop, footsteps, and then the rattle of bottles as a refrigerator door opened. He crept toward the back, hoping to get an opportunity to get to the back door. The frosted partitions would block the view, but he could see Callahan's form on the other side, so he knew that he too could be seen if Callahan looked this way. He crouched under the wood table in the center of the room. The phone rang.

Callahan walked back to the secretary's desk, and Marcus moved farther around the center of the space, now behind the bathroom wall.

"Hey. Yeah. I just came back from there. I'm checking the mail. Okay. Let me go grab a sandwich first."

Marcus looked around the wall. Callahan was facing the other direction. Marcus moved for the door, walking carefully on the hardwood floor that he feared would creak beneath him. He grabbed for the door as Callahan was hanging up. "Okay. I'll meet you there in fifteen minutes." Marcus was out. He took the back stairs down the four flights and pushed the giant steel door in front of him. He was now in the parking lot behind the building, and a red Porsche was parked right in front of him. He ran around the back corner of the building toward the street, toward his car.

The front door of the building opened just before Marcus came into view. He froze. There was nowhere to hide. He leaned against the building and looked down. Callahan walked right past him, and then right past his car, while punching buttons on his cell phone.

Marcus continued toward his car, watching Callahan walk toward Lake Street. He threw open the car door and hopped inside. "Did you see that?"

He looked around the empty car.

ABBY was gathering her bags and change from the boy behind the counter when the bells on the door clanged. She had just grabbed some napkins and straws at the side bar and was organizing her packages while walking toward the door, when a five-dollar bill slipped from her hand. She put the food on the closest table and bent down to get it. Someone bent down with her and his hand grabbed the bill before she had a chance.

"Here you go!"

Abby looked up at the friendly voice while reaching out to accept her money. Their eyes met. She froze. It was as if all the sounds of the world fell away.

He looked at her with a curious face, as though he were trying to place her. She waited without reaction, hoping he wouldn't make the connection. Then he smiled. "Well, hello. Abigail, right? I wondered if I'd ever see you again."

She didn't know what to do. She stared at him.

He stood then and pulled her up with him. "Remember me?"

She nodded with caution.

"Well, I should hope so. I'd be really insulted, otherwise." He smiled again. Like they shared something. The pounding of her heart felt so loud, she wondered if he could hear it. She knew she should speak but couldn't get anything out.

"You never called me," he teased.

Her stomach turned. Bile was rising in the back of her throat. Abby looked around the room. There were a lot of people here.

She faked a smile. "So sorry. I've gotta go!" She walked to the door without looking back, and the bells rang out loudly as she pulled it open with force.

Marcus had pulled the car up to the front of the building. Abby jumped in. "Go, go!"

He pulled out onto Lake Street. "Abby, didn't you promise to stay in the car?"

She was in a panic. "He saw me. He talked to me. He called me Abigail."

"What did you say?"

"Nothing! I didn't know what to do! I ran the hell out of there."

He tried to calm her. "It's okay. He almost saw me too, but I got out. Come on. Let's go back to your house. I want to check some things online."

"Oh, shit!"

"What?"

"I left the food. I bumped into him and just left it on the table! He's got to know I was scared. He's—"

"Abby. Stop. At this point, I'm not going to leave you alone. This will be over soon. I can feel it. Callahan had a file on his desk for Reggie's Bar. He's involved with the police in these forfeitures. I'm sure of it."

TRIP stood at the window and watched Abby get in a car and drive off. He couldn't see who was driving. He turned back and noticed her bagged food on the table. He knew that look. He knew fear. What did she know? He needed to finish this.

Trip sat at the table and opened Abby's bags. Two turkey and cream cheeses on multigrain. "Thanks, Abby," he muttered as he ate one of the sandwiches. He pulled a pen from his inside breast pocket and began making a list of what needed to be done.

Call Patrick—go Monday. Right before work.

Call Dominick.

Get Tanor's key.

And it was just that simple.

TWENTY-ONE

"ABBY, come here!" Marcus called to her from the guest room. He'd been on the computer for hours. Abby stopped working on her memo, though she'd barely begun, and took the steps two at a time.

"Look at this."

The screen was filled with the photo of a boy who looked no more than fifteen.

"Who's that?"

"Patrick Ellis. That's who was arrested at Quick Mart for alleged drug trafficking. So that's the guy who was here too."

"Where'd this picture come from? He looks so young."

"It's from his juvenile file. I've been going through Callahan's record from his time on the force more closely. We've seen him with the kid outside your place, and we know he didn't arrest him, so he's got to know him. I've

217

done a little digging. Looks like Callahan is one of two kids. Parents live up in Lake Forest. His father owns Callahan Construction."

"Well, that's huge."

"Yeah. Obviously comes from money. Mother has an architectural design firm—Weber Designs, LLC."

"Weber Designs. Like Weber Properties."

"Right. Mother's maiden name is Weber. He's got one sister. She's thirty-six, lives in Glencoe. Two small kids."

"So, he's obviously not related to this kid I've seen."

"Right. And I'm just trying to figure out the connection. See if it pulls this all together. It turns out Callahan arrested Patrick Ellis on three separate occasions back in 1999. Theft, a carjacking, drug dealing. The kid spent some time at the juvenile detention center. He was supposed to be held until he turned eighteen."

"So he would have gotten out, when? Last year?"

"Turns out he got out earlier, actually. I pulled up the boy's records from his time at juvie."

"I thought minors' records were sealed?"

"They are. But I'm not on the Internet here. I'm in the internal Intranet of the Chicago Correctional Facility. All the top brass at the department have access to the correctional systems. Duvane told me the code."

He turned back to the screen. "Anyway, this kid never had any visitors the first year he was there. Then, in 2000, he had three visits. The visitor signed in as TWC Industries. TWC Industries owns that Mercedes I saw Callahan driving yesterday." Marcus looked at Abby.

Abby went back to the big chair to process the information.

Marcus continued. "And here's the kicker. The kid got out a year early. Released in 2001, thanks to ..."—he began reading from the document—"*the testimony of the arresting officer who believes that he has been rehabilitated.*"

"So Callahan got the kid out three years ago. And now the kid owes him? Works for him?"

"I'm going to find that kid in the morning. I've got the address of the halfway house he was sent to. I'll start there. If I can find him, I think we have it. We get him to turn on Callahan, and maybe he can even name other cops."

Abby didn't let him finish. "But you'll stay here again tonight?"

He'd been at her place since Friday night, and it was a lot more comforting than her alarm system.

Marcus smiled. "Yes. And tomorrow, Abby, you go to work. You stay there, and if you haven't heard from me by the end of the day, you call me. I hope that I can talk to the kid, get enough information that I can have Callahan arrested by the end of the day. But I don't want you going home alone. And if anything happens and you can't reach me, call Duvane. You still have his card?"

"Yes."

"He knows all about you, Abby. We're both watching out for you."

ABBY and Marcus were both up by seven. Marcus came into the kitchen with his jacket on and put down the coffee he'd finished. Abby was getting some cereal and bowls for both of them.

"No, thanks," he said, looking at the cereal and then his watch. It was almost eight. "Probably best if your neighbor doesn't see me coming out of your place at this time in the morning."

Abby had to laugh. She could imagine the assumptions Mrs. Tanor would make if she saw Marcus leaving her place. "Oh, yes, go."

Marcus went to the coffee table, grabbed his gun, and put it in his ankle holster. "Now, you get to work too. I don't want you here alone."

"I know, I know. I just need to finish getting ready. I'll be out of here in about ten minutes."

"Okay, I'll call you later."

"Bye." She poured some milk on her cereal and heard him barrel down the stairs and let himself out.

Ten minutes later, Abby had eaten and dressed and was gathering up her paperwork. She had made some progress on the partnership memo, but it wasn't ready. She thought of bumping into Jerry, having him ask for it before it was done. She couldn't face that possibility. She might as well not turn it in. It would be proof that she'd slipped. She looked at her watch. Just finish, she thought. Nothing bad happens at eight o'clock in the morning. There was too much activity in the street, too many neighbors at home. She turned on her security alarm, sat down, and pulled out her draft.

Thirty minutes later, she put the papers in her briefcase and grabbed her coat. Things were turning around.

Bzzz. Bzzz. The noise startled her. Cautiously, Abby pressed the intercom button. "Yes?"

"Abigail, please come out. I need to talk to you."

"Who is this?"

"Uh. Patrick." She ran from the intercom to the window and peered out to the front gate. It was the kid. She ran back to the intercom.

"What do you want?"

"I need to talk to you. It's about Ali Rashid."

She didn't wait to hear more. She grabbed her briefcase from the table, put on her coat, and ran down the stairs and out to the gate. But the boy had moved away from the gate. He was now by the curb about six feet away. Abby remained inside the gate.

"What can you tell me? Do you know who killed him?"

The boy looked confused. Scared. He kept looking down the street.

"Please. Not right here. I…" He looked around and walked about ten feet farther away from her, toward the alley. He looked paranoid.

"Wait!" She opened the gate and hurried up to him.

"If you know something, please tell me. Are you working for Thomas Callahan?"

He stared at her, obviously surprised by the question. "I—I…" He looked down the block again and then smiled at her. A smirk really.

The tires of a police car screeched to a stop right next to them. The lights were flashing, though there were no siren sounds.

Abby, confused, but relieved to have a real officer, a man in uniform and a marked vehicle here to assist, turned to them for help. "Officer—"

Before she could finish her sentence, two officers jumped out of the car with guns drawn, telling them both to freeze.

Abby was dumbstruck. "Officer, this is a mistake!"

One of them grabbed Abby by the elbow and pulled her toward his car. The other officer did the same to the boy.

"Please, wait! Listen!"

The officer pushed her hands down on the hood of the vehicle and began to pat her down.

"Wait! What is happening? I'm a lawyer!"

The officers laughed. "Good for you," one of them said.

"And what do we have here?" His hand was in her coat pocket. He pulled out a big wad of bills.

"That's not mine!"

"And I think we've got something here as well," the other officer chimed in. He pulled a large bag of pills from the boy's jacket.

Abby looked at the boy's face. He had no reaction, as if he didn't even care what was happening.

"This is a mistake!"

"You have the right to remain silent." He handcuffed her, continuing with her Miranda rights, and pushed her into the back of the car.

Abby sat in silence as the officers drove them to the station. She looked at the boy. He was looking out the window.

"What were you going to tell me?"

He ignored her.

ABBY sat in the interrogation room with the arresting officers. One of them sat across from her at the table. The other paced the room.

"Officers, I don't know what you think you saw, but you didn't."

The man pacing the room cut her off. "We know who you are, Ms. Donovan. We know that you were just arrested with four thousand dollars in cash, and your little dealer was arrested, standing beside you with approximately four thousand worth of prescription drugs. Looks like clear-cut trafficking."

Abby opened her mouth to speak, but the officer put out his hand to cut her off.

"We know that you were recently at Dalcon Pharmaceuticals with unfettered access to their storage."

"What is going on here? How do you even know that? And why does that matter?"

"It matters because Dalcon Pharmaceuticals makes Medicone, an oxycodone formulation. And I'd bet money that the drugs we just found on the boy were Medicone."

"This is insanity. I'm an attorney. I'm representing Dalcon Pharmaceuticals in a product liability case."

The officer continued. "We know. We also know that the boy, your dealer, has been spotted outside your building on numerous occasions, upsetting your neighbors." He read from his notes. "A Mrs. Tanor, I believe?"

"Hold on a minute. I'm a senior associate at Simon & Dunn. I don't know who that boy is. I—"

The man in front of her chuckled. He spoke in a cool, even tone. "Ms. Donovan. You're obviously trafficking prescription drugs. Now, if you're just honest about the mess you're in, things will go a lot better for you."

She slapped her hand on the table. "This is insane. I don't do drugs or sell drugs or know anything about drugs."

The man by the door continued. "Well, what we know is that that kid has been seen loitering around your building on several occasions. You were also seen at a reputed drug location—one Reggie's Bar and Grill on January twenty-sixth."

Abby couldn't hide her rage. "You know that because I told the police I was there. I found that bar because I was trying to get home."

The man at the table cut her off again. He was still looking at her file. "Yes. And if you were at Reggie's for help, we're wondering how it is that you came across a dead body in the bathroom, never called anyone for help, and ran from the scene."

"I had to pee, okay? I found the woman in the bathroom. I couldn't find anyone who worked there. Some boys came in and attacked me. They stole my purse."

"Well, that's your story. Or maybe you're a strung-out lawyer trying to support a habit. We hear a lot of stories about professionals getting addicted to prescription drugs—trafficking to support their habit. You're in a high-stress job. Probably don't get much sleep."

The second officer broke in. "And I wonder what your fellow attorneys might say about your job performance? What your neighbors might say about you?"

Her head was spinning. She could just picture Jerry, her long time advocate, shaking his head in disbelief as he heard the news. Believing it because she had been slipping. Working less, more erratic. And her secretary, who'd been asking her why she was getting so many calls from police officers. Questions Abby had evaded. And Mrs. Tanor—she could just imagine. She'd think of that night when Abby forgot her keys; she'd think of Abby and David's breakup that Abby would never explain; she'd think of this boy who kept showing up, calling out to Abby. It sounded possible. Hell, if Abby didn't know better, she might believe the story.

The officer continued. "Maybe you went to Reggie's to make a buy, something went down, a woman was killed, and you ran."

She looked into their faces. She didn't know what to say. Tell them everything? Hope they believed her? Tell them about Marcus and Duvane? What if these guys were working with Callahan? "I want my lawyer."

TWENTY-TWO

MARCUS made a quick stop at home, changed into his own clothes so he no longer looked like anyone to fear, and drove to Rogers Park. The halfway house stood out between the three-flats on each of its sides. It was a wide, two-story brick structure with a big front porch and a black iron gate. The director, a squat, gray-haired woman, waddled to the front door to answer the bell.

"Hello, ma'am. I'm Detective Marcus Henton." He offered his badge, but the woman never looked at it. "I'm hoping you can help me find this boy." Marcus gave her the picture he'd printed from the police records. "I believe he was here in 2001?"

The woman nodded matter-of-factly upon review of the photograph. "Yes, Patrick. He was here for a time." She walked toward the office and Marcus followed. At the door to her office, she turned back. "Why are you looking for Patrick? What's he done?"

"I've spotted this kid at a couple of different locations that are under investigation right now."

"For what?"

"I'm not able to say. I'm not going to arrest him; I just need to speak to him. He might be able to help with my investigation."

The woman seemed satisfied and continued into the office. It was a mess. Her filing system involved lots of stacks. She walked along the small cleared path from the door to the desk and investigated several mounds of papers. Hundreds of photographs of teens filled the wall behind her desk. Marcus stared at the faces, looking for Patrick's.

"Well, of course he doesn't live here anymore." She was searching the filing cabinet toward the back of the room. "The state only required that he stay here for a year, and exactly one year to the day he moved out. He and another kid he met here got a place together. They've not kept in touch with me like I asked. But I keep my fingers crossed that they're staying out of trouble."

"Do you have their new address?"

"That's what I'm looking for."

Marcus waited.

"Here we go." She pulled a file and opened it on her desk. "Now this was in the spring of 2002. I can't say for sure that they'd still be there. You know how kids are. But this is it."

"That's great. I really appreciate the help."

She wrote the address on a Post-it.

"What did you think of Patrick while he was here?"

"Oh, you know. At the core, he was probably a good kid. But he hardly had a chance. Lost his parents young, shuffled around. Got into drugs. And you know what that leads to."

"Sure. Did he get a job when he lived here?"

"Oh, yes. They have to. That's part of the program. If anyone had a chance at a new life, I think it was Patrick."

"Why's that?"

"He had a guardian angel in that Mr. Callahan."

"Really? And who's Mr. Callahan?"

"Well, he was a police officer. I guess he took a special interest in Patrick. He helped him get out of the juvenile detention center early, and then once he got settled here, he offered Patrick a job. He was leaving the force and starting a real estate development company."

"And what was Patrick to do?"

"Oh, I don't know. Odd jobs, I guess. Make copies, maybe? Get coffee?"

Marcus took some notes.

"But Mr. Callahan paid him well. He even helped him get a car."

"Wow, that *is* nice. What kind of car was it?"

"Oh, just an older Cadillac. Tan, I think. Patrick loved it. If all my kids could have such people in their lives, we'd really have some hope."

"Yeah." Marcus put his pen and paper into his jacket. "I really appreciate your help, ma'am. Oh, and can you tell me the name of the boy he got a place with?"

"That would be Sam Williams." She went to her desk and sat. "Good luck, Detective."

MARCUS jumped in his car and headed toward Patrick Ellis's apartment. It was a few blocks from the lake. A three-flat. One of many lining the small residential street. Marcus got to the door and saw the labels for each unit. And there it was: "Williams/Ellis. 2B."

He rang the buzzer. No answer. He rang it a few more times. It was now nine fifteen. A voice came over the speaker. Groggy. Annoyed. "Yeah?"

"Patrick Ellis?"

"No."

"Is he available?"

"No."

"I'm sorry to bother you so early. I'm Detective Marcus Henton. I really need to find Mr. Ellis. Could you tell me where he is?"

"No."

"Son, he's not in trouble. But I really need to speak to him. Could you let me up?"

"No. You could be some psycho killer, dude."

"I'm not. I'll show you my badge if you just let me in. I just need to find Mr. Ellis."

"He left for work, like, a half hour ago."

"And where does he work?"

"He has a couple of jobs. Starbucks, up on the corner there." Marcus looked up the street and could see the sign. "Other shit. I don't know where he is." He let out an audible yawn. "Listen, dude. That's all I can say."

MARCUS stood on the corner in front of the Starbucks, talking to Duvane on his cell.

"Hey. I found the kid's apartment and his roommate said he left for work a while ago. I just came out of the Starbucks where he works, and he's not due here until noon. So I'm guessing he's working for Callahan right now."

"So what's next?"

"Well, I think it's a wild goose chase to try and spot him at a property. I could be running around all day and never see him. I think I should get back here when he's due at this job. I'm going to pay the medical examiner a visit. The same one signed off on both the prostitute's examination and Rashid's and his friend's. Maybe there's some way we can connect these two to Callahan. Or Reilly. And I'm going to see a property on Madison that Callahan had marked. See what I can find out."

"Good. Call me later."

"Duvane?"

"Yeah?"

"I think we should arrest Callahan today even if I don't find the kid."

"We don't have enough, Marcus. You're to nail dirty cops to the wall. This guy could lead us to them."

"Abby's in danger. I told her that I'd get this wrapped up today. We can arrest him for impersonating an officer. He's been at her place. And I'd bet Leon could place him at Reggie's too."

"Marcus, we need more."

"But maybe if we arrest him, and then go after Reilly, Reilly will implicate him. I don't want him on the street. Maybe even if we just put a scare in him—"

"I'll think about it. Just let me know what happens today and we'll take it from there."

TRIP was in his office, waiting for the call. He didn't have to wait long. Within fifteen minutes of arriving, his cell rang.

"Yes?" Trip didn't bother identifying himself.

"She's in custody."

"Good. Thanks, Dom."

"No, thank you."

"Just trying to do my part. So what's next?"

"Just waiting for the judge to sign off and we'll search her place."

"Perfect."

"How'd you find out about this?"

"You won't believe this, but I was dating her!"

"No shit. Well, she *is* hot."

"Yeah. Met her at the Drake, downtown. We had a great time. But then I found out she was using. I was going to break it off and then I saw her stash. When I saw Patrick's name and number at her place I was floored. I just knew I had to end it."

"Once a cop, always a cop."

"That's right. Anyway, maybe this will get them cleaned up."

"You done good."

"I just can't believe Patrick is mixed up in this. How's he doing?"

"He's fine. He acts like he couldn't give a shit about the whole thing."

"I'll talk to him. I'm going to get that kid on the straight and narrow if it kills me. I thought he'd been doing much better. When's the bond going to be set?"

"Just get him out of here. We'll let it go. We're more interested in her."

"Thanks man." Trip clenched a fist in silent victory and grinned. So predictable. He hung up the phone. "You *cannot* fuck with me, Abby," he spoke aloud, his voice triumphant. His pressure rose just thinking about it, but he surveyed the wall of pins and regained his composure. Now, he just needed to clean up a bit.

Trip opened the drawer beside him and searched for the right keys. He then went to the back closet, opened the safe, and pulled out a large bag of red pills. He grabbed his coat and drove to Abby's.

Forty-five minutes later, he and Patrick were in his car, parked in front of the twenty-third district station house.

"Good work, Patrick. See, I told you I'd get you out. No problem."

The boy put on his seat belt. "Yeah, yeah. What if I had been charged?"

"I told you that wouldn't happen. And if it had, I could have dealt with it. Had the charges dropped. But why even talk about it? Here we sit. Just like I said."

The boy looked out the window. "So when do I get my money?"

"Patience, my boy. What'd I say?"

"A thousand dollars."

"That's a lot of money. You sure I said that much?"

Patrick looked back at him, failing to see the humor. "Don't fuck with me, Trip. I just did you a huge fuckin' favor. Put my life on the line. I need that fuckin' money."

He tried to calm the boy. "Patrick—I was kidding. I'll take care of you."

Patrick looked out the window again and muttered, "You better." His knee bounced nervously and his foot twitched.

Now Trip was annoyed. "Or what?"

The kid raised his voice in response but kept his gaze outside. "Or maybe this little operation of yours goes to hell."

Little shit. Little fucking drug-addicted punk, Trip thought, shaking his head. His hand was being forced yet again.

The boy looked back at Trip. "You know that bitch asked me if I was working for you."

Trip's expression went flat. "What did you say?"

"Nothin'. Cops pulled up a second later."

Trip sat there, gripping the steering wheel. He slammed a fist against it, causing the horn to honk.

"What the fuck, dude? I'm supposed to be at work in ten minutes. Can we get out of here?"

Trip took a slow, deep breath and slicked his hands over his hair. "Okay, sure. But I need to show you something. Where's your car?"

"In that lot next to the chick's place. Behind that bar."

ABBY sat at the metal table with legs crossed, back straight, hands clasped around her knees. She was trying to remain calm, but the constant tapping of her heel against the floor was a giveaway. She had watched the clock on the wall, watched the hands moving around in circles. They were messing with her. She had asked for her attorney three hours ago.

The door opened and she stopped tapping.

"Well, this is a surprise!" He put the case down.

Abby couldn't help the embarrassed smile when Ted Gottlieb came into the room. She stood to greet him. "Hi, Ted. Thanks for coming."

"What's going on here, Abby?"

"It's crazy. But you've got to believe me, and you've got to get me out of here."

He pulled out his chair to sit and motioned her to do the same.

"Well, tell me all about it."

She told him everything. About what had happened the night she met Ali. About Marcus Henton and Callahan and how she and Marcus suspected that Callahan might have been the man she saw leaving Reggie's that night four weeks back. About Reilly and the other cops. About how Callahan found her at the Drake. About the kid who started showing up at her building, who they saw on the tape at Ali's. About the staged arrest in front of her building and about how she was working a pro bono case with Nate, and Callahan might even be the unnamed fourth assailant.

Gottlieb sat and listened, taking notes. "This is kind of crazy."

She watched his notes carefully to be sure he was getting everything down. "I know. But Marcus has heard from kids in the west side neighborhood he's working that Callahan has roughed up some kids, acted like he was going to arrest them, taken drugs and money and then let them go."

She paused, giving Gottlieb a chance to finish the note. "In fact, if Callahan is behind sending the kid to my place all these times and this arrest, and the money in my pocket, he's the one who set me up."

Gottlieb looked up from his legal pad. "And why would he be doing this?"

"I guess he wants to be sure I can't place him at Reggie's."

"But you said you couldn't."

"I know."

"So I just don't know why he'd be after you."

"I don't know. But I've been investigating him. I mean, not really him at first, but just what happened that night. We were getting close. He must know it."

Gottlieb didn't respond, and she wondered if he thought she was crazy. Or worse, if he thought she was some strung-out lawyer, doing all the things the cops alleged.

She continued to think it through out loud. "I went to the auction for Ali's place. The buyer ended up being Callahan's company. Maybe he found out I was there. And then I saw him yesterday and freaked. He must have known."

"What?"

"That I know what he's up to."

"And what exactly do you think that is?"

She sat for a minute. She had so many pieces. She started talking it through again, while looking at Gottlieb's notes. "What if Callahan was doing the same thing at Reggie's and Quick Mart?"

"What?"

"Creating the setup for an arrest, creating the basis for forfeiture of the properties? He's got a real estate company now. And lots of his properties were bought at auction."

"Abby, that seems like a whole lot of trouble and risk just to buy some run-down buildings in a bad part of town."

"What risk? Callahan's an ex-cop acting like a cop. He's got friends on the force. They all seem to be working together. If he's stealing drugs from kids on the street, he could be using that for the setups. And if he's stealing money from dealers and thugs, he could be using that money to purchase properties." She sat back. "It's like he's funding his enterprise through neighborhood crime!" She couldn't help but give a satisfied smile.

"Abby, listen. If you're right about Callahan, why haven't the police brought him in?"

"Marcus was going to find the kid today, hoping to get him to turn on Callahan. His boss wanted it all pieced together before they tipped him off to their suspicions. They want to get everyone that might be connected. There could be several police officers involved."

Gottlieb sat back, taking it all in. "You know, Mr. Rashid told me the police had intimidated him when they seized his building."

"How do you mean?"

"Well, I guess I can share this now that he's gone. The police threatened to mess with Rashid's immigration papers and he was terrified, Abby. He had legal asylum in the U.S."

"Asylum, why?"

"Because in Iraq he would be killed for being a homosexual."

"What?"

"He said the police told him they knew all about him and Miguel and his papers, and suggested they'd send him back."

"Oh, my God."

"That's why I agreed to help him for a reduced fee. I was going to file a civil rights suit against the officers and the city, alleging improper behavior. I hoped it would convince the prosecution to drop the forfeiture case."

"But you didn't."

"Didn't have the chance. I called the prosecutor and gave him a heads up to see if he'd reconsider going forward, but he just said he'd think about it. By Tuesday, you told me Rashid was dead."

Abby could hardly believe it. It made everything worse. "They killed him. They didn't want him to fight back. They've been saying murder-suicide, but I never believed it. What prosecutor were you dealing with?"

"Gary McDougal."

Abby slammed the table. "That's his name! I knew the face but couldn't remember."

"What?"

"Marcus followed Callahan Friday night and spotted him with that guy—McDougal. That would explain how Callahan was able to get Quick Mart to auction so quickly. He's got McDougal in his pocket too."

Gottlieb dropped his pen and shook out his hand. "Abby, this is a lot to process. I need to talk to Detective Henton. In the meantime, these cops are looking at you as a trafficker. They said you had four thousand dollars on you at the time of the arrest."

"The kid must have slipped it in my pocket when the cops showed up."

"That may be true. But possession of that much cash, even without drugs or contraband, can be considered evidence of criminal activity."

Abby rested her head on her hands at the table. "This is insane." Her thoughts turned to the office. The partnership memo. What a joke. If they found out she'd been arrested for drug trafficking, it would all be over.

Gottlieb continued. "We'll see a judge this afternoon and get you out on bond. I'll take care of it. But you're going to be here for a few more hours. I imagine they'll put you in a holding cell."

She slammed her fist on the table. "Goddammit!" Now she was angry. So angry that someone could so easily manipulate a situation, set her up, ruin her life. It felt like her head would explode from the rage. "You've got to get me out of here."

Gottlieb put his hand on hers. "I'll see what I can do. I think you're supposed to be in front of Judge Tobin at four."

"Four o'clock? It's only noon."

"I know, Abby. Let me see if I can get you in front of someone else a little earlier."

"You've got to find Marcus. Maybe he or Duvane can get all this taken care of."

Gottlieb packed up his things. "Maybe. I'll call him." He stood to go.

"Thanks, Ted. I can't believe this is happening. You've got to fix this."

"I'll do what I can, Abby. Try not to worry."

Her voice lowered, exhausted by the morning's events. "I'm supposed to be at work right now."

Gottlieb gave her a half smile, like he understood, but obviously he couldn't fix that. He headed for the door.

Abby stood to stop him. "Can you please call my friend, Sarah?"

He turned back.

"She's my closest friend at the firm. She should be in the office today. Just back from her honeymoon. You need to call her. You need to tell her what's happened. That she can't tell anyone. That she needs to cover for me, take care of things for me today, and I'll call her tonight. Her name's Sarah Wilson—well, Sarah Baker now. Please call her."

Gottlieb grabbed the door handle. "I will."

• • •

MARCUS sat at the table by the window, thinking about his meeting with the examiner, scribbling notes on a napkin. He had wanted a more specific time of death on the prostitute. Then, if Leon could identify Callahan as the one who sent him on an errand, his testimony, along with Abby's vague description, would be compelling. But Leon's credibility would be a major hurdle.

Nothing in the doctor's report had helped, and he seemed unable to give Marcus anything more specific. As they talked it through, it seemed logical that she had been killed with one of her stockings, but it hadn't been recovered. No prints, no DNA, nothing to finger anyone. Marcus had then gone over the findings on Rashid and his friend. The report had appeared cursory. Marcus had been unable to locate a weapon's test finding and had mentioned this to the examiner.

"I wasn't given a weapon to test," the examiner had explained.

"How is that possible?"

"I just wasn't."

"Then how could you determine suicide?"

"The gun was obviously close to the victim's head, given the wound. The weapon was found next to his hand. It wasn't rocket science."

Marcus had been annoyed. This man was clearly over-worked, underpaid, and phoning it in. "You just said you didn't get a gun to test."

"That's right."

"So we don't know whose prints were on the gun and whether the gun at the scene was even fired. How do we even know that it was found next to the body?"

"It was in the police report."

"So what happened to it?"

"I don't know. It wasn't given to me. I didn't test it."

"Didn't you question the officers about where it was?"

"Hey, they bring me evidence and I test it. I'm not the investigator."

Marcus knew that if Reilly was dirty, there might never have even been a gun found at the scene. He wrote *Reilly's gun* on the napkin and circled it. Then he thought more about the Rashid case. Reilly had a partner. Where was he in all of this? If Reilly had actually murdered Rashid and his friend, his partner was either in on it or not around. Yet another cop to investigate.

Marcus looked at his watch. He'd been waiting for about thirty minutes. He was antsy. He went back to the counter and asked for the manager.

"Excuse me. I'm looking for Patrick Ellis. I was under the impression he would be working now?"

"Yep. His shift started at noon. Can I help you?"

"I don't suppose you'd know where he is?"

"Nope."

"Is it normal for him to be late?"

"No, and I don't think he'll be working here anymore." The manager was obviously as annoyed as Marcus.

"Right. Thanks." Marcus headed for the door.

TWENTY-THREE

ABBY was lying on her cot in the windowless holding cell, staring at the cinder-block wall by her side. She stared into the tiny pucks and grooves of the wall, wondering what she could have done differently, wondering where Marcus was, wondering if Callahan had killed Ali.

The sound of the metal lock down the hall was followed by footsteps. She sat up. Marcus?

It was Gottlieb. "Well, come on then. We're going to see Judge Shepherd. The hearing is in ten minutes."

Abby got up. "I thought you said something about Judge Tobin?"

"Yeah, I was able to get us an earlier hearing. Shepherd's doing bond hearings at two o'clock."

Abby had been in the holding cell for an hour and a half. It had felt like a hundred. She couldn't believe this was her life.

"Now, don't worry about a thing." Gottlieb was holding the cell open for her. "We won't argue the merits of the case; I'll just point out that you have no prior record, strong ties in the community, a prominent position at Simon & Dunn, and we'll wait for the judge to set the amount. It's pretty standard by statute. It'll probably be twenty thousand."

"Oh, God."

"What?"

"This is public information, right? I could end up being in the news."

He patted her shoulder as they entered the crowded courtroom.

"Please don't mention my job," she said softly.

"I'll only bring it up if necessary."

IT was unreal. Like a dream. Being in court. The accused. The wrongdoer. Waiting for a judge to determine her fate. She wanted to scream at the top of her lungs. But ranting lunatics didn't get far in court. She sat in silence and let Gottlieb do his job. They were the third matter on the docket. It didn't take long.

"Okay, then. I've got the bond. Let's get you out of here." Gottlieb guided Abby through the crowd toward the giant double doors. And then she saw him: David. He was standing against the back wall, probably waiting for his turn with the judge. He looked bewildered. He'd obviously been in the room while her matter was in front of the judge. She watched him as his blank stare finally met hers. She couldn't control her reaction. The floodgates opened, and she covered her face as Gottlieb guided her toward the exit.

David rushed toward her as Gottlieb continued to try and pull her out of the room.

He called out to her. "Abby, what's happening?"

Abby turned toward him then, separated by the crowd of people standing along the back of the courtroom. "I didn't do anything, David! I swear. Don't believe it!"

A gavel pounded behind her, and the judge asked for order. David looked toward him. Gottlieb and Abby finally made it to the hall and found a bench.

"Who was that?"

Abby wiped her face repeatedly. "My ex-boyfriend, a prosecutor in the state's attorney's office, who's probably now wondering if I'm a junkie." The tears continued, but she acted as if they had stopped.

"Abby, you need to go home. Get some rest. This has been quite a day."

She closed her eyes and rubbed them hard as if she could clear away the chaos. "I need to find Marcus and tell him what's happened. Maybe he's found the kid. Maybe he can get this all straightened out."

"I called him earlier. I didn't get him, but I left a message about what happened to you and asked him to call me."

Abby sat, staring at her briefcase. Her memo was due today. She wiped her face again, looked at Gottlieb, and took a deep breath. "I've got to go to work."

"Abby, don't do it. You don't exactly look your best. It would be nearly three o'clock by the time you got over there. Just call it a day."

She wiped her face again, trying to improve the mess. "You don't understand. This partnership memo is due today. I have to turn it in. If it's late, I might as well forget it." She could hear her own desperation.

"Abby, come on. This is the computer age. Go home. E-mail it to your assistant. Let her deliver it for you." He stood and pulled her up to join him. "Come on. I'm putting you in a cab."

She didn't argue. She felt like she'd been punched in the stomach. She just wanted to curl up into a ball.

MARCUS sat in traffic on Wells between Division and North. He was going to check that Madison property and see what he could find out. It was now three o'clock, and he felt no closer to getting Callahan. He'd been chasing dead ends for two hours. This kid was key, he could feel it, but he couldn't find the little shit. He'd gone back to the kid's apartment, only to get nowhere with the roommate, and returned to the halfway house to talk more with the director for ideas of where to look. Nothing. He'd then gone to his neighborhood to find Leon and get him to identify Callahan, but he hadn't found him either. The phone rang. It was Duvane.

"I had the Reggie's forfeiture case checked."

"And?"

"The prosecutor filed for default judgment this morning. The owner's dead. Drive-by shooting in Garfield Park over the weekend. Both driver and passenger killed."

"Who was in the car with him?"

"His son."

"Shit. This is Callahan. He wanted that property. I saw a file on his desk. Abby and I went through this. He's getting rid of anyone who dares to challenge a forfeiture case he's interested in. And now Leon can't finger him either."

"Where's the girl?"

"At work."

"You need to watch her. We better pick up Callahan."

Thank God. Marcus hung up and noticed the flashing voicemail message on his phone.

He listened to the message from some attorney who said he was representing Abby on her drug-trafficking charge. *What!* Marcus made an abrupt U-turn, ignoring the horns and screeching breaks, and gunned the car up Wells Street toward Abby. He tossed the phone, cursing. He couldn't believe he'd let this happen. It took about fifteen more minutes before he was on Halsted, just east of Abby's place. He turned west on Roscoe and flew up the small street, looking for parking. Gottlieb's message had said they had a two o'clock hearing. She should be home by now. He slowed when he got close, looking for a parking spot, a nearly impossible feat in this neighborhood. He continued to the corner of Roscoe and Clark and scanned the lot next to her building where parking was prohibited. He'd risk the ticket. A tan Cadillac was pulling out of a spot. Wait. The kid had a tan Cadillac. The car was coming right toward him. He watched as it pulled out onto Roscoe. And then he could see the driver. It was Callahan—taking a right on Clark and heading north. Marcus followed.

ABBY stared at the computer screen. She'd finished the damn thing this morning, but as she re-read it one last time, it sounded stupid—it sounded as transparent and phony as it felt. In the last section, she was to describe why she thought she was ready for partnership, what she felt most confident about as an attorney, and what she would bring to the partnership. What a joke. She'd bring what—a criminal record? An ability to fuck everything up?

It seemed so stupid to worry about work right now. She didn't deserve partnership anyway. She didn't even want it. But she did. She had to. And she needed to stay focused on it, to assume that this ridiculous mess would get straightened out, that no one at work would ever find out. That Callahan would be put away. Maybe he was already in jail. But why hadn't she heard from Marcus? Didn't he know what had happened? She closed the document and drafted an e-mail to David. She couldn't bear having him think she was on drugs. But she didn't want to talk to him and hardly knew what to write. It was brief. Laughably so.

David—Saw you today. Sorry for the scene. I got arrested. Didn't do anything. I'm being framed for trafficking! Sounds crazy, I know. But I'm trying to get to the bottom of it. Please don't think the worst. Love, Abby

She hit *Send* and wondered if he ever thought of her anymore.

The doorbell rang. She breathed a little easier, thinking that Marcus was here. Hoping for good news, she ran down the stairs. "Who is it?"

"Mrs. Tanor." Abby's body went limp with disappointment. She opened the door.

"Hello, dear."

"Hi."

"May I come in for a moment? It's freezing out here."

"Yes, of course." Abby could feel the wind going through her leggings and sweatshirt.

"Abby, I saw you get arrested this morning. Dear, is it true? What they're saying? That you've been dealing drugs?"

"No! Come on, Mrs. Tanor. You know me."

"Well, I thought I did. But that boy's been coming around, and your boyfriend moved out—you haven't seemed yourself in months." And then she whispered, "And I saw some scary *black* man with big gold chains come over very late Friday, and the two of you left together on Saturday."

Abby shook her head. Mrs. Tanor had obviously jumped to all sorts of conclusions. Everyone would. Because, of course, none of them knew her well enough not to. She'd kept most everyone at arm's length and eventually pushed David away too. And now even he probably wondered about her.

"Mrs. Tanor, please believe me. I'm not doing drugs. I don't sell drugs. I know you think you saw some gangster here, but you're mistaken. I just can't tell you what's going on. It's not what you think." She wanted to say more, but she was scared of Callahan and dirty cops and didn't want to put Mrs. Tanor in any danger.

"Abby, I don't know what to think. I always liked you. But I need to feel safe in my home. Lately, a lot of strange things have happened around here. I think someone was in my house yesterday. I'm an old woman. I need to feel safe!"

"What do you mean someone was in your house? Did you call the police?"

"Well, no, because there was really no evidence. My doors weren't broken and I couldn't find anything missing, but it seemed cold, like a window or a door had been open for a while, and the drawer in my kitchen was open. I didn't open it."

It didn't sound like much. "Mrs. Tanor. I'm in trouble. I don't know why, but someone is trying to frame me. Please, don't believe what you hear. I'm going to get this all sorted out."

"Okay, dear." She offered Abby a hug, and though Abby would normally resist, she couldn't. They embraced and Abby held on. She closed her eyes, took a breath, and tried to pretend her mom was here, hugging her, making it all better. Mrs. Tanor pulled away and looked at her face.

"Dear, you look so tired. Get some rest."

Abby let her out and climbed the steps slowly, like each leg weighed a hundred pounds. The phone rang and she sat at the kitchen table, took a breath, and answered.

"Hello?"

"Abby! Holy shit. What the fuck is happening?"

Just hearing Sarah's voice, her concern, put her back into a state. She tried pushing down the knot in her throat, to explain it all. Sarah could obviously hear the struggle.

"Oh, hon. What can I do?"

She spoke through tears. "I'm in a real mess. I need help."

"Anything."

But Sarah couldn't help her with this. Abby pulled it together. "Just check my e-mails for me. Have my secretary go over my docket with you. I can't even think right now. I just don't want to miss any filing deadlines. If there's anything urgent, please take care of it or get someone from the case involved. I'll be in tomorrow. I really don't want anyone to find out about this."

"No problem."

"Thanks." Abby took a breath and tried to change topics. "So, how was Aruba? I've missed you."

"Oh, please, Abby. We can't actually talk about Aruba now. I've missed you too. I'm just worried."

"Don't. I'm working with a detective. Remember I told you about that man that chased me the night I took the wrong train? Turns out he's a good guy. He's been like my best friend the last week."

"Jesus. I can't leave you alone at all, can I? Gone just two weeks and you go off and find a new best friend."

They both laughed. It felt good.

Abby heard the faint sound of a buzzer through the wall, from Mrs. Tanor's place. She walked toward the window in the living room to see who was outside. Four uniformed officers stood at the gate, and Mrs. Tanor was heading toward them. To let them in, she guessed.

"Sarah, I gotta go." Abby hung up the phone before Sarah could respond and stood, motionless, wondering what would be next.

The officers entered the courtyard and walked toward Abby's front door. And then she heard the pounding. Her heart sank. What could make this worse?

She walked toward the stairs to go let them in. They began shouting. "Police. Open up. We have a search warrant."

She stood there, momentarily indignant. She had nothing to hide. Perhaps they would finally realize this was all a setup. But then it struck her. If she were being set up, who could she trust? What if these were not good cops? She thought of Isabel Ramirez. She ran back to the kitchen drawer to grab her pepper spray.

They continued shouting through the door. "We will forcibly open this door if necessary!" She opened the kitchen drawer. There, in plain sight, was a quart-sized ziplock bag full of pills.

She wanted to scream. The pounding on the door continued. This was getting worse and she didn't know if Marcus could fix it. What if she went down for this crime? Was it possible? She grabbed the bag and ran up the stairs and into the bathroom. She looked at the toilet and thought of all the crime dramas on TV. That never worked. She heard them on the stairs. They were inside.

She ran up the ladder steps and opened the hatch to the roof. It was freezing. The decking was slick with melted snow, now frozen. She carefully stepped onto the ice, closed the hatch behind her, slid to the knee wall connecting her

roof to her neighbor's, and climbed over. Their large barbeque grill was against the wall. Abby ducked behind it.
But she still had the drugs. What if they came up, found
her with these drugs in her hand? She thought of tossing
them off the roof, but then feared they'd find them in the
parking lot or worse yet, right outside her front gate. She
popped open the grill and dropped them inside. The hatch
opened.

TWENTY-FOUR

THE Cadillac was four cars ahead of Marcus. They'd been driving north on Clark for about two miles. Maybe he was headed right back to the kid's place in Rogers Park. He called Duvane. "I'm following Thomas Callahan. He's in a tan Cadillac. It's the kid's car."

"Where are you?"

"Clark Street. Now Clark and Montrose. Oh, shit. Hold on." The stoplight ahead turned yellow just as Callahan turned left and headed west down Montrose. The next two cars made it through the light, but the car in front of Marcus stopped at the line. Cars from Montrose were now driving through the intersection. "Duvane, I'll call you right back." Marcus tossed the phone aside and strained to see the Cadillac.

He couldn't wait. He swerved into the southbound lane and, with cars barreling toward him, darted ahead into the intersection. Horns blared and cars screeched to a halt. Marcus made the turn and looked around for trouble. No accidents. No police.

He floored the accelerator but couldn't see the Cadillac anywhere. It couldn't be that far ahead, and it looked like there weren't too many places Callahan could have gone. Within a block, there were only trees to the north—a thick forest preserve that seemed to go on for about a mile. The stoplight up ahead was red and there was no sign of him in the strip mall parking lots on the south side of the street. The preserve entrance was coming up on the right. After the light turned green, Marcus turned in to the entrance. It was worth a shot. The road was narrow and curved around through the dense, barren trees. Snow covered the ground all around him. Marcus took it slow. He saw the "Deer Crossing" and "No Dumping" signs just as the road began to straighten out and spill into a giant parking lot. A car was headed right at him: a black Mercedes. Tinted windows. Marcus could only see a shadow. But he knew. As it passed, he looked in his rearview mirror at the license plate. It continued past him back toward Montrose.

The Cadillac was right there, parked at the edge of the empty lot. Marcus pulled up beside it. There was no sign of the boy. He quickly hopped out and looked into the empty car. Needles, pills, a bag of powder, all in plain sight, all over the front seat.

ABBY froze behind the grill. She could feel the prickling pain of ice against her feet. Her socks were soaked. The hatch was open but she couldn't peer around to see what was happening. She heard a voice. Muffled. He was obviously closing the hatch. "Nothing up there." She took a breath

251

and slowly looked around the corner of the grill toward her roof deck. It was empty. She cautiously moved toward the hatch so she could hear them. She was freezing. What if there were more drugs? How had someone gotten into her place? Callahan must have been in her home. The thought of him, of kissing him, of waking up naked, created a taste she couldn't swallow.

She crouched above the hatch, listening for sounds. Nothing. Suddenly, there were voices in the courtyard. She moved over to the wall's edge and looked down at the four uniformed officers who were walking toward the gate, chatting casually, like they'd just ended a coffee break. One of them was talking about the Bulls game.

Abby sat on her bed, removing the socks from her painfully cold feet, with the phone cradled in her neck, and waited. It was Gottlieb's office. He was out. She asked for his voicemail and left him a message about the warrant and the drugs. She called Nate. His voicemail picked up. She couldn't keep her voice from cracking. "Nate, I need your help. I'm in trouble. If you get this, call me. If you get a call from Ted Gottlieb, he's my lawyer. I was arrested today." It sounded so foreign, so unbelievable.

TRIP was driving west on Montrose when the cell rang. He'd been waiting for this call. It was all falling into place.

"That's impossible!" He was talking to Dominick from the twenty-third district. He tried not to sound as flabbergasted and frustrated as he was. He'd just planted those pills this morning. The officer sounded annoyed, as if Trip had sent him on a wild goose chase.

"Well, I don't know what to tell you. I only know what I saw. Has she seen a judge yet?"

"Yeah, her lawyer got her into the two o'clock call. She's been out for a while."

"And who's the lawyer?"

"Ted Gottlieb."

Trip tried to hide his reaction. "Okay, thanks for the information." Trip hung up the phone and pounded on the steering wheel. This bitch was not going to fuck this up. He was too close. He popped open the glove box—he had enough stuff. He made a U-turn and headed toward the townhouse.

MARCUS was back on Montrose, frantically searching the road for Callahan. He grabbed the phone. "Duvane. Callahan's now in the black Mercedes. You need to grab him now." He rattled off the plate number for Duvane and waited. They had to get to Callahan before Callahan got to Abby.

"Okay, we've got officers heading toward Montrose now. What happened to the Cadillac?"

"He dumped it. Listen, you need to get over to the forest preserve that's just west of Montrose and Clark. I think you'll find the kid."

"What's going on?"

"Callahan. I lost him briefly, but he dumped the car. I saw the Cadillac after he left. No sign of the kid, but there were drugs all over the seat."

"I don't like this."

"Me either. And Abby was arrested today with that kid."

"Arrested? What the hell happened?"

"I don't know. I'm heading to her place right now. Call me the minute you get Callahan."

"Will do."

Marcus closed the phone and immediately reopened it and called Abby's cell. She answered after one ring.

"Marcus! Where have you been?" She didn't wait for the answer. "I was arrested! Cops just came here with a warrant and searched my house. I was hiding on the roof!"

"Abby, I heard about the arrest. I'm so sorry I didn't get to you earlier. I was just following Callahan. I'm on my way to you right now."

"Marcus, there were drugs in my kitchen drawer. It's just luck that I even found them before the police came in. I put them on the roof." Her voice was starting to crack.

"Abby, I'm coming. Don't move."

"I can't take this. I'm getting set up. You have to get Callahan and end this."

"We will. There are cops looking for him right now. They're gonna pick him up."

"Where are you?"

"I'm just about ten blocks from you. I'll be there in a few minutes. Sit tight."

"I can't sit in this place. I feel like a target. I'm going outside. I'll wait for you out there."

He could hear the panic in her voice. "I won't let anything happen to you, Abby."

She cut him off. "I'm not safe here. He knows where I live." She was obviously having trouble holding it together. "Even Mrs. Tanor is thinking the worst."

"Abby, I know this seems impossible right now. Just hold on—I'll be there in about ten minutes."

Marcus closed the phone and tried to gun it down Montrose, only to be slowed by traffic.

• • •

ABBY closed the cell. She looked around the room. She wanted to fall back on the bed and cry, but if she relaxed, something else would happen. She grabbed socks and shoes and headed downstairs. She was not going to be a sitting duck. She buttoned up her coat, put her cell in her pocket, grabbed a baseball cap, and headed out the door.

Headlights came toward her from the right, and people clogged the sidewalks to her left. The streets and sidewalks were filled with the five o'clock rush. The traffic, the noise, the movement, felt comforting. Marcus would be here in just a few minutes. She took some deep breaths and kept her eyes on the road, waiting to see his car.

MARCUS held the cell tightly in his hand. He was on Clark, just a few blocks now from Abby's place, but the traffic was thick and crawling along. He could see the top of her building. "Just hold on, Abby." He tapped the steering wheel anxiously. He was craning his neck to see what was holding up the cars in front of him. He couldn't see. Headlights, brake lights, streetlights, store signs—all glowed in the darkening sky. He slammed the horn. "Move!" he yelled. The traffic had not eased. He flipped up the cell and called Abby again.

TRIP flew down Roscoe toward the townhouse, lowered his window, pounded the portable siren onto the roof, and hit the light. It didn't make a sound, but the flashing got some attention as he came to a stop. A woman in a baseball cap was standing at the gate in front of Abby's place. He watched as she tipped the cap lower on her face and briskly walked toward the crowd on the corner. People crossing the intersection at Clark looked his way.

He jumped out, the badge dangling from a chain around his neck.

Abby turned toward him and their eyes met. Everyone was watching. Not moving. Abby tried to run but bumped into people. It was like they had created a human wall. She was trapped. He had her by the arm within seconds.

"Help!" Abby screamed out to the crowd as he pulled her toward the car.

Trip spoke loudly, wanting to be sure the spectators could all hear him as he pulled her toward his car, forced her body to lean over the back, and cuffed her. "Thanks, folks. This has been a tough one. Ms. Donovan, you have the right to remain silent."

"No! No!" She was resisting. She yelled out to the crowd. "He's not a police officer! Help me!"

Trip just laughed. "Oh, that's original. Anything you say can and will be used against you." No one in the crowd moved. He finished the Miranda rights as he pulled her back up and pushed her head into the backseat.

"No! Someone stop him!" He slammed the door. She was screaming and kicking at the door. He smiled at the watchful crowd and waved as he pulled the siren off the roof. It only took a minute. The crowd separated as he pulled into the intersection and headed south.

AFTER four rings, Marcus couldn't take it anymore. He stared past the traffic, at the slightest hint of a blue light, maybe a strobe, in the distance. Panic set in. The cars were moving again, and he swerved into the northbound lane to try and get by. It was gridlock. "Fuck it," he said. Marcus swerved to the side and abandoned the car. Horns blared.

He started running for the townhouse. He was a block away when the flashing light stopped.

He got to the corner and looked down the street. It was quiet. He didn't see Abby. He ran to the gate and hit her buzzer. No answer. He tried the cell again. Nothing. He called the home phone. Nothing.

He rang unit 8, Mrs. Tanor, repeatedly pushing the button until finally he heard the static of a connection.

"Yes?"

"Mrs. Tanor. This is Detective Marcus Henton speaking. I'm looking for your neighbor, Ms. Donovan. Could you help me?"

"Just one moment, Detective." The connection ended then and Marcus waited, wondering what was keeping her.

Mrs. Tanor's door opened and she came into the courtyard, wearing a long wool coat over what looked to be a nightgown. She didn't open the gate.

"I'm really sorry to disturb you, ma'am, but it's quite urgent that I speak with Ms. Donovan. I spoke to her just ten minutes ago, and she was here. Now no one is answering her door or her phone."

She looked him up and down. "Listen, I don't know who you are, but I've seen you here before. You leave Abby alone. She seems to be in a heap of trouble these days, and I'm guessing you have something to do with that."

"Mrs. Tanor, I appreciate that you're trying to protect Abby, but I am too. I *am* a detective." He pulled out his badge and identification and offered it through the bars. "Look."

She studied the identification and looked back at him, still unsure.

"Mrs. Tanor, I know Abby didn't do anything. She may have witnessed a crime, and she and I have uncovered some illegal activity." He stopped; it would be too much to try to explain it all now. "Please, I can tell you care about Abby, but she might be in danger. Can you please tell me if you saw her leave or saw someone come here, or better yet, can you get me into her place? She said that you have her spare. I really need to be sure she's okay."

Mrs. Tanor reached for the handle. He'd gotten through. "I didn't see her leave, and I haven't heard anyone come here. And I can hear the buzzer when someone rings her place. That has not happened in the last ten minutes for sure. Wait here." They were now in the courtyard just outside Mrs. Tanor and Abby's doors. "I'll go get the key."

"Thank you." Marcus paced the area and called Abby's cell again. No answer. Mrs. Tanor returned just a minute later. "Detective, it's not here."

"Are you sure? Where do you keep it?"

"I always keep it in the kitchen drawer."

"Have you used it recently?"

"No. Abby brought me the new set when she changed the locks just a couple of weeks ago. It's not here." He could tell that she was processing something.

"What is it?"

"I just told Abby that I thought someone had been here. Had been in my house. That drawer was open. I never open that drawer."

"When was this?"

"Yesterday."

"Mrs. Tanor, thanks for your help. I'll be in touch."

Marcus headed back toward Clark and stopped to talk to a threesome hanging out at the corner.

"Did any of you see a woman standing on this corner a few minutes ago? I was supposed to meet a friend and I can't find her."

The three chuckled. "Well, I hope we didn't see your friend, but we did see some girl get dragged into a car by a cop a few minutes ago."

The other chimed in, "Dude, it was wild. Total undercover operation. Not even a cop car. But he had the badge and light."

"Was it a black Mercedes?"

"Yeah!" they responded in unison.

Marcus ran for his car without another word, hearing only a sarcastic, "You're welcome!" coming from over his shoulder. He felt like his mind was getting cloudy. The panic was almost too familiar. Running through the streets. Feeling mayhem building around him.

His cell rang. Duvane spoke before he could say anything.

"Marcus. I'm standing in the middle of this forest preserve you sent me to."

"And?"

"And I'm looking at your kid."

"Have you questioned him?"

"Oh, no. He's dead."

He knew it. "Callahan's got Abby."

"What?"

"He got to her place just before me. Seems like he staged another arrest. Kids on the street said she was arrested. Put in a black Mercedes by an undercover cop."

"I'll get more officers on the street. We'll get him."

"He's gonna kill her."

"We'll find him. Hold on."

It seemed like minutes of deadly silence. Marcus got back to his car and headed south. Duvane came back on the line. "Okay, we've got an APB, added kidnapping."

"I'm heading south on Clark. Maybe he'll go to his office."

"I'm going to have officers check the other properties too."

TWENTY-FIVE

ABBY'S wrists burned where the handcuffs had scraped her skin. Her right shoulder throbbed from being thrown into the car. Lying on her side, she could feel the vibrations of her phone. She knew it was Marcus. She sat up slowly. Callahan watched her in the rearview mirror. She needed to see where he was taking her.

"Why are you doing this?"

He looked at her eyes through the mirror. "So tell me, Abby, how'd you get rid of the drugs?"

Abby didn't answer.

He smiled. "Not to worry. I've got some more."

She spoke softly. "I don't do drugs."

"Oh, yes, you do, actually. Such a shame too. Such a pretty lady with so much potential, just thrown away."

He's going to kill me, she thought. "Why are you doing this?" she asked aloud.

He ignored her question. "Why didn't you mind your own business?"

And then, before she could respond, "We had such a good time that night, Abby. I really thought that it might actually turn into something."

Abby cringed at the thought—at having spent an entire evening with this psycho and maybe even sleeping with him.

"Didn't you have a good time that night, Abby?"

She didn't answer but just stared out the window, avoiding his probing eyes in the mirror. She was watching the roads carefully. They'd gone south and were now heading west. She thought they were on Division. They were heading back to that neighborhood.

"Why didn't you call me?" He actually sounded earnest. "It's because of the boyfriend, isn't it?"

She didn't answer. Who was he talking about? She looked at him.

He must have seen the question in her eyes. "Well, I just assumed he was your boyfriend. You and I have this great time, share that hot kiss on the dance floor—I could tell you were into it—and then as soon as we see that guy out front, you blow me off. I'm sorry, but what could that guy have that I don't?"

He was grinning at her through the rearview mirror.

It started to come back. "David," she said, remembering. "Yeah, that's right."

Finally, someone had jogged her memory. They had been standing under the awning in front of the Drake, waiting for the valet to bring his car around. David was there, putting his fiancée into a cab for some reason, and he came over and introduced himself to Callahan and said hi. She remembered his worried expression and her embarrassment when David had asked to be introduced and she didn't know Callahan's full name.

"You picked that idiot over me! Come on, Abby. Really? What were you thinking?"

And then she couldn't help it. A little smile crept on her face. Such relief. David's car had arrived, and he'd offered her a ride. She'd accepted and left this psycho at the hotel. Thank God.

"What have I done? I don't know anything." She was watching out the window—trying to remain focused on where they were headed.

"Let's not play games, Abigail. There's no point. We both know you saw me coming out of Reggie's that night. You went to the Quick Mart auction. You were researching forfeitures. You started working with that Nathan Walters."

Her heart jumped when she heard him say Nate's name. She didn't want anyone else in danger.

"I didn't plan on killing anyone, you know. But that whore saw me plant the drugs. I couldn't let her go."

"Of course," Abby muttered.

Callahan looked back at her and smirked at her fake agreement.

"And then that little A-rab had to go hire a lawyer."

Ali? "Are you talking about Ali Rashid and his friend? You killed them too?"

"You mean his boyfriend? Oh, yeah. I didn't plan to. Fucker should have just let it happen. Usually these fucking foreigners don't know what to do. It's like taking candy. They can't fight it. Too much risk, too much money. But that little fuck went and got himself a fancy lawyer, and they were going to file suit and cause all sorts of grief. Couldn't have that."

Abby's heart sank.

"And you!"

She looked at him then.

"You brought this on yourself, Abby. None of this had to happen. Hell, once I met you and you didn't seem to recognize me, I actually thought for a minute that I might have found myself a…" He looked back at her. "I just planted the seeds in case you started nosing around. In case you could identify me. But you just couldn't stay out of it. So now I guess we'll have to move forward with you too."

"How can you do this? You're destroying people's lives. Stealing their property. Innocent people! You were a police officer once. Whatever happened to 'serve and protect'?"

"Oh, please. That faggot A-rab was probably a terrorist. I did the world a favor. That woman at Reggie's was a crackhead whore. Every person I ever set up was a piece-of-shit lowlife."

"What about Juan Domenz?"

Callahan fell silent for a moment. "Wow, you really have done your homework."

"Yes, and I know about the prosecutor in your pocket. But you're not going to get away with this. People know."

"Bullshit."

"You're a monster. How can you be so—"

"So, *what?* Don't judge me. You don't know anything about me."

"I know you're from money. Lake Forest. Every opportunity in the world."

"You don't know shit."

"I know you're a psychopath. And you'll never get away with this. No one will believe I'm a drug dealer. It's ridiculous."

"You know they will." Those killer dimples appeared.

No. Callahan didn't know about Marcus or Duvane. She just needed to survive long enough for them to get to her.

He pulled into a motel parking lot and stopped by the neon "Open" sign in the office window. "Wait right here, love. I'll be just a sec. And don't do anything stupid. The windows are tinted and you're safer in my car than out there." He smiled again like this was just as casual as a date, then got out and locked the doors. Abby watched the metal lock descend into the door.

She fell over onto the seat and rolled over, trying to give her hands room to move. If she could just reach into her coat pocket and get to her phone. She had new speed dials set up and Marcus was "1." Her hands flailed, pulling on her coat, trying to reach into her pocket. There. She could feel it. Now, if she could just feel the buttons, figure out which one would be "1" and which would be "Send." The driver's door opened. Abby froze. Callahan pulled the car around to the back of the building and parked. He hopped out, opened the back door, and got into the back seat. She worked to prop herself back up to a seated position.

"Now, Abby, let's just take off this coat," he said, opening her coat and pulling it down so that it covered the cuffs, "and take a look at this." He pulled out a gun and pointed the barrel at her eyes. "See this. I don't want to have to use it. Now just get out of the car with me and don't speak, and you'll be fine. Try to scream or make a scene, and I'll just shoot you. No one 'round here going to be any kind of witness." He opened the door, got out, and pulled her to do the same. It was freezing. She didn't see anyone in the parking lot. Her coat, now draped behind her back, covered the handcuffs, and she could feel the barrel of Callahan's gun pushing into her side as he grabbed a leather briefcase from his trunk and walked her up the stairs and into room 109.

The smell in the room immediately attacked her senses. Mold, dust, neglect.

Callahan flipped the switch on the wall, and a fluorescent ceiling light exposed the burnt-orange shag carpeting and dirty walls. He put his gun on the glass-topped table by the door, and moved to switch on the big television that sat upon a seventies-style cabinet along the wall. "Get comfortable," he offered, with a wave toward the large orange, brown, and yellow flowered bedspread. He turned to chain the door. Abby saw a bathroom just off to the left and clumsily ran toward it and shut the door behind her with her body weight. With her back against the door, she fumbled to lock the handle, and slid down to the floor.

She could hear him laughing. He raised his voice. "Abby, babe, there's nowhere to run. Don't fight it. It's going to happen. Just make it easier. Maybe you'll even enjoy it."

TRIP took off his leather gloves and opened the case. He pulled some latex gloves from the inside pocket, slipped them on, and began to line up some vials, needles, a rubber band, and some pills. He sat on the bed then, looked at his watch, and began to shuffle through the channels with the remote control.

In a raised voice, he began. "Now Abby, come on. You either come out here on your own or I bust the door down."

She yelled back. "You'll never get away with this."

"What? Buying foreclosed property? Hardly a crime."

"I am talking about murder, about setting up bogus forfeiture cases with stolen drugs, buying property with stolen money."

Trip nodded, impressed. She was smart. "Interesting theory, Abby, but there's no proof."

"And what about me? This is kidnapping."

"Well, actually, this is just a sad scene. A bright lawyer. Up and coming. But you know how stressful those jobs can be." Trip smiled and continued. "According to her neighbors, shady characters had been coming over, making a scene. Maybe even a repeat drug offender!" He mocked. "A police officer had been to her office. People were talking. She'd been arrested for trafficking. Perhaps she was just overwhelmed about her life falling apart."

He waited for an answer. She didn't say a word. He'd gotten to her. Bitch was not going to take him down. "Now, don't worry too much. We'll make this quick and painless."

ABBY was rolling around on the floor, pulling at her coat, trying desperately to reach the cell phone in the coat pocket. She looked around the bathroom for a way out. There was no window. Nowhere to go. But could she hurt him? Nothing. Just a pedestal sink, toilet, shower. The top of the toilet tank could be used to smash his head, but with the cuffs on, she was useless. Grabbing at the coat hanging behind her, she tried to get to her cell phone again.

There. She felt the buttons and got oriented. She hit "1" and "Send," and then the side button for the speaker. It beeped. No one approached. She counted to three and began shouting to Callahan.

• • •

MARCUS felt panicked. Not like he was working a case. More like his own sister had been kidnapped. He'd called her cell several times. Where were they? He had already driven by Callahan's office, but there was no sign of the Mercedes. He headed toward the west side. He didn't know where to go. The helpless feeling was all too familiar. What if she were already dead? He pounded the steering wheel with each dire thought.

He drove slowly along Division, looking down every side street, scanning every car that passed. It was dark. He gripped the cell phone in his hand and stared out the window. A group was gathered in front of a shop on the corner just a block ahead. He spotted Darnel. Maybe they could help.

But it had been almost a year now. He'd gained trust and respect in the neighborhood. These guys had helped lead him to Callahan in the first place. What would happen if he leveled with them? It would be a betrayal. Duvane would freak. Months of undercover work, blown. He pulled over anyway.

The phone rang in his hand. He almost jumped. Before he even said hello he heard Abby's voice. It sounded like she was a couple of feet away from the phone, but she was yelling. "So, Trip, you're from Lake Forest, from money. Why become a cop? Why not go into the family business?"

There was a pause and Marcus listened intently. "Come on Abby—tell me where you are."

She was talking again. "Why bring me to this seedy motel? The Shangri-La?! I would think you'd have higher standards!" Another pause. "No, don't!" Her voice sounded more panicked. "I'm going to the bathroom!"

Marcus jumped out of his car and ran up to the group of men on the corner. Darnel threw up his hand for a greeting. Marcus clasped the raised hand and gave the requisite half hug. The others were ready to do the same. Marcus ignored them. "Dude—where's the Shangri-La?"

The boys started laughing. "The Shangri-La!"

"Sounds like Marcus has found some company!" one of the men said.

"She got any friends, dude?" another said.

Darnel laughed too. "You got a hooker, dude?"

Marcus grabbed Darnel and pushed him against the wall. "Tell me where the hotel is, now!"

"Chill, man. It's just around the corner, there." Darnel pointed toward the place.

"Yeah, what the fuck, Marcus?" another said.

Marcus let go of him. "Thanks. Sorry, man. I gotta go."

"What the fuck, Marcus?"

Marcus ran back toward his car.

Darnel yelled after him, "Yo, Marcus! You need help?"

He didn't answer. He got in his car, took the left turn, and saw the sign down the road on the left. He pulled into the lot and drove around the back. There it was. The Mercedes. His heart was racing. He ran to the office, flashed his badge and a picture of Callahan, and got the information he needed.

Back at his car, Marcus called Duvane.

"They're here. Shangri-La Motel on Maple, just off of Western. Room 109. I need backup."

"Okay. Marcus, now wait for my guys. We don't want to lose your cover. This might not be over."

"We can't wait. He's going to kill her."

"Marcus—"

"She could be dead by the time they get here."

"Marcus, wait," Duvane said, angrier now, obviously trying to control him.

Marcus cut him off. "I've got a plan. I won't blow cover. Just get here as fast as you can." He hung up the phone before Duvane could say more. He looked into the backseat and saw what he needed.

TWENTY-SIX

TRIP looked at his watch. He'd lost his whole day to dealing with Patrick and now this bitch. He needed to get this done and get out of here. He leaned against the bathroom door. "All right, Abby. Last warning. Get the fuck out of the bathroom, or I'll kick the door in." There was no response.

Then, a sudden knock at the motel door. Trip grabbed his gun and pulled a silencer from his inside coat pocket. He went to the door, ready. He slowly pulled back the window curtain to see a massive black man with a large gold medallion around his neck standing at the door. Maybe he was just at the wrong room. Trip waited silently for a moment. Perhaps he'd move on.

The man pounded again. "Yo, blondie. I seen your car out front. I know it's you. Open up."

Trip didn't respond. He didn't recognize the voice or the man. He'd busted hundreds of guys that looked just like this over the years. He stepped back from the door, unsure what to do.

The man continued, and his voice got softer. He was leaning in like he didn't want to be heard by anyone else. "I saw you man. I saw you with Delia. I know what you did."

Trip froze. Someone else he needed to deal with. The man didn't wait for a response. He was speaking close to the door, in a hushed tone. "I don't give a shit, man. I just need a favor. I need a little action, man. Delia told me you liked to party. I'm shaking out here."

He looked around the room. And then he couldn't help but crack a smile. It was almost too perfect. Trip opened the door with his gun drawn. The man entered with hands raised and looked over at the drugs on the table. A big grin swept over his face. "Now that's what I'm talkin''bout."

Abby yelled, "Help!" from the bathroom. The man lunged at Trip, an elbow to the nose, and went for his gun. Trip kneed him in the groin and pointed the barrel into the man's temple. He fell back slightly, and Trip was able to point it at his face, but then the man kicked his kneecap and Trip stumbled. His hand knocked the table, and the gun flew. It landed by the foot of the bed, near the bathroom door. The man went for it. Trip grabbed the lamp next to him and smashed it over the man's head. The man fell to his hands and knees. Blood began seeping out of a two-inch gash in the back of his head. Trip kicked him hard then in his side. The man was barely conscious. Trip kicked him again. The man rolled onto his back. His eyes were closed. Trip kicked again, this time his head, and ran to the gun. The bathroom door opened slightly. He pointed the gun at the man's chest and pulled the trigger. A slight ping exploded from the silencer. Abby screamed and slammed the door.

Trip wiped the sweat from his brow and caught his breath. His kneecap was throbbing. His nose felt broken. He wiped his face. There was blood all over his glove. "Abby," he began again, patience fried, "get the fuck out here or I'm busting in." There was no response. He moved to the bathroom door and gave it a small kick with his good leg. He felt the weight of her body against the cheap hollow door. Abby begged him to stop.

He kicked the door again, harder this time. His leg went straight through the door. He bent over and looked through the hole. Abby was standing against the sink. He reached through the hole for the handle but she kicked and smashed his fingers. "*Fuck!*" He pulled back. He quickly reached through the hole with the other hand and unlocked the door.

He was in. He pulled her out by the arm. She stumbled as he dragged her past the man on the ground.

"You saw that, huh? Dumb fuck never even saw it coming." He pulled her to the bed and threw her down. "Now I've got a strung-out lawyer and her junkie dealer, found dead in a motel. It's perfect." She was crying, shaking her head frantically, still cuffed, totally helpless.

He got a needle from the dresser and rolled her onto her side so he could see her wrists. He stuck the needle in her vein. She screamed. He forced her face into the pillows. She was resisting. He pulled her back by the hair and with a controlled rage, spoke softly. "It's all over, Abby. Now shut the fuck up." He threw her head back toward the bed. Her energy was draining. She whimpered. Maybe just one more.

He grabbed another needle and jammed it in. Her eyes rolled back in her head.

He took off her cuffs, turned up the volume of the television, and scanned the room. It was a mess, but there was no sign that he'd been there. He pulled off the gloves, shoved them in his pocket, put his leather gloves back on, wiped down the gun, and placed it in Abby's limp hand.

He opened the door to find strobe lights illuminating the lot. Three police cars. Trip ran toward the stairs at the far end of the motel, away from where he'd parked, and went down and around to the back of the building. A high fence surrounded the lot, but two dumpsters gave him a boost and within seconds, he'd thrown his case over, hopped the fence, and run down the alley.

TRIP got out of the cab at his office building with cell in hand. He was limping. That fucker had really nailed his knee. He rang Reilly's house while slowly climbing the stairs. When he got to the office, the door was open. The lights were on. Reilly was there. Sitting at the conference room table. Waiting.

Trip held back his surprise. "Hey—I was just trying to call you at home."

Reilly sat forward. "What the hell happened to you?"

Trip looked down at himself. "What do you mean?"

"Look at yourself, dude. There's blood all over your face."

"Oh, shit." Trip walked to the bathroom sink. "I just had a bloody nose. It's all good." He took a minute to clean up his face and came back with a wet paper towel held up to his nose.

"Mike, you need to file a stolen car report for me. Say noon. Say it was stolen from the lot here."

"I'm not gonna do that, Trip." He slowly stood from the table.

"Mike, what the hell? I took care of it. Abby Donovan is not a problem anymore. Just report the Mercedes stolen, and I can't be connected to anything. Which means you're good too."

Reilly pulled his gun and pointed it directly at Trip. "You're under arrest."

Trip backed away from the barrel. "Fuck that, Mike."

Reilly stood firm and put both hands on the gun. "This shit has gone too far."

"Mike, relax. Have a drink. Don't be an asshole." Trip turned away from him and grabbed a beer from the refrigerator.

Reilly lowered the gun. "I don't need a drink. I've had too many drinks. I sat in a goddamn bar all afternoon, trying to figure out a way out of this mess. This is it." He raised the gun at Callahan again. "I'm serious. You're fucking under arrest."

Trip took a sip from the beer. "Mike, if I go down, you go down."

Reilly waved the gun with his words. "I may have taken some bribes, but I didn't know about murder." He was drunk. "I'm not going down for that. I'll bring you in myself and tell them everything."

Trip walked to his secretary's desk and began sorting through the mail. "You so sure?"

Reilly moved a few feet toward Trip. "I'm not doing this anymore. It's gone too far. I never signed up for this. I just needed some money for my mother, for Christ's sake."

Trip had prepared for this. He sat on the edge of the desk and crossed his arms. "Didn't you lose your gun several weeks ago?"

Reilly looked at the gun in his hands.

"Had to get a new one, right?" He enjoyed the confusion, the fear. Reilly's focus wavered. Trip continued. "I know where it is. And I know that your prints are the only ones on the gun. I know it was your gun that killed Rashid and his friend."

"Bullshit."

"Wanna test me?"

Reilly moved closer. "You killed that prostitute with your bare hands."

"Not really. I think her stocking killed her." Trip was smiling. "No physical evidence on the body right? Hmm, wonder where that is? Oh, I bet I know. But I don't think you'd like it."

Reilly lowered the gun.

Trip relished the victory. "That's right. Your only chance at remaining free is if I remain free."

Reilly didn't say a word.

Trip turned away from the barrel. He still had the power. He walked past Reilly and tossed the bloody paper into the garbage. "Now don't panic. I've taken care of our only problems. We're done. There's nothing and no one out there who knows anything. I'm walking out that door, and you're not going to stop me."

The front door opened. It was Lisa, his receptionist. She saw Reilly's gun, still drawn at his side. "What's going on?"

Trip remained calm. "Oh, hi, Lisa. This is my good buddy, Officer Mike Reilly. We're old friends."

Reilly didn't speak.

Trip continued. "Hey, Lisa, my car was stolen from the lot today!"

"You're kidding!"

"No. Must have happened sometime in the late morning. My buddy Mike here is investigating." He kept walking toward the back exit. Reilly just stood there, powerless. "Lisa, I'm taking a little trip. Just be a couple of days. I'll be in touch. You keep doing what you've been doing. Thanks, love!" He held the door handle. Reilly had remained still. Trip turned back one more time. "Mikey, I'll be in touch. You just make that call." Reilly looked at him, and Trip gave him a wink. "We're all good, buddy!" And he was off. Out the back and into the Porsche parked in the lot. The kid was dead, Leon too. And now with Abby gone and that giant black dude, everything should be fine. Reilly just needed to report the car stolen. Though he wondered about all those cop cars at the motel.

ABBY opened her eyes and saw the machines, the I.V. in her arm. Marcus was sitting on the edge of her bed, his head bandaged.

"Marcus," Abby whispered.

He broke in immediately. "It's okay, Abby. You're okay."

She looked around the hospital room.

"They got to us in time. The doctor said you'd feel groggy and nauseous, but you'd be okay."

Abby couldn't stop the tears. "I saw him shoot you in the chest." Her head began shaking again at the image. "I thought you were dead."

"I'm sure that's what Callahan thinks. Abby, I had on a vest. Nothing got to my chest. I just got whacked in the head a few times," he said, rubbing the back of his skull. "I came to as the other officers were arriving." He took her hand in his. "We're okay."

Abby tried to process it all. She sat up. "You're really okay?"

"I'm fine. I'm an idiot, but I'm fine."

"What do you mean?"

"Abby, look at me. I'm a big dude. I let that punk get the better of me. I should have killed him the moment I walked in the door."

She fell back against the pillows, exhausted, and wiped her face. "He admitted everything to me, Marcus. Killing that woman at Reggie's, killing Ali Rashid and his friend. Planting the drugs at my house."

"Yeah, he killed the kid too—Patrick Ellis. Duvane found him at a forest preserve this afternoon. And Leon and his dad were killed over the weekend."

"Jesus. It's over, right? He's arrested? I get my life back?"

He didn't answer right away, and Abby sat up straight. "What?"

"We've got him, Abby. We've got enough to nail him to the wall. We just need to find him."

"What?"

"He got away. Before the backup arrived. We haven't located him yet."

Her whole body tensed. It wasn't over.

"Abby, stop. I can see it on your face. It's going to be fine. I'll get this guy. You rest. It'll be over soon."

"How can I rest? I was arrested today, my home was ransacked by police, I found drugs in my house. I was kidnapped, drugged, left for dead. I thought I saw you die." She was yelling now. Unable to control her anger, her fear. "Why are you even here? You need to get him!"

Before Marcus could respond, someone said, "I don't think so." They both turned to the voice at the open door, where a big black man in his fifties, wearing a long wool coat, stood. He continued. "Henton is staying right here."

Abby looked back at Marcus. "Abby, meet my boss, Assistant Deputy Superintendent Robert Duvane."

The man came over to the bed and offered his hand. "A pleasure to meet you, Ms. Donovan. I've heard wonderful things from Henton here, and we couldn't have broken this case without your help."

She didn't know what to say. A small "thanks" was all that came out.

Duvane continued. "Marcus's got ten stitches in the back of his head and a concussion. We're still waiting on the lab reports for all the rest. He took a pretty good beating, unfortunately."

"Oh, my God. Marcus, are you okay?"

"I'm fine."

Duvane broke in. "He needs to be in his own room, resting. But he insisted on sitting here with you. Waiting for you to wake up."

She looked at Marcus again. He took her hand. "I'm *okay*."

She turned away from both of them and stared out the window.

Marcus turned to Duvane. "Give me a minute here?"

"Sure. I'm waiting for you outside, though, Marcus. We need to talk. Ms. Donovan?" Abby turned to his voice. "Again, glad to meet you, and I want you to know that we're going to get this guy. There's an officer right outside your door. We're not going to let anything happen to you again."

Abby turned back toward the window. Who was going to get him? The only police she trusted were the two in the room. For all she knew there were dozens of dirty cops on the force. How could she feel safe?

"I know what you're thinking, Abby."

She cut him off. "I'm not safe here. As soon as he finds out that I'm not dead, he's going to come after me."

"You're not going to stay here. I've taken care of it."

Before she could respond, Nate walked into the room.

"Hi there," he said.

She smiled and relaxed back into her pillow a bit.

Nate went for her hand, but she pulled him in for a hug and wouldn't let go. She held on to him as she spoke, "Marcus, this is my good friend, Nate Walters."

"Yes. We've met. In fact, you're going home with Nate."

"What?"

"I don't want you here, and I don't want you at the townhouse. Nate and I have talked. He lives up north. You'll be safe there. This whole thing should be over in twenty-four hours, Abby. Callahan's Mercedes was reported stolen at noon. It just popped up in the system an hour ago. He thinks he's covered his tracks, and there's no one left. We've got the bus and train stations and airports covered just in case. We'll keep an officer here, and as far as anyone knows, you're spending the night. But really, he probably won't even know you're here. As far as he's concerned, we're both dead."

She looked back and forth between them. "How did you even—"

As if they both knew the question, they responded in unison: "Gottlieb."

Nate continued. "Your lawyer called me. And then I talked to Duvane, and he told me you were here. Abby, the detective here didn't tell me everything—just that you were hurt and that he wanted you out of town. So you're coming with me because I want to know what the heck is going on."

"You won't believe it."

Marcus broke in. "I don't know about that. Didn't you tell me he goes after dirty cops?"

"Oh, that's right." Abby got excited. "Nate, we know who the mystery cop is in the Ramirez case."

TWENTY-SEVEN

T RIP pulled into the long gravel drive and parked off to the left by the garage. The Jaguar was nowhere in sight. He checked inside the garage. Not there either. Good. He was in no mood to deal with his dad. He grabbed the front door handle and winced. Bitch probably broke his finger.

He walked in the unlocked front door and was immediately greeted by Felix, their boxer. Just to see that slobbering face heading his way relaxed him. He leaned forward to accept the attack of love. Felix licked his face compulsively. He probably smelled the remnants of blood.

Trip's mother came walking into the front hall from the kitchen, wearing a big grin. "Trip? Well, this is a surprise. You just missed dinner."

Trip broke away from the dog and gave his mother a hug. "Yeah, I know, Mom. I just felt like getting out of the city. Thought it would be nice to come up here for a couple of days. Do you mind?"

"Of course not, dear. Your dad's back in Florida. Golf match. He'll be sorry to have missed the visit, but I'd love the company."

"You're the one I want to see anyway, Mom." Trip gave her that charming smile. The one she'd helped cultivate.

She smiled back. "Well, come on in. You hungry?" She led him back to the kitchen. With all the activity of the day, he hadn't eaten since breakfast. It was now eight thirty, and he was starving.

His mother opened the fridge and pulled out the leftovers. "Well, this is a first, isn't it?" She didn't make eye contact. They were good at avoiding any big confrontations. "I mean, I usually have to plead to get you up here for dinner once a month."

Trip sat at the breakfast table and looked out the window into the dark night. "I know, Mom. I thought it would be a nice surprise."

"It is, honey. I just want to be sure you're okay." She brought him an opened Amstel Light.

He felt some relief. She cared. She always reserved judgment.

"I'm okay." He took a sip of the beer and thought back on the day. "Everything should be fine."

"Should be?" A plate of salmon, spinach, and couscous landed in front of him. "Should still be hot. Cassie had just put this up." She sat at the table with him, waiting for more.

Trip plowed through the food while his mother waited. "It was just a difficult day, Mom, but I think that I've dealt with everything." He hoped. Abby had to be dead. As long as Reilly called in his Mercedes as stolen before noon, there was no chance he could be connected to anything that had gone down. He should be fine. And he'd created great insurance for dealing with Reilly. But he just wanted confirmation, and Reilly wasn't answering his phone. He tried to relax.

"Work?"

"Huh?"

"When you say you've dealt with everything, I assume you're talking about work. Is it going well?"

"Oh yes. Real estate developing can be stressful—you know that. But the market is awesome. Every building is turning a huge profit. And one job just seems to lead to the next. I've got a plan, and I've stuck to it. It's coming together."

"Trip," she reached out toward his face, but he pulled back before she could touch him. "Your nose looks swollen! Like it might be broken."

He faked a laugh. "Oh, yeah. It probably is. My assistant smashed the door in my face today. It was pretty funny. Hurt like a bitch, though."

"So why are you really staying the night, son? I don't see a bag."

Trip sat back and looked at her, searching her expression for what might work. He took a sip of his beer again and began. "I just broke it off with this girl. She was a little psycho, actually. Couldn't take no for an answer, and I was thinking about how she was likely to pop over tonight or call my phone, and I thought I'd get out of there."

"I never heard about this girl."

"Yeah, it didn't last long. I found out she was doing drugs, and I broke it off. Too bad too. I really thought she was a keeper. A lawyer, pretty. You would have liked her. Except for the drugs."

"Well, good for you, baby. Sounds like a bad egg." She put the Tupperware back in the refrigerator, and Trip resumed eating.

"Well, how about doing some property runs with me tomorrow? We could spend some time together."

"Sounds good to me." No better way to stay out of sight for a day or so.

"I have to head out to a property in the morning. Then perhaps we could go visit that property you wanted me to look at?"

He needed to talk to Reilly before he went anywhere near his properties. But he'd deal with that wrinkle when he knew more. "Sure."

"Dear, I love having you here." She kissed the top of his head. "Makes me feel safe."

Trip put his hand on hers. "Me too."

"Okay, then, I'm going up, honey. Turn off the lights, okay? I'll set the alarm."

"Will do. Love you, Mom."

ABBY sat in the overstuffed armchair, wrapped in a giant chenille blanket, and stared at the flames of the fire. She was dazed. It was hard to reconcile the serenity, safety, and warmth of this moment with the events of the day. She still felt nauseous. A faint whistle came from the kitchen, and a moment later, Nate appeared with two mugs.

The hot chocolate was almost too hot to drink, but the warmth of the cup felt good in her hands. Abby glanced over at the photos of Nate's family on the table next to her.

"Thanks again, Nate, for bringing me here."

He stoked the fire and went to the chair across from her and sat.

"Of course, Abby. You're like family to me."

She was still looking at the pictures of his wife and baby. "They're both so beautiful. You've done very well here," she added, looking around the room.

"Yeah, we love this old house." He smiled at the room. "It's been nothing but dust and debris since we moved in, but it's a great old place."

It was a huge living room. The fireplace mantel was massive, and it looked like the entire piece was made of stone. "And I love those doors," Abby said, nodding toward the back wall. Two giant French doors obviously led to the backyard. "I just feel a little weird being here. I haven't even met Meg yet."

Nate smiled. "I know. I thought she might still be up, but she often falls asleep after putting Lizzy down. She's still getting up a couple of times each night, so she's pretty much exhausted all the time."

"And she won't mind finding me here tomorrow?"

"No. I've told her all about you. And I'll tell her you're here before I leave in the morning. I'm sure she'll be glad for the company."

Abby didn't say any more. She drank her hot chocolate and stared at the flames.

"Abby, I can't believe the mess you're in. It's unbelievable."

She looked at him then. "I feel so stupid. I don't know how I let myself get set up like this. This wouldn't have happened to Denny. He was too smart."

"Abby, you're smart too. This could have happened to anyone. It was random."

"Well, I don't think it could have happened to *anyone*. It's not exactly a normal situation."

"It sounds like this happened because you were trying to help a friend, to do the right thing."

"Yeah, but I got him killed."

"It wasn't your fault, Abby."

She couldn't respond. The words seemed empty. She felt empty. Silence began to fill the space between them.

"Abby, talk to me."

She looked at him for a clue as to what he meant.

"You're not the girl I knew in high school."

Thank god. That's what she had been running from.

"You were confident, outrageous, full of big dreams. And now..."

This didn't feel like a compliment. She turned her gaze back toward the fire and closed her eyes to stop the tears from coming. "And now?" she nearly whispered.

"You just seem so alone...and sad." He waited for a response.

She didn't have one. She sipped her hot chocolate.

"What happened with your boyfriend? Your eyes actually lit up when you told me about him."

She tried to answer but couldn't find the right words.

"Did you love him?"

She nodded.

"Why did you let him go?"

She thought about the quickest way to answer the question. "He didn't really know me."

"What do you mean?"

She looked at Nate now, ready to see the change in his expression that would surely end this line of questioning.

"He didn't even know about Denny. I told him I was an only child."

He almost laughed. But it wasn't a joke. "Why?"

There was really no reason not to come clean at this point. She'd already lost it all. "I...he..." The words felt trapped in her throat.

"Abby."

She knew he was going to try to make her feel better. She couldn't take it anymore. She put the mug down on the table with force. A splash of chocolate jumped the rim. "I killed him." As soon as the words escaped, she looked away from Nate, unable to face him.

Nate sat forward. "No you didn't. He was killed by a drunk driver."

She shook her head. He didn't get it. It was too late to turn back now. She looked at him and forced the words to come. "I'm the reason Denny is dead."

"No one blames you, Abby. I don't understand."

"They should blame me. If they knew, they would."

"Knew what?"

She couldn't look at him. She stared into the fire. "We weren't out together that night, Nate."

Nate didn't respond, and Abby looked at the confusion in his face. "He was at the library, studying, of course. I was drunk and didn't want to get in trouble with Mom and Dad. I called him to come get me. He was on the road that night because of me."

Nate sat back in silence then, taking in the information. She held her breath and awaited the anger that would follow. "But Abby, even still..."

He still didn't get it. She felt angry. He needed to see. "We were fighting in the car. He told me I was acting like a screw-up. I told him he was an asshole. What an asshole, right? Big brother, the one who was about to graduate at the top of his class, the one who was nice enough to come get me so I wouldn't have to call Mom and Dad—he was the asshole."

"Abby, you can't blame yourself for his death. It was a tragic accident."

"But I was fucking with the radio!"

"What?"

"Trying to tune him out. And he went to turn it down and I slapped his hand away. We would have seen that car. I distracted him. I caused the accident."

Nate didn't say anything. She knew. She knew that Nate finally understood. He'd probably hate her, but there was some sense of relief in saying it out loud. Finally.

"All these years…" he put down his mug and stood.

"I killed your best friend, Nate. I killed my brother." She couldn't look at him. She waited for him to leave. It was what she expected. What she deserved. The blame.

But he didn't leave. Nate came over to her chair and forced her to stand up and look at him. She couldn't do it. She was afraid to see his eyes.

His arms locked around her and she tried to pull back. He held her tight. She went limp, but he wouldn't let go. She froze, not sure what to make of this.

He whispered in her ear, "Abby, I don't blame you. You were a kid."

Abby sobbed into his shoulder. "I'm so sorry, Nate."

He let go then and held her back so she would see his face. "Yes, you got drunk. But you were a teenager. Screwing up is expected."

She kept shaking her head, unable to take the pain of sharing the truth.

"You called your brother. You didn't get behind the wheel yourself. That was the right thing to do."

Abby couldn't respond.

"Is that why you've done all this?" He let her free of his embrace, and she fell back into the chair. Nate stepped back to his seat and waited.

Abby stared at the carpet as the tears dropped off her chin. She wiped her face. "When I finally woke up in the hospital, and Mom and Dad sat at the side of my bed and said that Denny was dead, I just couldn't tell them. Mom's eyes were so red and swollen. I knew she'd been crying for days. Dad could barely even look at me. But they kept hugging me and saying how grateful they were that I was alive. I couldn't tell them. I couldn't bear to have them hate me."

"They wouldn't have—"

"They would have blamed me. They had a right to. It was my fault. Nate, he was in that car because of me. We didn't see that man speeding toward the red light because of me!"

Nate tried to speak again, but she cut him off. "But I couldn't tell. I just didn't know what to do. And I tried to think about Denny. What would he do? He wanted to be a lawyer, like dad. Dad loved that. I thought maybe I could give him that. Maybe make him proud, maybe make Denny proud. The next year I signed up for debate. It made them so happy. I quit singing. I got serious about school. It seemed like every time I made a decision based on what Denny would have done, it helped."

"You've been trying to live his life."

"Doing a great job too, aren't I?"

Nate smirked and shook his head. It reminded her of Denny. "Is there anything you like about being a lawyer?"

Abby didn't answer right away, and Nate laughed. She had to smile too. "I'm thinking!" She wiped the tears. "Actually, I've enjoyed a few things. When I feel like I'm helping people, I like that. But most of the time, it's just a lot of game playing. And none of this feels natural. It's like I've been playing a part."

"Is that why you say your boyfriend didn't know you?"

Abby nodded. "We were engaged. Did I tell you that?" She didn't wait for the response. "I loved him. I still love him. But you can't marry someone if you're not going to really let them in. I couldn't do it. I was too afraid. He used to prosecute DUIs for Christ's sake! He was always telling me stories. How could I tell him that I was one of those stories? That I was—"

"Abby, look at me."

She did.

"We all make mistakes. But Denny wouldn't want you living his life. He was so proud of you."

"There wasn't anything to be proud of. I was a fuck-up."

"He thought you were awesome. He thought you were talented. Abby, you've got to forgive yourself."

This was so unexpected. All these years, Abby had been sure she knew what people would think of her if they knew the truth. But here was Nate. He hadn't yelled. Hadn't even gotten mad. It was overwhelming. It felt good to finally be free of all the secrets.

"I couldn't go through with it, Nate. The wedding. I kept putting it off. Kept putting the job first. David got sick of it. Sick of me. I couldn't blame him, but I just couldn't choose him, you know?"

He obviously didn't know.

"I had to choose Denny."

They sat in silence for several minutes.

"Abby, thank you for telling me."

She stared into the flames, watching them dance and hiss and crackle. She watched the smoke rise up the chimney. She felt lighter. "Thanks for not hating me, Nate."

"Abby."

She looked at him then. At his warmth and ease.

Nate leaned forward and smirked like he had a secret. "You know, Abby, maybe all this happened for a reason. I mean, it's pretty random that we found each other after all these years. Everything that's happened to you in the last month is pretty random. Maybe Denny had something to do with it."

She smiled at the thought of her brother pulling strings from above. She took a deep breath. It was finally over.

TWENTY-EIGHT

MARCUS was dressed, sitting in the corner, waiting. The sun was coming up and filled the room with light. Duvane burst through the door.

Marcus stood immediately. "Thank God. Let's get the hell out of here."

"Doctors gave you the all clear, right?"

"Yes, yes. I'll be fine. We need to find Callahan."

"On that note, I have a surprise."

"What?"

"Come with me."

THEY arrived at the eleventh district station house and went to the second floor—to the viewing room adjacent to the interrogation room. There, behind the glass, sat Reilly. Hunched over, with his head on the table, sleeping.

"What time did you get him?"

"It was about nine o'clock last night. He was spotted in the evidence room, going through the stuff from the Rashid murder-suicide case. I had him held. After a few hours, he fell apart. Told me everything."

"Well, let's go."

Duvane and Marcus entered the room together, and Marcus emptied the contents of a folder on the table. Reilly's wallet, phone, and keys fell to the table. Reilly woke from the noise.

Duvane started. "Pick up that phone and call Callahan. Speaker phone. Find out where he is."

Reilly's nerves were shot. Marcus didn't have time for any games. "Whatever he told you to do, say it's done. Your only shot at not going away for all of Callahan's crimes is full cooperation."

Reilly dialed the phone. They all listened to the ringing. Callahan picked up on the second ring. He was obviously groggy.

"Uh, hey, Trip. Hope I didn't wake you."

"Mike, what the hell? I called you like ten times last night. What's the status?"

"You're good. I put a report in the system for your car. Said that you reported it stolen at noon."

"And the girl? Is she dead?"

Reilly looked at Marcus, who nodded. "Yeah."

"What about that big fucker that was with her?"

Marcus smiled. He wanted to rip the phone from Reilly's hand and spew venom at Callahan, but he controlled himself and gestured the correct answer.

"Dead too."

"And what about all those squad cars at the motel—what was that about?"

"Some drug bust."

"Well, that's good news." His voice cleared like he was waking up. "We're good, baby!"

Reilly continued. "I need out, Trip."

Callahan didn't respond.

"Trip, come on. You don't need me anymore. I did what you asked. You're covered for yesterday. Just give me back my gun."

"Mikey, relax." There was a pause then.

Reilly looked at the phone like maybe Callahan had hung up.

They heard Callahan talk to someone in the background. The voices were muffled. It sounded like he said he'd be right down.

Finally, Callahan spoke into the phone again. "Mikey, you there? Okay, we're done. I've got enough buildings at this point. Business is good. I don't have time for this bullshit."

Reilly opened his mouth to respond.

"But I'm not giving you that gun. That's my insurance. I'm not an idiot."

"Fine." He looked up at Marcus and Duvane. Marcus motioned him to keep talking.

"Take care of yourself, Mikey." The phone went dead.

Marcus was busting. "You didn't ask him where he was!"

"It would have been a giveaway. He would have known."

Duvane broke in. "He's right, Marcus. But here's the good news. He should feel perfectly safe. Totally covered. We'll stake out his office, his properties, his apartment. The moment he surfaces, we've got him."

"But meanwhile, Abby's living in limbo. And what about the press? If a reporter got the E.R. reports from last night, this would be a story. We need to nail this guy now." Marcus grabbed Reilly by the collar and forced him up to face him. His feet practically came off the ground. "Where do you think he'd be?"

"I don't know! I'm sure I don't know half the shit Callahan was into. Maybe he's got a girl."

"Did he have any properties out of town?"

"Not that I know of."

Unsatisfied with Reilly, Marcus tossed him away and slammed his fist against the wall. Reilly stumbled back and tripped over the chair. No one spoke.

"Oh, shit. Yes! Duvane, let's go!" Marcus was already heading for the door.

Duvane followed. "What is it?"

"His parents. They live in Lake Forest. Sounded like he said he'd be right down. As in, he's on the second floor...of a house? It's breakfast time."

Reilly stood there, clearly wondering if he had any hope. "What about me?"

Marcus didn't even turn around. "You're busy."

They left the room and instructed the officer outside the door to confiscate his things again and guard the room.

THE morning sun streamed through the windows. Abby woke feeling surprisingly well rested. She looked around at the spacious and meticulously decorated room and took in the view out back—the big pile of construction debris, partially tarped and covered under a fresh blanket of snow, the patio directly below her, the large yard surrounded by a new cedar picket fence, and beyond the fence, the thick blue line across the horizon—Lake Michigan. Even without her glasses, it was a breathtaking property.

She wanted to stay here forever. No stress, no memories, no fear. It was like it had all washed away. She felt lighter. Almost like the last few weeks had just been a bad dream.

Finally, she felt free. Free of the weight of her secret. And it was okay. Nate knew everything, and he still loved her. Maybe everything did happen for a reason. Maybe Denny really did want her to live her own dreams. She had the sudden urge to tell her parents the whole story. They might blame her, but now she wasn't sure.

Maybe she could even come clean to David. What must he be thinking? She wondered if he'd seen her e-mail yesterday. What a relief to learn that David had actually driven her home from the wedding. She wondered what they'd talked about. More questions filled her head. The end of that evening was still a haze. If she could just tell him why she'd let him go, tell him how sorry she was, how much she had missed him. Maybe he'd react like Nate.

No. It didn't matter now. David was engaged. He was happy. She couldn't mess with that. She'd put him through enough.

Abby fell back onto the bed and closed her eyes, exhausted. She had to end the charade. She couldn't even worry about work. She'd probably messed that up too, but she didn't care.

A baby started crying down the hall and Abby listened as Nate's wife, Meg, soothed her. The sounds got louder and she could hear them go downstairs. She took a look in the big mirror above the dresser. She was a wreck, but there was little she could do to fix it.

ABBY walked through the living room, now flooded with sunlight, and smelled the remnants of burned wood in the fireplace. She followed the sounds of Meg and the baby through the dining room off to the left. Straight ahead she saw the kitchen and heard Meg. She entered tentatively.

"Hello?" It felt so strange to meet this way. Meg was standing by the sink, and the baby was in some sort of bouncing chair on the countertop, watching her mommy.

Meg turned to Abby and immediately came to her with a big smile. "Hi, Abby!" She pulled her in for a hug without hesitation. "Nate has told me so much about you. I couldn't wait to meet you. I'm so glad you're here."

Something about her voice, the expression on her face, told Abby that she probably knew everything. Maybe not the whole Callahan mess, but certainly the Denny stuff. Abby didn't care.

"I hope you don't mind meeting me in such a weird way."

"Oh, please. I don't care." She spoke to the baby then. "Lizzy, this is Abby. Say 'Hi Abby.'"

Abby said hi and reached for her tiny hand.

"Come on." Meg turned, grabbing Lizzy and her bouncing chair, and Abby followed them to the large, round table by a giant bay of windows. The room was bright and filled with morning sun.

"I spend so much time in this house with this little terror," Meg continued, as she carefully placed the baby and the chair on the table, "I'm just glad for some adult company. I've been on leave for four months. The only people I talk to are the workers, and most of them don't speak English."

Meg seemed to be as laid-back and easygoing as Abby had imagined and hoped. "Nate mentioned that you're doing some work here. It looks beautiful."

"Thanks. We feel so lucky to have found it. The previous owners had lived here for sixty years. They took great care of it, but when we came to see it, it was like walking into a time machine. Nothing had been updated in, like, forty years. It was pretty funny."

"Well, you've obviously already done this room," Abby said, looking around at the sparkling stainless appliances.

"Yeah. We're almost done with everything now. I've been working with this wonderful design firm. The woman has a great eye, and she's so easy to deal with. We've just got to finish the basement at this point."

"How long did all this take?"

"It's been, like, eight months. It wasn't so bad when I was still at work, but once I had the peanut here and we've both been home, it's, like, 'Stop hammering!'"

Abby offered Lizzy a Cheerio from the pile of cereal on the table. Lizzy accepted the offer and grabbed Abby's finger. Meg got up from the table then. "So, you hungry?"

She couldn't even pretend. "God, yes!" But then she felt bad. "Please don't wait on me. I can help myself. You've got someone else to worry about."

Meg stopped her. "Oh, don't worry about it. You hang out with Lizzy. Looks like she likes you. I'll make us some coffee. And how about an egg sandwich? I've got some ham and cheese and good muffins."

"Sounds wonderful. Thank you."

"You're welcome. And Abby, please stay as long as you want. I really wouldn't mind at all."

"I appreciate that. I'll think about it." She hoped that this whole mess would be over today, but until they caught Callahan, she was happy to stay right here.

• • •

MARCUS turned off Sheridan onto Deerpath. "Wow. Nice digs," Duvane offered.

"Yeah. Should be just another block down." Each home was unique. Most looked stately and old, like they were built in the early 1900s. They saw the number 502 on a gate and knew they had to be close. Just up here. One more. A giant hedge flanked an eight-foot-high iron gate. The gate was open. A circular gravel drive led them to the front door. A red Porsche with gold hubcaps was parked out front. Marcus recognized it from the parking lot behind Weber Properties. He couldn't forget those hubcaps.

He pointed at the car and mouthed to Duvane, "He's here."

They parked behind the Porsche and walked to the door. Marcus reached for the doorbell.

Duvane stopped his hand. "Now I know this guy got the better of you yesterday, but you're going to stay cool, right?"

Marcus replied impatiently, "Of course."

"Callahan has no reason to be jumpy. At least not until he sees you. Maybe you should stay out of sight for a minute. Let me go in. Keep this scene calm. Get him cuffed without some sort of panic."

"Yeah, okay." Marcus wanted to see the look on his face when the cuffs went on, but he knew that as soon as Callahan saw him, the wheels would turn, and panic would set in. They had to play this right. He stepped back from the entry and remained hidden from sight, with his gun drawn. Duvane rang the bell.

A woman in a black maid's uniform opened the door. "Yes?"

"Excuse me, ma'am. I'm looking for Trip Callahan. I believe that's his car?"

"Yes, sir."

"Could you let him know that an old friend is here to see him?"

"I'm sorry, sir. But he just left. He and his mama went off together. Just about fifteen minutes ago. Should I tell him who came by?"

"Can you tell me where they went?"

"No, sir."

"Ma'am, this is an official police matter." He flashed his badge. "You need to tell me where they are."

"I'm sorry, sir. I don't know."

TWENTY-NINE

MEG brought the sandwich over to Abby, along with a few pieces of fruit. The smell of brewing coffee filled the room. Abby thanked Meg and took a bite. Cheese dripped from her mouth. Lizzy watched and giggled.

"See, we're both messy eaters!" Abby said to Lizzy. The baby now had oatmeal covering most of her face and hands. "Yum!" Abby added with exaggeration for Lizzy's entertainment.

She turned to Meg, back at the stove. "This is great."

Meg was working on her own. "Good. I make one for myself almost every day." Sounded like a much better start than the Dunkin' Donuts muffin Abby usually ate.

"I see why."

The doorbell rang. Abby perked up. Marcus. Hopefully, he had some good news.

Meg looked toward the hall. "Shoot. Abby, would you watch the stove for me?"

"Sure." Abby got up from the table, with sandwich in hand, and took over at the stove. She listened to Meg's slippers shuffle along the tile in the hall.

"Hi, Margaret! I forgot you were coming this morning," Meg said.

A woman's voice replied. "I hope this is a good time."

"Of course. Come on in."

And then Abby heard the woman again, "And you remember my son? I think you met when he picked me up here a couple of weeks ago?"

Meg replied. "Sure, hello again. Is it Thomas?"

"Good memory. But everyone calls me Trip. You're Meg, right?" the son asked.

Abby almost dropped the spatula. A chill crawled up her spine and into her scalp. Her heart pounded wildly. She surveyed the room. Lizzy in her chair; the egg, sizzling in front of her.

"Well, come on in," she heard Meg continue. The footsteps on tile got louder and louder. "Would either of you like some coffee? I was just making breakfast for Lizzy and my friend, Abby."

Abby darted into the dining room. She could still hear them.

"Hey, Abby, this is my…Abby?" She heard Meg go to the stove and move the frying pan off the heat. "Well, that's weird. I'll introduce you in a moment. So, who wants coffee?"

Both voices said "Me!"

Abby peered into the doorway. Callahan and his mother were standing by the stove with Meg. Lizzy was looking at her, smiling and cooing and reaching out toward her. Abby tucked back out of sight, tiptoed through the living room, slid along the tile in the front hall, and ran upstairs. The guest room was straight ahead. She grabbed her cell and called Marcus.

"Henton here."

"Marcus, he's here!"

"What? Abby? *Callahan?*"

"I'm at Nate's house and Callahan just walked in the front door!"

"He's at Walters' in Wilmette!" she heard him repeat.

"Where are you?"

"Duvane and I just left Callahan's parents' house in Lake Forest. We're not far. We're on the way! Don't move, Abby. How could he know you'd be there?"

"I don't think he did. I can't believe—"

"Stay out of sight. We're coming!"

Abby closed the phone and went back into the hall and listened over the railing. She needed to know if he knew she was here. She could hear them chatting but couldn't quite make out the words. She went down a few more stairs to hear better. Then a few more.

TRIP took his coffee, walked to the window, and looked out into the backyard. Just hearing the name Abby had his blood pumping. It had to be a coincidence. She's dead. He looked around the room. Whose house was this, anyway?

"So, Meg," he began casually. "How's motherhood?" He sat at the table with Lizzy and offered her a Cheerio.

"It's great," Meg offered with a big smile. "Maternity leave is a tad challenging, but motherhood is great."

"What do you do?"

She brought her coffee toward the table where Lizzy sat. His mother followed. "I'm a lawyer."

"Oh," he continued, leading her right where he wanted. "Is your husband one too?"

"Isn't that how it always seems to go? Yes. Though we don't work together."

"I know several lawyers in the city. What's his name?" Trip took a sip and looked around the room for clues.

"Nate. Nathan Walters."

The coffee caught in his throat, and he coughed. He looked around and brushed his right foot against his ankle holster. It was there.

His mother reached over and touched his arm. "Are you okay?"

"Yeah, the coffee just went down the wrong pipe." He turned back to Meg. "I don't know that name. You said you have a friend visiting?"

"Yeah, an old friend of Nate's. She should be right back."

"Is she single?" his mother joked. "I'm always on the lookout for a nice girl for my son."

Meg played along. "Well, from what I've heard, Abby is single and quite a catch. So, who knows?" She smiled at Trip.

His mother's smile faded when she turned to him. "Trip, you look pale. Are you feeling okay?"

His head was spinning. He ignored his mother. Reilly said she was dead. He had to know for sure. He continued to stare at his coffee mug as he addressed Meg. "I know an Abby. I wonder if it's the same one."

"I don't know. Abby Donovan? She and my husband grew up together in Georgia."

Trip froze with his coffee halfway to his mouth. His tongue went dry. "No. Not the same." He put down the mug

305

and got up from the table, heading for the hall. "Excuse me for a moment, I need to use the bathroom."

"Sure. It's right under the stairs in the hall."

HE knows. Abby scurried out of the hall to the dining room when she heard Callahan walk toward the bathroom. His footsteps got louder. He wasn't going to the bathroom. He was looking for her. Abby moved farther into the dining room, looking for a place to hide. She ducked under the table. Lizzy spotted her through the doorway and began making noises while lifting her arms toward Abby. "Shhh," Abby softly pleaded.

"Abby?" Meg spotted her.

Her heart was pounding. Abby cautiously stepped into the kitchen.

TRIP turned back when he heard her name. He walked back into the kitchen just as Abby entered from the dining room. They stared at each other.

"Looking for me?" Abby stood between Meg and his mother.

"Oh, hello!" His mother stood immediately and offered her hand. "You must be Meg's friend."

Abby did not reply.

Trip stepped back toward the women. He never took his eyes off Abby.

"What's going on here?" Meg asked.

"Are you surprised to see me?" Abby asked.

He smiled and began to bend down.

"Stop!" Abby yelled. "Meg, please take Lizzy and get out of here. Callahan, it's all over. The police will be here any minute. Don't do anything stupid."

"What's this about?" his mother insisted.

"Your son kidnapped me yesterday, ma'am. Drugged me and left me to die in a motel room."

Meg nervously stood and began lifting Lizzy from her chair.

Trip laughed and shook his head.

"That's absurd!" his mother responded. "Trip?"

"Mom, remember I told you about that lawyer I was dating. Here she is."

"*What?*" replied all the women.

"Meg, get out of here!" Abby shouted.

Trip grabbed his gun from his ankle holster and pointed it at Meg. "Don't move."

"Trip, what are you doing?" cried his mother.

"Don't!" Abby cried.

"Shut up! All of you!" Trip's gaze remained fixed on Meg, and he held the gun with both hands, pointed at her face. "This bitch has caused me more problems..." His hands felt shaky. "Just shut up!"

Lizzy started crying, and Meg tried to soothe her.

Abby spoke. "You want me, Trip. Not anyone else."

He was still looking at Meg and the baby, but he could see Abby in his periphery.

"So come and get me!"

He turned to Abby's voice and fired the gun, but she was gone. The bullet shattered the window behind them. Meg and Trip's mother screamed. Lizzy cried harder and louder. Trip ran into the dining room.

DUVANE and Marcus slammed the car door shut just as the shot rang out. He looked back at Duvane. "Did you hear that?"

Both men pulled their weapons, instinctively crouched toward the ground, and scurried toward the house. Marcus motioned to Duvane. He'd head around the back as Duvane began looking through the front windows.

Marcus went to the backyard and peered through the windows. He looked into what appeared to be a study. No sign of life. Suddenly, he saw Callahan with gun drawn, creeping around the corner. Marcus stood firm, pointed his gun, and yelled, "Freeze!"

Callahan turned to the voice and fired. Marcus ducked as the bullet shattered the glass window between them. He looked back. Callahan was gone.

Marcus ran farther along the building. He saw nothing in the living room, so he continued past the dining room and came up to the kitchen windows. Two women were huddled in a corner, one holding a baby. Marcus knocked on the glass and motioned for them to open the door. "Police," he mouthed. The older woman quickly opened the door.

"Where are they?" Marcus whispered.

She shook her head frantically. "I don't know."

The younger woman chimed in from the corner. "He has a gun. Abby said he kidnapped her!"

"Both of you—don't move. Get back on the ground. Don't come out until I say."

Marcus silently stepped into the dining room. He caught a glimpse of a shirt in the hall.

"Freeze!" Marcus yelled again. Callahan turned and fired at Marcus, who fired back and ran toward the man.

Another gunshot rang out, and a window shattered. Marcus went into the front hall and saw Duvane clutching his arm on the ground outside. Marcus turned to the empty living room. He shouted, "Thomas Callahan, you're under arrest! Don't make this worse for yourself!" Marcus slowly moved through the room with gun at the ready and continued. "There are a lot of innocent people here. Your mother for one. A baby. Don't make this any worse." He walked through the dining room and looked back into the kitchen area at the women in the corner.

"How could this get any worse?"

Marcus turned to Callahan's voice. Callahan was standing just inside the dining room by the hall, with his gun pointed at Marcus. Marcus's gun wasn't aimed at him. He made a slight move. Callahan cocked the trigger.

"You're supposed to be dead."

Marcus moved slightly to face him. "Surprise."

"I guess I'll have to kill you both again."

Marcus didn't move. "I wish you wouldn't do that." The bathroom door under the stairwell began to open.

Callahan chuckled. "Yeah, I bet you do." He lifted the gun slightly, closed an eye to perfect the shot, and straightened his firing arm. Abby was behind him. Lifting something big and white over her head. *Whack.* The weight of it came down hard against Callahan's head. Abby dropped it. Callahan collapsed on the ground, dropping his gun. The white object shattered as it hit the tile floor. Marcus moved in with his gun pointed at Callahan, rolled him onto his back, and put all of his weight on top as he pulled out his cuffs.

ABBY fell to the ground.

"Abby!" Meg's cried out from the kitchen.

"It's okay!" Marcus shouted toward the kitchen. Meg and Callahan's mother ran into the room. Lizzy was still in Meg's arms.

"Trip!" His mother ran and crouched at his side. He was regaining consciousness.

Marcus forced Callahan to stand and ushered him outside. Callahan's mother followed. "What's happening?" She was pleading for information as they went out the front door.

"Abby!" Meg ran to her, and they hugged.

"Meg, I'm so sorry!" She looked at Lizzy then, flushed and puffy from tears. "Lizzy! Hey, baby girl. I'm so sorry! I'm so sorry!" She was shaking her head. "I can't believe I brought this into your house." She couldn't speak anymore.

"We're okay! We're okay!"

Abby looked around at the shattered porcelain surrounding them. "I broke it."

"What is that, anyway?"

"The lid to your toilet tank."

Meg let out a chuckle. "Are you telling me that you nailed him with my toilet?"

Abby smiled then. "Guess I did."

THIRTY

WHEN the doorbell rang the next morning, Abby looked out the front window from the hall. It was Marcus.

Nate shouted, "I've got it!" from the kitchen. Abby went back into the guest room, grabbed her things, and walked down the hall to the nursery. Meg was sitting in a chair, rocking Lizzy.

"Okay, I'm heading out. Thanks again for the clothes," she said as she posed in the blue business suit.

"Hey, that looks good on you!"

"Well, it's lucky for me we're the same size."

"Well, at one point we were. Take your time returning it. I've got some baby weight to lose anyway."

Abby walked into the room and sat on the edge of the bed. "Meg, you look beautiful. And you're the nicest person on the whole planet. After everything that happened here yesterday, I..." She didn't know what else to say. "Thank you for everything."

Meg stood then. "You know what they say: A traumatic event brings people together! I can tell we're going to be great friends. Now get out of here. You're late."

"Okay. Thanks. Thanks for everything." She planted a kiss on Lizzy's head. "Bye, baby girl!"

Nate and Marcus were chatting in the front hall at the foot of the stairs. "Hey, guys."

"Hey there, Abby, you ready?"

"Yeah." She gave Nate a big hug. "Thank you for everything," she whispered.

Nate pulled out of the embrace and held her arms in a firm grip. "Hey, we're family, right?" She nodded in agreement. "Good. Don't forget it. I'll call you later."

Marcus opened the passenger door for her and started up the car.

"Well, what have I missed?" Abby inquired.

"It's been quite a twenty-four hours, my friend."

"Yeah?"

Marcus pulled out onto Sheridan Road and headed south for the city. "Where to start? Okay, first, Isabel Ramirez came into the station yesterday afternoon. She identified Callahan in a line-up. We called in another guy who I knew was at Reggie's the first time Callahan and his cronies came in; the brother of one of my contacts on the street. He identified the three officers and Callahan as well. They're all in custody. They're now the primary suspects in Leon's drive-by shooting, and the plan is to charge Callahan with the murders of that prostitute, Ali Rashid, and his friend as soon as you come in to give your statement."

"All good stuff."

"And we got a search warrant yesterday afternoon for Callahan's business. Several officers have already spent hours gathering paperwork and computers and everything that might help. They'll be going through the arrest records and evidence connected with every property he's acquired through auction. His phone records and e-mails are being scoured. Any contacts with Chicago police will be investigated."

"Good."

"And Reilly is anxious to do whatever he can to lessen the charges against him, so you can bet he'll be testifying against Callahan."

"And of course I will too."

"Yes, I think Callahan will go away for a long time."

"What about bail? If he gets bail, you have to tell me because I'll leave town. I wouldn't feel safe."

"I wouldn't worry about that, Abby. With all of the charges and evidence they're piecing together, a judge will know what a flight risk he'd be. And besides, his father came into the station yesterday."

"Yeah?"

"One would guess that a powerful family would be protecting their own, lawyering up. But it turns out Trip Callahan is not exactly the golden child. The father came in to see him and said good-bye. Told the officers he was washing his hands of him."

"Wow. And what about the charges against me?"

"Duvane personally saw to it that the entire case was tossed. It's really over, Abby." He put his hand on hers. "And I couldn't have done this without you, you know. Really, I give you all the credit here. And I wish I had protected you better."

Abby put her other hand on his. "You did fine."

He looked over at her. "You saved my life yesterday, Abby."

It didn't feel that way. It felt like being with Marcus, working this case, had somehow saved her life. She smiled. "You like my toilet-lid move, eh? Gonna use that one sometime?"

"I might!"

They continued down Sheridan and cut over to Lake Shore Drive. Within minutes they had a perfect view of the skyline and the Drake Hotel, perched right there at the curve, straight ahead.

"And what about the prosecutor you saw with Callahan?"

"We're just starting to build the case against him. Not sure yet how much he knew, but Duvane's getting a warrant for his personal financials, and the state's attorney has put him on leave pending the investigation. It's going to take a while, but we'll get them all."

"Wow. Are you still undercover? Will you stay with Internal Affairs?"

"For now. Amazingly enough, my cover's still intact. And according to Duvane, there's still a lot of work to be done."

"I'm glad you'll be staying in Chicago. I've gotten used to having you around."

He smiled. "Me too."

They drove in silence past Navy Pier and took a right on Monroe toward her building.

"And now you can get back to work too. Must be a relief."

She gave a halfhearted "yeah."

He pulled over under the L tracks on Wabash in front of her office.

"Thanks for the ride, Marcus."

"Hey, it's the least I could do. I'll be in touch," he said in his most professional tone.

She leaned over then and gave him a big hug. "Friends?"

He smiled and hugged back. "Friends."

"So that means we actually start hanging out sometimes? Go get a beer or something?"

"I'd love it."

"And if you ever need someone to bounce ideas off of, or to do a little covert research, I'm your girl!"

He laughed then. "Yeah, yeah. Get out of the car already."

IT was about ten o'clock by the time Abby got to the lobby. She hadn't shown up to work now since last Friday—three days without a word, other than Sarah trying to cover for her. She'd never even gotten that partnership memo turned in. She might even get fired, but she felt at peace. She really didn't care what happened at this point but thought the partners deserved—no, *she* deserved—for them to know the truth.

She had called ahead and asked Dorothy, Jerry's secretary, when he'd be free, so she knew she could get a few minutes right now. She headed straight to his office and knocked on his open door.

"Abby, please come in. I was going to call you in here today. I never got a partnership memo from you."

She entered and shut the door behind her. "Yeah, about that. I need to tell you something."

BACK at her desk, Abby organized a to-do list for getting through the work that had piled up since Monday. She couldn't wipe the grin from her face. The shock on Jerry's face was priceless. The firm was never going to fire her now. The media would be all over this story within hours, and Abby's role was sure to shine light on her firm. They would never want to be thought of as the big firm that fired her for solving some kind of crime ring and putting a murderer and several dirty cops behind bars. The firm would want to put her on posters as the face of justice. Jerry was probably already sharing the story with every other senior partner he could find.

It felt good to have the firm behind her again, but nothing felt quite as good as finally being ready to live her life. She couldn't live for Denny anymore, and she'd finally realized that she didn't have to. When the dust settled from all of this, she was sure she'd cry again about letting David go. They were kindred spirits—more than she'd ever let him know.

But she would not cry today. Today was for new beginnings. For setting in motion a game plan and charting a new course. She was determined to find her own way, and this desk would not hold her for much longer.

ABBY was finishing up for the day when a new e-mail popped up from Seth, the eternal cheerleader of the firm's associates. The regarding line said only: *HAPPY HOUR CELEBRATION*. Abby opened the mail:

> *Hey, everyone. Sarah's back from her honeymoon, and it's not official yet, but the word at the water cooler is that one of our own may soon leave the lowly rank of associate to become a partner. We need beer. Clark Street Ale House. Five o'clock. Be there.*

Abby shook her head and smiled. Jerry had already given her the heads up regarding the whole partnership issue. She looked down at her calendar. The afternoon was clear. And then she saw one more new e-mail. It was from David. She held her breath and opened the message: *Hi, Abby. Thanks for the note. I don't think the worst of you. I know what happened. We should talk. Can you meet?* He knew what happened? But how could he? And then, before the excitement of talking to David again took over, she reminded herself aloud, "He loves someone else now." She wrote back:

Thanks, David. Looks like that matter's all cleared up. Thank goodness. I'm happy to talk whenever you've got the time. Take care.

Maybe she could face him tomorrow.

And then she noticed them. The flowers from Ali. Still sitting in what was now brown water, surrounded by dried-out petals on her desk. She sat back and took a deep breath. So much had happened. So much had changed. And it had all started because of Ali. He'd saved her life in every way. She looked back at the calendar. Just four weeks had passed since that fateful night.

ABBY, Sarah, and her husband, Rick, stood at the end of the bar, with their drinks in hand. Abby suggested a toast to Sarah and Rick's marriage, Sarah suggested a toast to Abby's survival, and Rick suggested a toast to Neil's rise to partnership, which gave them the biggest laugh. They all looked over at Neil, who was off in the corner, holding court among the younger eager beavers. "Let him have it," Sarah said to Abby, as if she needed reassurance.

"Absolutely. I'm moving on," Abby advised with confidence. She took a deep breath and welcomed the major change in direction she was now willing to make.

"Hi, everyone." The sound of his voice sent her pulse racing. Butterflies fluttered. How could she even look at him? Sarah and Rick looked up and got off their stools with enthusiastic greetings. Abby remained frozen. She couldn't turn around. She heard him congratulate the newlyweds and order a beer.

"Hi, Abby."

She took a breath and turned to face the voice she knew so well. "Hi."

"How are you?" He looked serious.

Sarah put her arm around Abby. "She's great."

Abby smiled. "Yeah. Everything's good."

"I'm so glad."

She knew she had to say something. "David, I'm sorry about that crazy scene at the courthouse on Monday."

"I just came from a meeting with Robert Duvane. Looks like I'll be prosecuting those officers. Abby, I can't believe what you've been through. I wish I'd known."

She didn't know what to say. Everyone was connected.

David turned to Sarah and Rick. "You said this is a celebration?"

"Yes," Sarah raised her glass. "To Neil's rise to partnership," she offered with sarcasm.

Abby raised her glass. "Sarah and Rick's return is the real cause for celebration."

Sarah raised her glass even higher. "No, we're really celebrating Abby's bad-ass survival skills!"

"Hear, hear!" Everyone agreed and took a sip.

David turned to Abby again. "Neil's a partner? How do you feel about that?"

"Great, actually."

"Really?"

"We'll be back," Sarah blurted. She grabbed Rick by the arm and headed off to the other end of the bar.

David sat on the stool next to Abby. She nervously took another sip of her beer.

"Are you really okay with Neil becoming a partner?"

Abby put down the glass and finally met his eyes. "I know it's a surprising answer. But a lot has happened. He can have it." She felt lost in his eyes; she wanted to come clean, but she couldn't. "And you? I hear that congratulations are in order for you too?"

"For what?"

"For your pending marriage?"

He looked at his beer. "Oh, that." He opened his mouth to speak but didn't.

Abby wondered if she should even ask.

David took another sip and then looked at Abby. "That's not going to happen."

Abby could feel the rush of red to her cheeks. "What?"

He relaxed back into his chair. "We broke up at Sarah's wedding."

"Really?"

"She said she could tell it wasn't over between you and me. She said I was staring at you all night."

Abby couldn't look away. She stared into his eyes and took a deep breath before she responded. "Wow."

"Yeah, wow." They both took a sip from their beers. David continued: "You want to know something else?"

Abby sat up taller. "What's that?"

"I was at the Blue Note last Friday."

"What?"

"When you sang?"

Abby covered her face. "I'm so embarrassed."

"Abby, don't be." He pulled her hands from her face and held them. "I think I saw more of you that night then you let me see in years. You were amazing."

Without knowing it, he gave her the courage. She looked into his eyes. "I'm so happy you're not engaged."

"And why's that?"

She took another sip and continued. "Because I want you to spend the rest of your life with me." She was shocked at her own bravado but refused to turn away. "If you still want to." She waited for a response.

David was obviously flustered and hardly knew how to react. "Either you've had a lot to drink or a lot has changed."

She gestured to the full beer in front of her. "Well, this is my first beer, so I guess a lot has changed." Abby looked into those light-blue eyes and could see the love was still there.

AUTHOR'S NOTE

I BEGAN writing *The Green Line* in 2004, when my oldest child was just three years old. He's now eleven. It's been an arduous, exciting, invigorating, and exhausting adventure. Many people helped me along the way. My sincere thanks go to Karen Osborne, D. C. Brod, Julia Buckley, Cynthia Quam, Martha Whitehead, Kathi Baron, and John Pogue. Their feedback, insight, tips, and encouragement carried me through the ups and downs. I'd also like to thank Win Golden of The Julia Castiglia Agency. Her enthusiasm for the project gave me confidence that publication was not just a pipe dream. Many thanks also go to everyone involved in the book's production: Richard Klin, Gwen Gades, Derek Murphy, and the whole team at Thomas & Mercer. Finally, I thank my family. My husband, parents, siblings, and kids gave me unwavering support and encouragement to keep writing and to never give up.

The seeds of this story were planted more than a decade ago. Living in Chicago for much of my twenties, I was a constant traveler on public transportation. I once sat as a silent hostage and watched as three young men verbally terrorized a fellow passenger for no other reason than their own amusement. It was a crowded train, but every one of us, all witnesses to the rudeness, the insults, the unbelievable vulgarity, feared them and did nothing. Another time, an older, mentally unstable woman looked into my eyes and uttered the words I used on the first page of this story: "If I had me a gun, I'd just shoot all them white people." Ninety-nine percent of the time, my rides were safe and uneventful, but I never forgot those moments, and after unintentionally boarding the Green Line once in the middle of the day, back when I didn't know Chicago well and knew only that I was headed toward the most dangerous parts of the city, I wondered what might have happened if it had been late at night.

Though I don't share much with Abby Donovan, there are a couple of parallels. I too was an associate at a large law firm in downtown Chicago, and I researched and wrote a law review article about civil forfeiture that was published in the late 1990s. I read countless stories and cases of innocent owners who were stripped of personal property with no due process. It was shocking to me that we actually have laws on the books that disregard the guilt or innocence of property owners, laws that are fully enforceable and utilized by law enforcement all over the country. Although Congress passed a reform bill in 2000 that improved the situation in some cases, there are still countless disturbing elements of this widely used procedure.

Finally, Chicago's numerous law enforcement scandals over the last several decades were great sources of inspiration while researching and writing this story. Of course, the story is fictional, and my assumption is that the vast majority of police officers are, in fact, the good guys, but soon after finishing *The Green Line*, a *Chicago Tribune* article reported on the sentencing of a former officer in conjunction with one of the worst misconduct scandals in the department's history. The officer, and nearly a dozen other officers, had assisted in stealing hundreds of thousands of dollars in cash from suspected drug dealers and others after making illegal traffic stops or illegal property searches. Though the officer faced up to thirteen years in prison, he and the majority of others involved received less than six-month sentences.

About the Author

 E.C. Diskin received a B.S. from Texas Christian University and a law degree from DePaul University College of Law in Chicago. She lives in Oak Park, Illinois, with her husband and two kids. This is her first novel.

For more information, go to www.ecdiskin.com